SIDE ONE

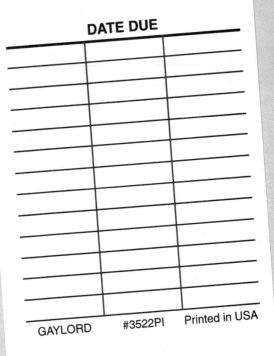

DATE DUE

GAYLORD   #3522PI   Printed in USA

THE NEW ADVENTURES OF
STAR TREK: DEEP SPACE NINE®

The Left Hand of Destiny, Book Two
by J. G. Hertzler & Jeffrey Lang

Unity
by S. D. Perry

Worlds of Star Trek: Deep Space Nine, Volume One
by Una McCormack; Heather Jarman

Worlds of Star Trek: Deep Space Nine, Volume Two
by Andy Mangels & Michael A. Martin; J. Noah Kym

Worlds of Star Trek: Deep Space Nine, Volume Three
by Keith R. A. DeCandido; David R. George III

Warpath
by David Mack

Fearful Symmetry
by Olivia Woods

COLLECTIONS

Twist of Faith by S. D. Perry;
David Weddle & Jeffrey Lang; Keith R. A. DeCandido

These Haunted Seas
by David R. George III; Heather Jarman

FROM POCKET BOOKS
AVAILABLE WHEREVER BOOKS ARE SOLD
ALSO AVAILABLE AS EBOOKS
www.startrekbooks.com

STAR TREK
DEEP SPACE NINE®

FEARFUL SYMMETRY

OLIVIA WOODS

Based upon STAR TREK®
created by Gene Roddenberry,
and STAR TREK: DEEP SPACE NINE
created by Rick Berman and Michael Piller

POCKET BOOKS
New York   London   Toronto   Sydney   Dahkur

Pocket Books
A Division of Simon & Schuster, Inc.
1230 Avenue of the Americas
New York, NY 10020

This book is a work of fiction. Names, characters, places, and incidents either are products of the author's imagination or are used fictitiously. Any resemblance to actual events or locales or persons, living or dead, is entirely coincidental.

First Pocket Books paperback edition July 2008

POCKET and colophon are registered trademarks
of Simon & Schuster, Inc.

For information about special discounts for bulk purchases,
please contact Simon & Schuster Special Sales at
1-800-456-6798 or business@simonandschuster.com.

Cover art by John Picacio; cover design by John Vairo, Jr.

Manufactured in the United States of America

10 9 8 7 6 5 4 3 2 1

ISBN-13: 978-1-4165-6781-3
ISBN-10:   1-4165-6781-X

For A. and A.,
sister and brother

"All my victims. It always comes back to that, doesn't it? All my crimes."

Prologue

The world receded behind an infinite vista of radiant white, until all that remained was the beating of his heart—the steady rhythm that kept him anchored to his life on the linear plane. He found his hand, long brown fingers flexing above his open palm, just as he had done during his original encounter with the Prophets. And like that first time, he came to understand that he was not alone.

But he had intuited from the start that this was not to be another meeting with the wormhole entities. His sudden need to experience the Orb that had guided him here had come from his vague sense of a different sort of connection, one deep in the center of his being . . . something that transcended even the most intimate relationships of his linear life. As his awareness continued to spread outward, he started to recognize those who were already assembled here: seven others who had, like him, been drawn by necessity to this place that was not a place, at a time when there was no time. He walked forward into a circle of Emissaries.

A gathering of men named Benjamin Sisko.

They looked at one another across the whiteness, men from different universes; each one, like him, born by design, and each of whom in time—despite how differently their lives had unfolded—had met his destiny on a world called Bajor.

Ben felt the void at once, a cold and yawning emptiness very close by, like a missing piece of his soul. To his immediate right, there was a break in the circle. Someone was missing.

"I take it," he said, "that we're here to do something about the hole in our ranks."

"Not us," said one of the others. "You."

Ben's gaze fixed upon the speaker, a clean-shaven civilian wearing the formal attire of a Federation diplomat, and as their identical eyes met, his counterpart's life and the world from which he came were suddenly an open book: Ambassador Sisko of the UFP Diplomatic Corps, who had lost his wife Jennifer on Cardassia Prime during a suicide attack by Kohn-Ma terrorists, even as he was trying to negotiate the withdrawal of Cardassia's military forces from Bajor. . . .

Ben heard his heart beating faster. He focused on the sound, followed it back to his true self, realizing that it would be all too easy to become lost in the alternate lives arrayed around him. "I don't understand."

"He was your responsibility," someone else said. Ben turned and focused past the break in the circle, where another counterpart was gesturing toward the vacant space between them. What appeared to be a dagger was sheathed in the sashlike belt of his gaudy metallic uniform: Fleet Captain Sisko, the military governor of Bajor under a Terran Empire that never fell, the livid scar across his right, sightless eye the only legacy of the father who had betrayed him. "It was your task to reach him, to convince him to take his place among us."

"What are you talking about?" Ben asked. "I never even met our counterpart in that reality. How is *anything* about him or that universe my responsibility?"

"You ignored the signs," the imperial said.

"What signs? Every crossover was their doing, except for the first one, and that was entirely by accident!" As he spoke, the events of that original contact came back to him: Nerys and Julian's runabout mysteriously malfunctioning as it entered the wormhole, out of control until it emerged, inexplicably, in the alternate universe of the Intendant.

Then he paused, comprehension slowly dawning . . . along with the terrible realization that he had been blind to a pattern that had been there before him all along.

"It wasn't an accident at all," Ben said. "The Prophets wanted our two universes to connect."

"You're starting to understand," said another civilian, this one full-bearded and wearing a blue laboratory jumpsuit: Dr. Sisko of the Daystrom Institute, whose discovery of the wormhole years after the terrible accident that had claimed the life of his sister had led, not to strife, but to a new renaissance of art, science, and philosophy—and to a spreading social revolution in which the free exchange of knowledge and ideas was catalyzing a gradual dismantling of the familiar galactic nation-states in favor of a loose but stable interstellar sprawl. "Every other crossover was initiated by their side, just as you said," the scientist continued. "And more tellingly, they all occurred by transporter. But your Kira and Bashir's runabout went through the wormhole to get there and back that first time, and you never stopped to consider the possibility that it wasn't a random event, or that your two universes seemed unusually permeable in the Bajoran system after that first event. You never wondered why no one in that universe ever opened *their* Temple Gates, despite the presence of a Sisko in that continuum. Not even after you learned the truth about your origins . . . that Benjamin Sisko does not exist by accident, in *any* universe."

"The Sisko of the Intendant's dimension," Ben realized. "He was supposed to have become their Emissary."

"That's the only reason any of us exist," said still another counterpart, his uniform an odd amalgam of Starfleet and Militia design: Colonel Sisko of the Celestial Union—from the universe where Bajor was the nucleus of a vast planetary alliance that stretched from Cardassia to Earth—who had discovered the wormhole at the height of a savage and protracted war with the Tholians . . . a conflict that had claimed the lives of both his parents. "We're each born onto a path we're meant to walk," the colonel continued, "but his life—his reality—made him the most reluctant of us, the one least open to accepting the role we're all meant to fulfill."

"Cowardice" was the judgment of Admiral Sisko, widower and hero of Wolf 359, whose Federation had long ago absorbed the Klingons, the Romulans, the Cardassians, even the Tzenkethi and the Breen. "The fear to believe in ourselves has always been our greatest enemy. That was where *you* came in."

"You're telling me I was supposed to have gotten through to him somehow."

"Not alone," said Sisko of the Borg, his mechanically aided voice reverberating as it passed through his dull gray lips. "Never alone. But it was your job to keep your eye on the ball." Ben repressed a shudder at seeing the fate he knew he himself had only narrowly escaped. But his revulsion was tempered by fascination—that in a universe where the collective had overrun Earth and then pushed on through the Federation toward Bajor, the Prophets' plan for Benjamin Sisko had still come to fruition, even for one so wounded in body, mind, and soul.

"But why me?" Ben wanted to know. "You all seem to have understood my task when I didn't even know I had one. Why wasn't it one of you?"

"Because next to him, you were the slowest of us to accept who you really are," came the answer from the Sisko whose life seemed most like his own . . . until the death of his only son aboard the *Saratoga,* a loss from which he never recovered. Broken and consumed by grief, it destroyed his marriage, his career, and almost his will to live. But time and destiny eventually swept him to Bajor, and thus to the truth, as they had for every other Emissary. "Helping him would have helped you to reach a better understanding of yourself much sooner, to think outside your comfort zone, so you could have better prepared your Bajor for the trials ahead."

And there it was—as it had been during the throes of the rapture that had led to his rediscovery of B'hala, and again during his tutelage in the Temple—a fleeting glimpse of the pattern that held the Tapestry together, spanning past, present, and future . . . now coupled with the real possibility that he himself was responsible, because of actions he had failed to take, for putting it all at risk.

"What happens now?" he asked.

"Our most immediate concern," the admiral said, "is that the deserter's continuum is now vulnerable to the threat from your side."

"What threat?"

"You'll know soon," said the scientist. "Events are proceeding quickly in both realities."

"The damage may already be too great for the outcome we're hoping for," warned the imperial.

"If the circle isn't complete, the Tapestry will unravel," the colonel countered. "That musn't happen."

"What must I do?" Ben asked.

And they told him.

"Are you all right?" Opaka Sulan asked after she had closed the Orb casket.

Ben nodded, but it was mostly reflex. The truth was, he was overcome with a profound sense of loss. Some of his previous experiences with the Tears had left him feeling either exhilarated or drained, physically and emotionally. But this was something else, something more disturbing; this time in the Orb's embrace he'd felt whole in a way he'd never experienced before, a near completeness that, in its aftermath, lingered only as an echo—a memory that was now painful to recall, because it reinforced his utter isolation on the linear plane.

"Drink this." Opaka held out a goblet of water she'd poured from the decanter that rested on a narrow table by the door. "It will help."

Ben accepted the water gratefully. He drank it in one shot, savoring the cooling sensation in his gut. He looked around the room for some indication of how long he'd been in the Orb fugue, but of course there was no sign.

The underground crypts that had been created to conceal the Tears until they could be safely returned to their shrines were windowless and offered no hint of the passage of time.

"The candles," Opaka said, taking back the empty goblet. At first Ben didn't understand what she meant, but then he realized she had read the question in his face and was offering him a clue to the answer. Now that he focused on them, he saw that the candles in the room were noticeably shorter than they were when the former kai of Bajor had led him to this place.

"Have I been here all afternoon?" he asked.

"Nearly so," Opaka confirmed. "As you've no doubt realized by now, the Orb of Souls can be taxing—far more so than any of the other Tears. It is the least understood of the Nine, and the most unsettling. Encounters with it are exceedingly rare, for few meet its gaze willingly; even those who are called to it, as you were." She paused, studying his face. "Did you find what you sought?"

Ben didn't answer immediately. Opaka, of course, knew better than to ask him specifics—Orb encounters were considered too personal to share, requiring each seeker to decode them as best he could. This one, however, had far less ambiguity about it than his previous experiences.

Finally he told her, "I learned what I needed to know. I'm just not sure I can do what's being asked of me."

The stout woman lowered her eyes. Her lips curled slightly upward, but she offered no comment.

"What?" Sisko asked. "No sage words of advice to trust my own judgment, to walk the path that's been laid out for me?"

She looked at him, arching an eyebrow. "When have you ever known me to tell you what you already know?"

"Then how about telling me what I *don't* know?"

Opaka regarded him a moment longer, concern knotting her brow. Then she reached up and grasped his earlobe between her thumb and forefinger. She closed her eyes. "Breathe," she told him, the way she had when they'd first met. "Breathe . . ."

Ben blew air out his nostrils, then took it back in slowly. He waited, still fascinated even after all these years by the ability some Bajorans possessed to read each other's inner state, a sensitivity that extended even outside their species. Jadzia had once speculated it was simply a limited form of "touch-empathy." Maybe that's all it was. Maybe.

Opaka opened her eyes and released him. "It's all right to be afraid," she said quietly.

"I'm not afraid," he assured her.

"Not for yourself, no. But you're deeply concerned about the consequences of the choices you must make."

He shrugged. "I've lived with that concern my entire adult life."

"But not like this."

Ben exhaled and glanced at the ark of the Orb of Souls. "No, not like this." He looked back at his old friend, grateful she was here with him. There were very few people in his life who had any real understanding of the burden he bore as the so-called Emissary of the Prophets, and none more so than Opaka, who eight years ago had started him on this strange journey of self-discovery and daunting responsibility. "There's something I need to ask you," he said.

Opaka waited.

"What can you tell me about the Sidau Orb fragment?" When she failed to reply immediately, Ben said, "I saw the look on your face when Lieutenant Ro first told us about it, two months ago. You know something. What?"

Opaka sighed. "What I 'know' may provoke more questions than it answers," she said at last. "I first heard about it long ago, in connection with a much-revered kai from many hundreds of years past, Dava Nikende. He supposedly kept an object that fits the description Ro Laren gave us: a single, tiny green stone set in an ornate golden bracelet, which Kai Dava wore around the palm of his hand until he died. The Vedek Assembly has always considered the story apocryphal; it was never anything more than a folktale—an unlikely rumor, at best." Sadness seemed to overtake her. "At least it had been, before the Sidau massacre." She paused to wipe the tears forming in her eyes.

"I'm sorry," Ben said softly.

Opaka took a deep breath and regained her composure, but her mournful countenance remained. "Since then, I have been searching the Vedek Assembly archives for some forgotten insight into the artifact's origins . . . or its fate."

"And?"

"I've told you that an encounter with the Orb of Souls is a rare event. Kai Dava was one of the few people known to have been called to it. Archival references to that encounter only slightly predate the earliest mention of the object he supposedly carried . . . the *Paghvaram*."

" 'Soul key,' " Sisko translated and turned his head toward the Tear's ark. "Then the fragment is from the Orb of Souls. Dava must have—"

"No," Opaka said gently. "Not unless our understanding of Dava Nikende is so flawed as to be complete fallacy. He revered the Tears. He even foresaw the need to conceal the Orb of Prophecy and Change, centuries before the occupation, so that it would be safe from the Cardassians and here to receive you when you came to us. For him to damage a Tear would be unthinkable . . . and none of them bear the evidence of such a crime."

"Then what is this thing that three hundred people died for?"

"I wish I knew," Opaka whispered.

"Emissary?"

Ben and Opaka both turned. Yandu Jezahl, the tall, dark-haired theologian who had been placed in charge of the crypt, stood in the doorway, her expression grave. "What is it, Vedek?" Ben asked.

"Forgive the intrusion, but we've received a communication from your wife," Yandu said. "She said it was most urgent that she speak with you. She seemed quite distressed."

Oh, no.

"We've routed the call to a companel on this level. If you'll follow me . . ."

Ben's first thought was that something had happened to the baby. But when Kasidy appeared on the comm screen with Rebecca sleeping peacefully against her chest, that initial dread dissipated quickly. The anxious look on Kas's face, however, gave rise to new fears. "Kas, what's happened?"

"I just heard from Ezri," she told him. *"Something's gone wrong aboard the station. That Jem'Hadar that's been living up there—he attacked Nerys and Lieutenant Ro, Ben. They're both badly injured."*

Taran'atar? "Have they contained him?" Ben asked.

Kasidy shook her head. *"Ezri said he fled the station. Commander Vaughn went after him in the* Defiant.*"*

Damn. "Kasidy . . . I have to—"

"I know what you have to do. Call us when you have news."

"Are you sure? You and Rebecca—"

"We'll be fine," Kasidy assured him. *"Nerys needs you more than we do right now."*

"I love you."

"We love you too."

He waited until he was certain that Kasidy had cut the connection, and then he released the anguish building inside him, pounding his fist once against the panel.

A hand touched his shoulder. Warm. Strong. Reassuring. He looked into Opaka's face and she offered him a slight, encouraging nod, urging him to go.

Ben took a deep breath and started marching toward the long stone stairway that led back to the surface.

1

"My name is Iliana Ghemor," the Cardassian woman said. "I'm a former agent of the Obsidian Order, the intelligence arm of the Klingon-Cardassian Alliance, in what to you is an alternate universe. Now I'm part of the rebellion organized by the Terrans of my continuum, whose objective is to overthrow the Alliance and live free of tyranny. My assignment was to assassinate the Intendant of Bajor, Kira Nerys. I aborted that mission when I learned of a plot that involved individuals from your side. I crossed over to stop it."

"What was the nature of this plot?"

"To replace her with someone even worse."

"Who?"

The Cardassian's eyes narrowed. "You aren't very good at this, are you?"

"Who was planning to replace the Intendant?"

"You're not really an interrogator. Your technique is terrible."

"This isn't an interrogation. I'm just here to ask some questions."

"Whatever you want to call it, we don't have time for this. You have to let me speak to your captain."

"I'll look into that. Who was planning to replace the Intendant?"

The Cardassian sighed. "Your reality's version of me. My counterpart. Years ago, she was surgically altered to replace your Kira. I believe she has already crossed into my universe, killed the Intendant, and taken her place."

"If that's the case, why are you still in this universe?"

"This is pointless! I already told Commander Vaughn all of this! Just let me speak to Captain Kira."

"I said I'd look into it. Why are you still in this universe?"

"Because the device I used to make the crossover was destroyed . . . and because I need your help to stop my counterpart from carrying out her objectives."

"What are those objectives?"

"I'll reveal that only to Captain Kira."

"You'll reveal it to me."

"Wouldn't you rather know why that creature turned against you? What do you call it—a Jem'Hadar?"

"We already know that someone who looks like Captain Kira was communicating surreptitiously with Taran'atar for the past three months, using a very sophisticated method of brainwashing. We know that Taran'atar supplied information to this individual that enabled her to carry out the massacre of a Bajoran village more than ten weeks ago. And we know that Taran'atar attacked Captain Kira and Lieutenant Ro before fleeing to the planet Harkoum, where, by a strange coincidence, we found you."

The Cardassian smiled. "There are no coincidences. And you didn't 'find' me. I rescued two of your officers."

"We also recovered a large cache of data on the genetic experimentation that was being conducted at the Grennokar prison facility on Harkoum—experiments on living Jem'Hadar subjects dating back more than three years."

"Is there a question you want to ask me?"

"Are you responsible for Taran'atar's betrayal?"

"No."

"Were you involved in the Sidau massacre?"

"No."

"What proof can you offer that your story is true?"

"I can offer it to Captain Kira."

"What are your counterpart's objectives?"

"I'll reveal that only to Captain Kira."

The Cardassian's face froze as Lieutenant Ezri Dax touched the control interface, pausing the playback before she strode away from the wardroom screen and took her place at the conference table. "I'm sorry to say the rest of the interview was more of the same," she told the room. "The subject volunteered no additional information, and just kept repeating her demands to speak directly to the captain."

Kira stared at the unsettlingly familiar visage on the screen. She gave herself a moment to compose her features before swiveling her chair to face her officers: Dax, Commander Elias Vaughn, Dr. Julian Bashir, Lieutenant Samaritan Bowers, Lieutenant Nog, and Ensign Prynn Tenmei. "We may as well start with the fundamentals," she said, focusing her attention first on Bashir. "Your report, Doctor?"

From his place at the far end of the table, Deep Space 9's chief medical officer slid a padd toward Kira across the illuminated surface. It stopped precisely in front of her. Not for the first time, the captain caught herself envying Bashir's genetic enhancements. "Based upon my examination of our guest, I've managed to verify three salient facts," he began. "One: that she is a healthy Cardassian female approximately thirty-four years of age. Two: using our medical records of Legate Tekeny Ghemor to compare genetic profiles, I can confirm that this woman is indeed his daughter. And three: that analysis of her quantum resonance signature proves beyond any doubt that she is not native to our continuum. When I ran that signature through our database, the computer came up with only one match."

"Let me guess," Kira said. "The other Bareil Antos, the one who crossed over from the alternate universe almost three years ago."

"That's correct," Bashir said.

"I wasn't aware it was possible to differentiate between people from different universes that way," Bowers said, his deep brown forehead creased with interest.

"It's a relatively recent discovery," Bashir explained to the tactical officer. "Most of our knowledge comes from an incident involving our former strategic operations officer, Lieutenant Commander Worf, from about seven years ago when he served aboard the *Enterprise*. An anomalous trans-spatial event led to the temporary intersection of more than three hundred thousand parallel universes, each with its own unique quantum signature."

"All right," Kira said. "She's who she claims to be. The question is, can we trust anything she says beyond that?"

"She came to our aid on Harkoum at considerable risk to her own life," Tenmei pointed out.

"True," Kira acknowledged, offering Tenmei an approving nod. Ordinarily the *Defiant*'s conn officer wouldn't be required to attend a briefing like this one, but Tenmei was one of the witnesses to the events on Harkoum, as well as being Taran'atar's captive from the moment he fled the station, and Kira had wanted her participation. "But is there any reason to think that her actions weren't calculated precisely in order to earn our trust?"

"I'm sure they were," Vaughn said. "But that in and of itself doesn't make her a liar."

"All of our interactions with the alternate universe have involved some level of deceit by their side," Dax reminded the group. "And as a Cardassian, she was born into the ruling authority that enslaves most of the species we think of as comprising the Federation. For all we know, the real Intendant is still alive and this is all part of another elaborate plan on her part to seize power over there."

"Or a prelude to an invasion of our side," Bowers added.

"We're getting a bit ahead of ourselves, aren't we?" Bashir asked. "We need to consider our visitor as an individual and in the context of recent events, not just our history with her continuum."

"With all due respect, Doctor," Nog said, "that's exactly the mistake we made with Taran'atar."

Bashir's eyes narrowed at the Ferengi engineer. "Taran'atar's recent actions were beyond his control," the doctor said, and Kira was surprised by the certainty in his voice. "As you know perfectly well, Nog."

"I think we all share strong feelings on that particular subject," Vaughn cut in before Nog could reply, casting a warning glance both at him and at Bashir, "and we'd do well not to let those emotions influence our thinking. The fact remains, our guest has so far acted in good faith."

"Except when it comes to elaborating on her claims about our universe's Iliana Ghemor," Dax said. "You gotta admit, Commander, it's a pretty wild story to accept on the face of it. The fact that she refuses to say anything more except to the captain is reason enough to be cautious. For all we know, she may be hoping to win us over just so she can finish what Taran'atar started."

His knife in my chest. My blood on the deck. Kira pushed the memory away.

"We've *been* cautious," Vaughn said. "We've had her confined for a week now on suspicion alone, under surveillance and under guard, and we've yet to make a ding in her shields. Unless the captain intends to authorize more forceful methods of interrogation, we've run out of options."

A shocked silence fell over the table. "Is that what you're proposing?" Kira asked pointedly. "A 'more forceful' interrogation?"

"No," Vaughn assured her. "Even if such action weren't unlawful and abhorrent, she's done nothing to deserve such treatment. I'm simply trying to make the point that short of taking such extreme action, we've reached an impasse with our guest. But we've yet to find any direct evidence linking her to Taran'atar's recent behavior or the Sidau massacre, nor ruled out the possibility that everything she's been telling us is the truth."

Kira felt a headache coming on. She closed her eyes and massaged the ridges of her nose. "Status of Lieutenant Ro's investigation?"

"Ongoing," Vaughn answered. "She's put Major Cenn in charge of the criminals we rounded up on Harkoum, but so far they've had little to say that's useful regarding their missing ringleader."

"That ringleader supposedly being our side's Iliana Ghemor," Kira said.

"If our visitor's story is to be believed, yes."

Silence settled over the wardroom again, and Kira saw a troubled expression seeping into Bashir's face. "Your thoughts, Doctor?"

Bashir hesitated, then took a deep breath. "I was just remembering my own experience in the alternate universe, and what it felt like to be trapped in a world that was so familiar, yet was so horrifically different. I don't know if I've ever felt so afraid or so lost."

Kira knew exactly what Bashir was talking about. She'd felt it too on that same occasion. "And you think our visitor may be feeling the same way?"

"I think she's doing her best to earn our trust, Captain," the doctor said. "Maybe it's time we considered trying to earn hers."

Kira took a moment to weigh the opinions she'd heard, then reached a decision. "Lieutenant Dax, please inform security that I'll meet with the visitor in my quarters tomorrow morning at oh-nine-hundred hours."

Dax looked at Vaughn, then back at Kira, her brow furrowed. "Me, Captain?"

"Have you become hard of hearing, Lieutenant?"

Dax blinked. "No, sir."

"Then that'll be all. Meeting adjourned." As her staff rose and started to file out, Kira said, "Commander Vaughn, stay a moment."

Vaughn stopped and turned back to face his captain, knowing that a storm was brewing. He considered re-seating himself, then decided it would be best to remain standing. Kira's formality through most of the meeting—

as well as her atypical decision to delegate a task to Dax that ordinarily would fall to him—had set the tone for whatever discussion would follow. He'd heard the thunder; now he braced himself for the lightning.

Kira was leaning forward in her chair, fingers laced in front of her chin as she waited for the other officers to vacate the wardroom. She looked weary—physically exhausted and emotionally drained, none of which was surprising: Despite the risky regenerative treatments Bashir had reluctantly authorized—under Kira's direct order—to speed up her recovery, she was still the recent victim of a savage attack that had damaged her heart beyond repair. The organ that now beat beneath her healed chest was a biosynthetic replacement that, odds were, she would need for the rest of her life.

The same attack had shattered the spine of Ro Laren, who, like Kira, should have been convalescing but had instead thrown herself into some kind of investigative overdrive. Technically off duty, Ro was refusing to see anyone, but judging by the round-the-clock computer activity from her quarters, she was anything but idle. Vaughn had known many headstrong individuals in his long life, but Kira and Ro were in a class by themselves.

Not that he could blame either of them: Despite the lethal damage Taran'atar had inflicted, Vaughn knew that the Dominion observer's apparent betrayal had hurt them more. That same betrayal had launched Vaughn and the crew of the *Defiant* on a chase deep into the Romulan protectorate of the Cardassian Union, to a world where Taran'atar had taken Prynn as a hostage until he could join his new master. Vaughn resisted the impulse to rub his mended arm, still sore from his bone-breaking confrontation with the Jem'Hadar soldier.

For long seconds after the wardroom doors closed behind the last of the departing senior staff, Kira said nothing. When she finally spoke, she did so without looking at him. "You want to tell me what the hell happened out there?"

Vaughn frowned. "Captain?"

"With Taran'atar. With the *Defiant*. With Prynn." She turned to face him, standing up slowly. "I read your after-action report. I also read Ezri's, and Sam's, and your daughter's. And what I'm left wondering is, after all the questionable actions you took while I was out of commission . . . how is it you're still alive, Commander?"

A dozen answers came to the tip of Vaughn's tongue, competing for expression. He could have told her he'd survived because his tactics had been sound, or because his lifetime of experience gave him the edge he needed, or because Taran'atar had clearly been struggling against whatever had been done to him. Every answer would have been the truth, but none of them were honest. And it was his honesty Kira wanted. It was what she required. And it was nothing less than she deserved.

"I was lucky," he answered.

"Damn right you were," Kira said. "You put yourself, your crew, and the *Defiant* at risk, and you failed the mission."

"Respectfully, Captain, although Taran'atar did get away, Ensign Tenmei was recovered, vital intel was obtained, a criminal enclave was routed, and we returned to the station without a single fatality."

"Is that supposed to mitigate your actions? Going after Taran'atar yourself, first after he'd taken your daughter hostage and again after believing he'd killed her? Never once contacting Starfleet to apprise them of the situation and request assistance? Your judgment was, at best, questionable, and at worst—"

"I was in command," Vaughn said firmly. "I took what I believed were the correct and necessary steps to resolve the crisis. If you're unhappy with how I do my job—"

"You made it personal, Commander!"

He met her gaze. "Haven't you ever made it personal, Captain?" Vaughn asked quietly.

Kira's eyes narrowed. Her jaw tightened. Then she turned her back to him. "Get out."

"Captain—"

"You're relieved of duty until further notice, Commander. Dismissed."

Vaughn blinked. At the age of 102, he thought he was long past being surprised by anything, but this turn of events had taken him completely off guard. He wanted to talk this out with Kira, explain himself, but the captain acted as though he had somehow betrayed her trust.

Is that what I've done? he wondered. *Was I too close to the situation to make the right calls?* The delay in reporting the incident to Starfleet Command had seemed like the prudent thing to do; there was too much they still didn't know at the time to risk making the situation worse by entrusting it to well-meaning men and women who had no experience with Jem'Hadar outside the context of the Dominion War, and who couldn't relate to Taran'atar as anything other than a deadly enemy. Someone who had gotten to know Taran'atar as an individual, Vaughn believed, stood the best chance of achieving the mission objective: capturing him alive. Because throughout the chase—even when he believed Taran'atar had tricked him into killing Prynn—Vaughn had been convinced that there was more to what was going on than met the eye.

But though that belief had been borne out, the mission had been anything but a resounding success.

If Prynn hadn't been involved, was there anything I'd have done differently? Would this crisis already be over?

As he pivoted away from Kira's back and marched out of the wardroom, Vaughn wondered if he had finally outlived his usefulness.

2

"I'm done arguing with you, Lieutenant," Simon Tarses said tersely. "Your physical therapy was supposed to have begun yesterday. I let you take a pass on it once because you gave me your word as an officer that we'd begin today. You can't decline therapy again."

Ro Laren looked up from the massive interface console that currently took up the space where her couch used to be. "Watch me," she said and went back to the file she'd been reading when Tarses had interrupted her.

"Lieutenant, you can't expect to walk again unless you do the work," Tarses said, stooping to pick up one of the discarded legs from the powered exoframe she was supposed to be wearing. "If anything, you're taking a step backward. What are you doing in a wheelchair when you should be using this?"

"It slows me down," Ro said. "Chair's faster for what I'm doing, easier."

"Unacceptable," the doctor said. "I'm giving you a direct medical order to stop whatever you're—" Tarses dodged the bowl of replicated *moba* slices she threw at him. It crashed against the wall behind him, splattering the bulkhead. "Hey! What the hell's your problem, any-way?"

"Right now, just you," Ro said. "So I suggest you get lost, before I pick up my spice pudding."

"You can't just—" Tarses ducked as the pudding came at him and covered her door in a gooey mess. "That's it! I've had it! Maybe Doctor Bashir will have better luck with you."

"Don't bet on it," Ro said through her teeth.

"Don't think this over, Lieutenant."

"I'm reaching for my tuna salad . . ."

Tarses bolted from her quarters without further ar-gument. Ro shook her head. *Medics. They just don't get it.* Making a mental note to have someone from main-tenance come up to deal with the mess, she sighed and tried to refocus her thoughts on the task she had set for herself.

Obsidian Order agents, doubles, alternate universes, stolen artifacts, and massacred innocents—all of them were elements of a very improbable story, when you got right down to it. And yet, Ro was convinced they were all connected in a web of someone's making. Whether that someone was truly the long-missing Iliana Ghemor remained to be seen. The real mystery was what the still-unproven architect of recent events was trying to achieve, and what the overall pattern of the web would reveal when she finally reconstructed it.

Her borrowed interface console was active with real-time links to the station's main computer, the Bajoran Central Archives, and Memory Alpha. Padds were strewn everywhere—on the console, on the carpet, in the rep-licator, on the couch that had been pushed to one end of the room to make room for the new equipment she'd persuaded Nog to set up in her quarters. Those padds displayed open files on everything from Bajoran prophecies, to the Obsidian Order, to the personal histories of dozens of individuals—not just station personnel, but persons of interest on Bajor, on Cardassia, in Starfleet, and elsewhere—the living and the dead. She allowed herself a grim smile. Tarses might have the medical authority to keep her officially off duty during her rehab, but nobody could do a damn thing about how she occupied herself in her quarters. And there was no way in hell she wasn't going to stay involved in the investigation. If that meant putting off a full recovery from her injuries, that was her own damn choice to make.

Ro noted the time and glanced over her shoulder at the array of monitors mounted atop her console. On one of them was the surveillance feed into a locked and guarded cabin halfway around the habitat ring—the current home of the Cardassian whom Dr. Bashir had positively identified as the alternate Iliana Ghemor. Their visitor had been making good use of the limited access she'd been granted to the library computer, researching the history files that were widely available on the public comnet. As she watched, security personnel arrived right on schedule to escort Ghemor to her meeting with Kira.

A second monitor showed Major Cenn, the Bajoran Militia liaison officer, questioning one of the twenty-one surviving mercenaries who had been captured on Harkoum. Nearly a dozen different species were represented among the prisoners, and thus far none of them had offered up any useful information. This one was a female Kressari. Cenn wasn't having a great deal of success with her either, but that wasn't surprising; Kressari had hard, textured skin that made their emotions difficult to read for outsiders. You might learn a lot from watching the changing color of their eyes, or from listening carefully to the inflections in their speech, but if the suspect was communicating as little as this one was, then it became difficult to develop an effective interrogation strategy based on exploiting the subject's emotional state.

The third monitor displayed one of the audiovisual records embedded in the data cache Vaughn had recovered from Grennokar, showing a pair of Cardassian doctors performing open-brain surgery on a live Jem'Hadar soldier. Ro had sent captures of the men's faces to the station's closest ally in the Union military, Gul Akellen Macet, who had eventually sent back confirmation of their identities: Drune Omek and Strell Vekeer were two scientists once attached to the Obsidian Order, but both had dropped out of sight not long after the intelligence group's collapse, over five years ago. Even more interesting, though, was that according to the timestamp on the recordings, these men had been routinely cutting into Jem'Hadar skulls almost from the day Cardassia had joined the Dominion—two years after Omek and Vekeer had both vanished—with the apparent goal of trying to decipher the code behind the soldiers' genetically mandated loyalty to the Founders. Ro had so far gone through seven of the horrific recordings. Each time, the subjects would go into violent, fatal seizures. Sometimes they died instantly, sometimes slowly. One had convulsed for more than two hours before it finally expired. The surgeons seemed utterly indifferent to the suffering they were witnessing. They merely watched and recorded their observations, sometimes adjusting their equipment as the gruesome scenes played out.

The last monitor was standing by with a menu of every datafile that had passed through Taran'atar's companel since he'd taken up residence on the station: information on Sidau village, the wormhole, the Orbs, the alternate universe, and any personal or official log that mentioned those items. She'd already gone through the material half a dozen times.

Ro turned away from the console and gazed up at the enormous freestanding viewscreen that dominated the back wall of her quarters, so big it completely obstructed both viewports. She had masked the display when Tarses had come calling, and now, alone once again, she tapped it back on. Here she studied the ever-expanding structure of her hypothetical web—carefully arranged images of people, places, and dated events, with notes or questions beneath each one, many of them connected by red lines denoting relationships among them. At the center of them all, radiating lines to practically every other item on the screen, were two images. One was Captain Kira. The other was the grainy capture of the nearly identical face Nog had extracted from the reconstituted activity log for Taran'atar's companel: supposedly the Iliana Ghemor of this universe.

Iliana had been off the grid for sixteen years. Most of what they knew about her—and it was very little—had come from her now-deceased handler within the Order, Corbin Entek, when he kidnapped Kira six years ago and attempted to convince her that she was, in reality, Iliana—part of a convoluted scheme to expose Iliana's father, Legate Tekeny Ghemor, as a dissident.

But Iliana's fate had never become known.

It made her counterpart's claim about the true identity of their enemy a compelling one, to say the least.

Ro picked up the padd that had been resting on her lap. She considered the face it displayed and once again she keyed the bookmarked segment of the audiofile she had discovered earlier that afternoon in the station's databases.

"Your daughter is alive, Ghemor. I know where to find her."

She paused the playback of the three-year-old recording and stared at the image on the padd's tiny screen. With grim resolve, Ro touched the upload command and added the speaker's face to her web: Skrain Dukat.

Ro might not have any personal experience with Bajor's late former prefect, but she knew him by reputation well enough not to take anything he ever said at face value. The man was notoriously self-absorbed, at times to the point of believing his own lies, and therefore gauging his truthfulness was always problematic. In this instance, the gul had been addressing Tekeny Ghemor, at a time when the former legate was aboard the station, in his final days of life, suffering from an incurable illness. Kira had been recording her sessions with the exiled dissident as he undertook the final rite of *shri-tal,* in which dying Cardassians passed on their secrets to loved ones, ostensibly to be used against their enemies. Dukat, who at that time had been the Dominion's puppet ruler of the Cardassian Union, had obviously been sufficiently concerned about what the old legate might divulge that he'd made a pilgrimage to Ghemor's deathbed, hoping to coerce his return to Cardassia before he revealed too much. Kira had the foresight to leave her recorder running during the visit and captured the claim Dukat had made about Iliana during his final appeal to the dying man, which Ghemor had valiantly rejected.

Dukat and Iliana—they were connected somehow.

Slowly and deliberately, Ro keyed a vivid red line to extend from one face to the other.

With one guard marching in front of her and one behind, the two armed and uniformed humans escorted Ghemor down one of the curving main corridors that ran through the station's enormous habitat ring.

Human security guards. The thought almost made her laugh. As an abstract idea it was one thing. The reality was something else entirely. These Starfleet humans bore little resemblance to the barely civilized thugs that made up most of Smiley's rebellion; they seemed to have more in common with Cardassians . . . and that likeness was not a hopeful sign.

She and her escorts abruptly halted in front of a door. The lead guard, a red-blond female, tapped the chime once.

"Enter," came the response, in a voice that was unsettlingly familiar. The door opened into a well-kept Cardassian-designed stateroom. It was furnished to Bajoran tastes but was far less decadent than those Ghemor was used to seeing. Its sole occupant, another Starfleet officer, knelt in front of a small shrine against the right-hand wall. Arms half extended at either side, her slightly cupped hands faced forward at level with her head.

"The visitor, Captain. As ordered," the leading guard said.

The captain's arms dropped and she slowly rose to her feet. "Thanks, Neeley," she said as she extinguished the shrine's two small candles. "Wait outside, please."

Both guards took a half step backward, and Ghemor

took that as her cue to cross the threshold. When the door closed behind her, she said, "Thank you for seeing me. I apologize if I've interrupted anything."

The captain turned, and Ghemor saw the face that until now she'd known only in a very different context. The earring was different, and the coppery hair was a little longer, but those details did little to negate the uneasy feeling, despite what she knew to the contrary, that she was standing in the presence of Bajor's Intendant.

"I was just praying," the Bajoran replied with a hint of a smile. Not the predatory smirk of her counterpart, but a disarming look of self-deprecating humor.

"For what?"

"I'm sorry?"

"When you pray," Ghemor said, "what do you ask of your gods?"

The half-smile was back. "I don't ask them for anything. I look inward for the virtues the Prophets have taught us to cultivate. Wisdom . . . strength . . . hope."

Not the answer she expected. "Meditation, then."

Her host shrugged and strode toward her. "Labels don't matter. What counts is the act of exploring one's *pagh*."

"Did it work?"

"It's a process, not a goal." She stopped in front of Ghemor and nodded curtly. "Captain Kira Nerys, commander of Deep Space 9."

"Iliana Ghemor."

Kira's brow furrowed slightly. Then she seemed to realize she was staring. "You'll have to forgive me. Last time I saw that face, I was looking into a mirror on Cardassia Prime. Seeing you in person is a little . . . disorienting."

"I know exactly what you mean."

"I imagine you do."

Ghemor slowly circled the room, absorbing what it told her about its owner. As she expected, it said very little; Kira was evidently wise enough not to reveal too much about herself to anyone, even within her personal space. A few things stood out, though: the modest shrine was the only religious icon in evidence, testifying to the seriousness with which she took her faith without feeling the need to flaunt it; simple but comfortable furnishings spoke to her appreciation for the need to unwind occasionally, but not to the point of sloth; a few pieces of Bajoran arts and crafts confirmed her pride of heritage; and the fresh flowers on the dining table betrayed a softer side she wasn't ashamed of.

Something shiny on a trinket shelf next to the sleep-chamber door caught Ghemor's attention. She stopped dead in her tracks.

Her mother's bracelet.

She thought she was prepared for anything this continuum could throw at her: friends and enemies with their roles reversed; dead people who were alive; subtle similarities and gross contradictions. . . . She'd read and heard enough about the alternate universe to think nothing would surprise her, that she wouldn't be taken off guard by anything she encountered. Yet here, among the possessions of this strangely benign version of the Intendant, was Kaleen's bracelet.

Ghemor picked it up; it felt absurd to ask permission first. It was whole, pristine. Unsullied and undamaged.

"You recognize that?" Kira asked.

Without taking her eyes off the bracelet, Ghemor nodded. "My mother had one just like it. How is it that you—?"

"On this side, the widower of Kaleen Ghemor was a dissident, secretly working to reform Cardassia," the captain explained. "Years ago I was abducted by the Obsidian Order and made to look like his long lost daughter as part of a plot to expose him. We both escaped, and as a token of the bond that had developed between us, Tekeny Ghemor gave me the bracelet he'd hoped to pass down to his daughter."

Ghemor didn't respond, but in fact she knew that story quite well. Before she'd crossed over to this universe, she had learned a great deal of things, but she wasn't ready to share all of it. Not yet.

Still not looking up, she asked, "Is your Tekeny still alive?"

"No," Kira said. "He became stricken with Yarim Fel syndrome and died a couple of years later, believing his daughter was dead. I keep the bracelet to honor his memory. . . . What's so funny?"

Ghemor was laughing. She couldn't help herself; the respect in Kira's voice when she spoke of Tekeny was the final irony.

"*My* father," Ghemor began, "was the brutal, ruthless head of the Obsidian Order for almost a quarter of a century. It's because of him that I became an operative, and it's because of him that I turned against the Alliance. In a way, I suppose he's responsible for my being here."

"And your mother's bracelet?"

She saw it vividly in her memory: melted around a burned, blackened wrist. She remembered screaming as Ataan pulled her away from her mother's smoking body, telling her they needed to get away . . .

"I'm not sure what became of it," Ghemor said. "I haven't seen it in years." She gently set the bracelet down and turned to face Kira again. "So how do you want to begin?"

Kira gestured toward a chair on one long side of the dining table. Iliana seated herself, while the captain took the chair opposite her. "Why are you here?"

"That's the wrong question."

The Bajoran frowned. "Then what's the right one?"

"What really happened to the Iliana Ghemor of this universe?"

"Do you know?"

"I know some things," Ghemor said. "For example, I know her deep-cover assignment to infiltrate the Bajoran resistance involved not merely making her look like you but also suppressing her real identity and replacing it with yours."

Kira didn't answer immediately. She seemed to be growing agitated. Finally she said, "I was fed that lie once before, and nothing ever came to light to back it up."

"It wasn't a lie," Ghemor said. "Not all of it."

"I suppose you're going to tell me it happened at Elemspur Detention Center."

"That's right."

"Except I was never at Elemspur. I was never replaced by a Cardassian operative."

"But you *were* a target for replacement," Ghemor said calmly. "Do you think that the underlying resemblance between you and my counterpart—between you and *me*—played no part in the assignment she was given?"

Again Kira hesitated. "When you rescued Vaughn and Tenmei, you told them Gul Dukat had betrayed the Obsidian Order's plan to have Iliana replace me."

"That's right."

"Why would he do that?"

"I have no idea," Ghemor lied, "and I can't say that I care."

"No idea," Kira repeated, clearly skeptical. "None at all?"

"If I was to guess, I'd say it had something to do with your mother. . . . Meru, wasn't it? As I understand it, she was his comfort woman for a time." She watched Kira's expression darken. *I seem to have touched a nerve. I'll have to remember that.* "It's true, then?"

"Yes," Kira said quietly. "But she'd been dead for years by the time Iliana was sent to Bajor. She wasn't in a position to influence him on my behalf, if that's what you're suggesting."

"You underestimate my people's capacity for sentimentality," Ghemor said. "But maybe you're right. Maybe it was less about helping you than it was about hurting someone else. Or maybe there's a different explanation entirely. Do you think it makes any difference now?"

"Let me tell you what I think." Kira angrily pushed away from the table and stood. "I think you're working for the Intendant. I think she's the one behind all of this, and that you're here spinning this insane tale to distract us from whatever it is she's really up to. Or maybe your job is to deliver us into a trap."

"Perfectly logical," Ghemor conceded. "And also perfectly wrong."

"Then what happened to your counterpart? Where has she been all this time? And what does she want now?"

"I don't have all the answers, Captain. But I do know that she's completely insane and extremely dangerous. She still thinks she's you."

"After all this time? Sixteen years?"

"That's one of the reasons she's out of her mind, Captain. She was never reactivated. The galaxy is very different from the one she remembers, and you've been living the life that she believes should have been hers."

"This is all about getting to me? That's why Taran'atar tried to kill me and my chief of security?"

"There's much more to it than that," Ghemor said. "I told your interrogator, Lieutenant Dax, that I believe my counterpart crossed into my universe with the intention of replacing the Intendant."

"And?"

"I don't believe she has any intention of stopping. She plans to keep going—eliminate every Kira Nerys in every universe she can reach. And she thinks that little trinket she murdered a village to get hold of is the key."

Kira stared at her. Ghemor held her gaze, watching her face as the revelation sank in.

"You can't be serious."

"Do I look as though I'm joking, Captain?"

Kira sat back down. "Even if you're telling the truth, what do you expect me to do about it?"

"Isn't it obvious? I failed to stop her. I need your help to go after her."

"Why should I trust you?" the captain asked.

"You don't have to trust me," Ghemor said. "You just have to believe me."

"Believe you? I still don't believe you about Elemspur, and you want me to—"

"It happened the week you stopped blaming yourself for the death of Dakahna Vaas."

Kira gaped. Ghemor was almost amused by her speechlessness.

"That's right, I know about Dakahna. She was your partner the day she was lost on the mission to raid the geological survey station in the hills outside Tempasa. Her death was eating you from the inside out for months afterward . . . until Elemspur."

Ghemor paused. "So now, Captain, here's the question you need to answer: Does my impossible knowledge of this dark and deeply personal chapter of your life make me more trustworthy . . . or less?"

Kira had maintained her composure throughout, but now there was a glimmer of hatred in her brown eyes, and Ghemor knew she had overplayed her hand.

The captain tapped her combadge. "Kira to Neeley. Take our guest back to confinement."

3

"All right, let's say she's telling the truth," Dax said, clasping her hands behind her back. "What then? What are our responsibilities? If it really is our Iliana that Taran'atar has followed into the alternate universe, do we leave them for the other side to deal with? Or do we have an obligation to go after them for the crimes that were committed here?"

"Those are all excellent questions," Kira said, sounding a little short of breath as she paced Ro Laren's quarters. Ezri remembered how Julian had warned Kira that the accelerated regen treatments could take their toll on her, especially if she insisted on returning to duty too soon. Clearly that's what Dax was seeing now, and she wasn't the only one to notice.

"Are you all right, Captain?" Julian asked.

"I'm fine," Kira said sharply, turning to face him, Dax, and Nog, whom she had summoned to a hastily convened meeting in the security chief's cabin. "I'm not prepared to undertake an incursion into the alternate universe without provocation, and certainly not on this woman's say-so. What we need is someone who can corroborate her story. She claims to be working with Smiley's rebellion. We need a way to contact them." Kira zeroed in on her chief of operations. "We already know how to transport over there. It must be possible to establish communication between our two universes."

Nog blinked in surprise, then slowly nodded. "It may be. We still have the specs Chief O'Brien made from his analysis of Smiley's dimensional transport module. If I can adapt its quantum targeting system to our subspace array, I should be able to home in on her continuum, then establish a two-way real-time audiovisual lock with Terok Nor. It'll take time, though, Captain. Maybe a couple of days."

"Get to work on it immediately, then."

"Aye, Captain." Nog gave her a sharp nod and left the cabin.

"What do you want to do with our visitor?" Dax asked.

"Nothing," Kira said. "At least, not until we can reach the rebels on Terok Nor."

"You don't plan to continue questioning her?" Bashir asked.

"I don't trust her, Julian. She obviously knows much more than she's saying, and she's giving up only scraps of information at a time. She's playing some game, and I'm not allowing it to continue until I've figured out exactly what it is."

Dax cleared her throat. "Captain, if I may suggest, Commander Vaughn has considerable experience in this area. He may be able to—"

"Commander Vaughn isn't available."

"But, Captain—"

"Let it go, Ezri," Kira said, keeping her voice gentle but firm.

Dax forced down further protests, but just barely. She wished that whatever was going on between Kira and Vaughn would resolve itself soon. There was a dangerous climate building aboard the station—an unspoken feeling that everything was coming apart—and Dax, even in her capacity as acting X.O., was feeling powerless to combat it.

"Captain, this doesn't make sense," Ro said suddenly.

Everyone turned to look at the chief of security, hunched over the abusurdly wide interface console with its multiple monitors. It made Dax wonder why Ro needed the huge viewscreen standing behind her, especially considering that it had been dark since their arrival.

The officers stepped around the console to get a look at what was perplexing the chief of security. The monitor displayed what Dax recognized immediately as a classified report from Bajoran Intelligence. "What doesn't make sense, Lieutenant?" Kira asked.

"I've been reviewing the records of your abduction by the Obsidian Order six years ago, and I'm finding several items that just don't add up." Ro tapped the monitor. "According to this, Corbin Entek's plan to convince you that you were really Iliana Ghemor was set in motion when Alenis Grem of the Bajoran Central Archives contacted you to ask about a seven-day period, ten years prior, when you were supposedly incarcerated at Elemspur Detention Center."

"That's right."

"The report further notes that, using the information from the archives, Security Chief Odo subsequently tracked down someone who at that time was believed to be your only surviving cellmate at Elemspur, one Yeln Arvam. This Yeln claimed to recognize you from the detention center, which made you curious enough to go investigate Elemspur firsthand and gave Entek's people the opportunity they needed to kidnap you."

"Yes, and Yeln had disappeared by the time I was rescued from Cardassia. The investigation wasn't conclusive, but it was believed that Yeln himself was a Cardassian agent planted on Bajor to help carry out the deception. There was some speculation he was even the one who altered the archive records." Kira was growing irritated; she obviously didn't appreciate being reminded of how utterly duped she'd been. "What's your point, Ro?"

"My point, Captain, is that there's no evidence the archive records were ever altered in any way. Don't get me wrong—it wasn't an unreasonable assumption given what little was known. But as you say, the investigation was inconclusive, and the lack of corroborating evidence led to what I now believe was some flawed speculation about what actually happened."

The captain scowled, and Dax recalled Odo's irritation at having the investigation taken away from him by Bajoran Intelligence following Kira's return to the station. She remembered that he hadn't been happy with their final report, either, and made his feelings known to Kira, wanting to launch an investigation of his own. But by that time Nerys had wanted to put the whole ugly business behind her and rejected his offer, telling him she was satisfied with BI's findings and considered the matter closed. Odo hadn't pressed, respecting her wishes but clearly unhappy with her decision.

Now, six years after the fact, Ro was confirming that

Odo's instincts had been right all along. But if that was true . . .

"What are you saying?" Julian asked. "That Captain Kira really was at Elemspur, despite the fact that she has no memory of it?"

"I don't know," Ro said. "All I can tell you is that unless the archive records were altered in such a way that the tampering remains completely undetectable, they appear to be authentic. Then there's Yeln Arvam himself to consider."

"What about him?" Kira asked.

In response, Ro touched a control and activated another monitor, bringing up an occupation-era image of a young man with thick black hair and small eyes. "This image was taken twenty years ago. Is this the man you spoke to?"

Kira studied the familiar face. "It looks like him, yes."

"Well, it isn't. The one you spoke to was definitely an impostor."

"And you know that because . . . ?"

"Because the real Yeln—this man—died at Elemspur Detention Center almost four years after this image was taken . . . during the exact week you were supposed to have been there."

"The records show that?"

"Yes, and they're supported by DNA samples the Militia collected when the mass graves at Elemspur were unearthed shortly after the end of the occupation."

"All right, so the Order didn't invent him," Dax said. "That doesn't prove the captain was there too."

"No, it doesn't," Julian agreed. "But if the archive files were altered, why bother to re-create Yeln Arvam? They could have invented anyone."

"Exactly," Ro said. "That suggests to me that the Order stuck as closely to the truth as possible when they put their operation together. And if that's true, then we need to ask what else was presented to then-Major Kira that was also true."

Kira paced the room, thinking. "He knew about the *hara* cat."

Dax's brow furrowed. "Captain?"

"Entek," Kira said. "On Cardassia, while he was still trying to convince me that I was really Iliana Ghemor, he reminded me about a *hara* cat I once killed during the occupation, after I mistook it for a Cardassian soldier. It was a . . . difficult moment in my life, something I'd never told anyone. Entek said it was just a memory the Order had put in my head. He'd already showed me a preserved corpse that looked like me, the way I did during my days in the resistance. I knew it had to be a fake, but then when he told me he knew about the *hara* cat, I started to doubt myself. Even after Julian proved medically that it was all a lie—that I was Bajoran and always had been—I still wondered how Entek could have known about the *hara* cat."

"Maybe Ro's right, and Entek told you the truth—up to a point," Dax speculated. "Maybe it was something he had imprinted in your mind when you were being surgically altered to look Cardassian. He could then use it against you at a moment of his choosing, present it as 'proof' of his story."

"Maybe," Kira said. "But what if it was a real memory? What if Entek knew about it not because he fabricated it, but because it was one of the memories he transferred to Iliana sixteen years ago? What if I really was at Elemspur?"

Julian shook his head. "Another fine byzantine plot courtesy of the Obsidian Order."

"Except we still don't have any concrete evidence," Dax said. "Anyone who might be able to confirm these conclusions is long dead."

Ro glanced knowingly at Julian, and after a moment, he looked at Kira and Dax, a smile spreading across his handsome face. "Not everyone," he said.

"Really, Doctor," Garak said from Ro's comm screen. *"Flattering as I find your faith in me, I'm afraid that in this case you severely overestimate the depth of my inside knowledge into the Order's activities during my exile."*

The difficult year Garak had lived on postwar Cardassia was etched deeply into his face, Kira thought. He'd lost weight, and his hair, black since she'd met him, was turning gray. Part of her was surprised he'd made himself available to answer their inquiries when Bashir had attempted to reach him. But despite—or perhaps because of—his tireless work helping restore his devastated homeworld, the man who once claimed to be nothing more than a simple tailor seemed almost to welcome the momentary distraction the doctor was now offering him.

"I don't think I've ever overestimated anything about you, Garak," Bashir answered. "You never made a secret of the fact that you still had contacts in the Order during that time, tipping you off to things the organization was up to. You admitted as much when you came to me with your information about Major Kira's abduction."

"Yes," Garak acknowledged, looking chagrined, *"for the all the good it did me. Blackmailed by Commander Sisko into returning to Cardassia, an almost certain death sentence,*

only to find myself in the awkward position of being forced to kill a former associate."

"Not to mention extracting a leading member of the dissident movement," the doctor reminded him.

"I found the whole affair quite embarrassing."

"But why get involved in the first place?" Bashir asked, folding his arms. "You had nothing to gain by informing us of Kira's kidnapping."

Garak smiled. *"Are you suggesting that my innate sense of gallantry wasn't motive enough?"*

"And currying favor with Sisko never interested you until Cardassia allied itself with the Dominion," Bashir went on, ignoring Garak's attempts to deflect him. Kira was impressed; Julian was obviously long past the point of letting Garak get away with *that.* "You knew about the plot against Legate Ghemor from the beginning, didn't you? And by telling us about it, you effectively set in motion your own little counter-op, knowing Commander Sisko would try to rescue Major Kira and, in the process, save the legate. You were trying to help the dissidents."

Garak's smile widened. *"I always said you had a vivid imagination, Doctor."*

"Well, I have you to thank for that, don't I?"

"And you're most welcome."

"So assuming you knew about Entek's plan all along," Dax cut in, "what do you know about Iliana Ghemor?"

"Not as much as the captain would like to know, I fear."

"What the hell does that mean, Garak?" Kira said.

"It means that the Obsidian Order's most effective weapon has always been the truth, especially when they could make that truth appear to be a lie. And in this instance, the truth is that Iliana Ghemor was indeed sent on a mission to replace you exactly as Entek described it, and that you were indeed at Elemspur."

"Garak, this doesn't make sense," Kira said. "If there was someone with my face on Bajor all these years, don't you think *someone* would have noticed it?"

"*Most certainly, Captain. Which, particularly in the context of your current situation, forces us to conclude that wherever Operative Ghemor was all these years, it was not Bajor.*"

"Where, then?"

"*That I don't know, which leads me to believe that no one in the Order knew what became of her, either. Not even the late, lamented Corbin Entek.*"

The alternate Iliana's claim came back to haunt her. "Dukat," Kira said, expelling the name like a curse.

Garak's head tilted fractionally to one side. "*What an intriguing notion, Captain. A pity you have no way of testing that hypothesis; I would be extremely interested in the results. Still, I won't shed any tears over it. Will you?*"

Kira eyed Garak carefully, her mouth spreading into a smile. "Thanks for the suggestion," she said. "You know, it's funny . . . Tekeny Ghemor once warned me that I should never trust you, Garak."

"*The legate was an excellent judge of character.*"

"Not always. Take care."

Garak nodded to her and vanished from the screen, replaced by the Federation Seal.

"What was that all about?" Dax asked.

Kira was already marching toward the door. "I have to go to Bajor."

"You're going to Elemspur?" Ro asked.

"I am going to find out the truth," Kira said, "wherever it leads me."

4

Major Cenn Desca strode into the Ferengi bar against his better judgment, and in doing so he caught himself wondering, not for the first time, just what the *kosst* he'd gotten himself into.

On Bajor, as a Militia officer under the direct command of General Lenaris Holem himself, Cenn had always been in his element, dealing with domestic security issues ranging from conducting forensic analyses and criminal profiling to participating in field operations that had exposed underground enclaves of nihilistic Pah-wraith cultists and rooted out occasional resurgences of the Circle. Living and working aboard the space station, by contrast, while no more complicated in Cenn's estimation than life on Bajor, was nevertheless . . . well, *weirder* by several orders of magnitude. From the dizzying and ever-present complement of aliens, to the bizarre histories of its most prominent residents, to the frequent nearby manifestations of the Celestial Temple itself, being on Deep Space 9 often felt like the surreal consequences of a night spent drinking far too much *copal*.

So it wasn't without some measure of irony that he found himself entering Quark's, which seemed to function as the station's raucous hub of social activity. He'd been scrupulously avoiding the place since his arrival two months ago, and it was only today, as he decided to take a working lunch during his investigation of the Harkoum mercenaries, that he realized how tired he'd grown of taking his meals from replicators. Unfortunately, the Promenade's Bajoran restaurant was temporarily closed while the owners were planetside attending a wedding. Cenn didn't think he was ready to try the Klingon restaurant, or any of the other alien eateries. Quark's, however, having a real kitchen in addition to replicators, boasted a varied menu that included Bajoran dishes.

Unfortunately, Cenn seemed to have chosen a busy time of day for the self-styled "bar, grill, embassy, gaming house, and holosuite arcade"; every table was taken, even those on the second level. Paradoxically disappointed and relieved, Cenn started to go, resigning himself to yet another inadequately spiced *ratamba* stew from the Replimat . . .

"Hi, handsome. Get you anything?"

Cenn turned. Facing him was the shapely and diaphanously draped torso of the tallest woman he'd ever met—at least two meters. She was also green.

In his mind, Cenn answered, *Well, I was looking for a vacant table, but you don't seem to have one available.* What came out of his mouth was, "Um . . ."

The woman smiled and took Cenn's arm, leading him toward the bar. "You look hungry. Come have a seat over here and relax while I get you a menu. I'm Treir, by the way. How about a drink to get you started?"

"Um, sure. . . . Synthale?" Cenn said, managing to remember that he was still on duty.

"Coming right up." Treir left him on a stool, next to a bald, broad-bodied alien with tiny ears, a small high-set nose, a wide downturned mouth, and no chin. The alien was nursing a drink. He nodded to Cenn as the major sat down.

Treir reappeared on the other side of the bar with a full mug and a menu. "Here you go. If you're looking for something Bajoran, it's in the front. Personally, I recommend the *foraiga*. But if you have a sweet tooth, the *tuwaly* pie is absolutely decadent."

"*Foraiga* sounds . . . wonderful," Cenn said without looking at the menu, uncharacteristically mesmerized by the woman. *Pheromones, maybe?* Not that she wasn't stunning, but he was usually a lot more subtle when he felt attracted to someone sexually.

"Good choice," Treir said, taking back the menu. "It'll be just a few minutes. Enjoy your drink while you wait, and don't hesitate to let me know if you need anything else."

Cenn enjoyed watching her walk away before she disappeared into a back room. He leaned toward the alien sitting next to him. "Please tell me there aren't more like her around here."

The alien, who was in the middle of a long draft from an enormous stein, made a thumbs-down gesture and kept right on drinking.

"Thank the Prophets," Cenn muttered. With Treir's departure, he felt his head starting to clear and decided he would try to get some work done. He took out the padd tucked in his belt, turned it on, and considered, once again, the short list of names he'd assembled the night before.

Of the twenty-one mercenaries captured during the *Defiant*'s raid on Harkoum, seventeen had been remanded to Militia custody as of this morning and were on their way to Bajor. After days of researching their backgrounds and questioning each one individually, Cenn had concluded that the majority of them were not much more than hired guns with little useful information about their fugitive employer or her objectives. They had little to say of substance, but what they knew they gave up freely in the hope that it would earn them leniency from Bajoran authorities for whatever complicity they had in the deaths at Sidau, as well as the host of lesser charges the Federation would level against them for the various illegal activities they'd staged from Harkoum.

But the remaining four mercs—two males, a Romulan and a Lissepian; and two females, a Kressari and an Efrosian—were far less forthcoming, and the threat of bearing the full weight of Federation justice for their noncooperation seemed to concern them not at all. Cenn's instincts told him that they warranted much closer scrutiny; he'd come to suspect that these four were their leader's lieutenants—an inner circle of coconspirators whose loyalty had not been rented, but earned somehow.

Cenn had run their DNA through the Federation security database in the hopes of learning something about the four that would assist him in the next phase of interrogations. He discovered that all of them were under suspicion of various illegal activities but that each of them had, over the course of the last eight years, dropped out of sight, their whereabouts unknown. He had tried checking with the Cardassian authorities as well but came up empty.

"You're Major Cenn!" someone said with particular enthusiasm. At first Cenn thought it was his drinking companion, but when he saw that the wide-shouldered alien still had the brim of his stein firmly affixed to his mouth, Cenn looked up and saw an extravagantly dressed Ferengi staring at him from behind the bar with a toothy grin.

"You know who I am?" the major asked.

The Ferengi set down the glass he'd been drying. "It's always good business to know your customers before they walk in the door." He said it as if he were quoting some profound kernel of wisdom. The Ferengi placed an orange hand over his chest and continued, "Besides, I happen to be a close personal friend of Lieutenant Ro, and she speaks very highly of you. It made me wonder when you might find time in your busy schedule to visit my humble establishment. Welcome to Quark's."

Ah, the proprietor. Of course. "Thank you," he said curtly. He knew that the lieutenant had an inexplicable fondness for this creature, but he also knew Quark's wider reputation.

"Would you care to see a menu?" his host asked.

"I've already ordered, thanks," Cenn said, his eyes dropping back to his padd.

"Perhaps, after you've eaten, you'd care to partake of a round of *dabo*? If you're not familiar with it, it's a wonderful game, very easy to learn, and requires a minimum opening wager of only—"

"It's really not my thing."

"Then maybe a holosuite program?" Quark said. "We're proud to offer a variety of simulations catering to *every* conceivable taste. If you'd like to make a reservation—"

"Another time, perhaps."

"Well, keep in mind that Quark's is also Bajor's official liaison to the Ferengi Alliance, and we offer a full array of diplomatic services, including—"

"No, thanks," Cenn said, starting to lose his patience. "I'm trying to work."

"Oh, of course," Quark said. "How goes your investigation?"

Cenn kept his eyes on his padd. "I can't discuss it."

"You're looking into those mercenaries, right? I understand most of them were transferred to Bajor this morning. The ones you held on to must be *very* interesting."

Cenn looked at him, his eyes narrowing. "I said, I can't discuss it."

Quark held up his hands in a gesture of acquiescence, then moved away to fill a drink order. Cenn shook his head and took a sip of his synthale before turning his attention back to his work.

Moments later, he became aware that Quark was leaning way over the bar, trying to get a look at the padd.

Cenn set the the device facedown on the bar. "Do you mind?"

"Not at all," the Ferengi answered and snatched up the padd before the major could stop him.

"Hey!" Cenn cried, grabbing Quark roughly by the lapel.

Quark's eyes shifted from the padd's screen to the fist in which the fabric of his gaudy jacket was gathered, and when he looked up at Cenn, he actually had the temerity to sound offended. "Easy on the material, son. Where I come from, jackets like this don't come cheap."

"Give me back the padd, *now*," Cenn said through his teeth, one hand on the butt of his holstered phaser.

"All right, all right," the Ferengi said soothingly.

"Here you go." Quark handed back the device, looking at Cenn as if he was appraising a new piece of merchandise, which only infuriated Cenn more.

Quark slowly moved away and opened a drawer under the bar. He started rifling through it, occasionally taking out an isolinear rod and holding it up to the light while he spoke. "You know, Major, I realize you're still new here and probably under a great deal of pressure, but as you may have heard, I've been on this station a very long time—longer, in fact, than anyone else since the Cardassians left." Apparently finding the rod he was looking for, Quark turned and inserted it into the companel behind the bar, tapping in a sequence of keys. When he finished, he returned to the bar and leaned toward Cenn. "And do you know what I've learned in all my time here?"

Cenn glared at him. "Do I look like I give a *kosst*?"

Quark went on as if he hadn't spoken. "It's this: In a crisis, help can sometimes— Wait, I've got a better one: When in doubt, tug on the lobes of your elders. You know, that's not bad. I should write that one down." He started looking around for a stylus.

"It's a wonder no one's killed you yet," Cenn muttered.

Quark waved the idea away. "People love the bartender; Rule of Acquisition Number 147. Why do you think I took up mixology in the first place?"

The companel behind the Ferengi chimed, and Quark offered him another toothy smile before going to check it.

Cenn decided he'd had enough. *No* foraiga *is worth this.* He got off his stool and announced, "I'm leaving, Mister Quark. Please tell Treir that I canceled my order." He started to walk out.

"You haven't paid for your synthale," the bartender reminded him.

Cenn stopped, cursing under his breath as he turned back. "Fine. Take my thumbscan so I can get out of here."

"That won't be necessary," Quark said, downloading data from the companel into a padd of his own. "Much as I detest the custom, the first drink is always on the house."

I should just shoot him and be done with it. "Then why did you—?"

"Because," said the Ferengi, presenting the padd to Cenn, "I needed another moment so I could show you this."

The major looked at the device. He blinked in surprise, unable at first to believe what he was seeing. Quark had evidently run the names from Cenn's padd and, according to the results, somehow established that the four mercenaries were linked by one key past experience that he knew wasn't shared by any of the other mercs: they had, over the last eight years, each been convicted of assorted crimes against the Cardassian Union. Moreover, they were all interned in the same detention facility and had until today been numbered among the many thousands of inmates who were believed killed when the Jem'Hadar had started slaughtering Cardassians during the final days of the Dominion War.

"Letau," Cenn said, reading the prison's name off the padd. He looked up at the Ferengi. "How'd you do this? The Cardassians weren't able to help me."

"Yeah, that's a shock. They're *so* organized these days," Quark scoffed. "It's a wonder Laren is able to get as much as she does from Gul Macet half the time. Lucky for you, though, I still have a few links to a little-known records office in the Cardassian justice system. What's left of it, anyway. And in my experience," he added, tapping the padd with a blue fingernail, "people like this often meet in prison."

Cenn was speechless. Quark might have actually provided him with the break he needed.

Treir returned, setting down a steaming plate of *foraiga* and offering Cenn a smile and a wink before she went away again. "Oops," the Ferengi said. "Looks like it's too late to cancel your order."

"No problem," Cenn told him, eagerly retaking his stool. "Thank you, Quark. I mean that. I owe you one."

Quark smiled in a manner that Cenn found distinctly unsettling. "I'm so glad we got off on the right foot."

"We aren't going behind the captain's back," Dax said, trying to keep the irritation out of her voice.

"I didn't say we were," insisted Nog. "I said it *feels* like we're going behind the captain's back."

"We're preparing options for her, Nog," Bowers said. "That's what good officers are supposed to do."

"We're just doing it discreetly," said Tenmei, her tone conveying how dubious she thought their proposed undertaking was.

"It isn't as if we're having a secret meeting," Julian said, nodding toward Kira's office, where the captain had been on the comm for the last twenty minutes. "We're in plain view of her, for heaven's sake."

"And if she wants to know what we're discussing, I'll tell her," Dax said, standing at the head of the ops situation table, around which the five of them had gathered. "But she has enough on her mind right now. It's our job to anticipate her needs, and the more we can do in that regard without troubling her, the better it'll be for all concerned."

"So what's the plan?" Bowers asked.

"First things first," Dax said, turning to Julian. "How do things stand with the neuro-pulse device you and Nog created to reverse Taran'atar's brainwashing?"

"We learned a great deal from the data cache Commander Vaughn brought back from Harkoum," Julian said. "Working with Ensign Leishman, I've been able to make considerable refinements on our original design."

"How considerable?"

"Leishman believes she isn't far off from being able to modify combadges to generate the pulse on command. It'll still be necessary to activate it within five meters of Taran'atar in order to have any effect, but it'll no longer be necessary to carry an unwieldy extra piece of equipment, as it was with our prototype."

"Good work," Dax said. "Let me know when you're ready. Nog, how's your progress on the dimensional comlink?"

"Slow going, to be honest," Nog said. "We can't replicate the dimensional transport unit, so I have to try building one from scratch based on the specs, then run simulations to confirm that it works, *then* take it apart again to adapt it for communications."

"Dimensional transport unit?" Tenmei asked.

"It's the modular device that Smiley—the alternate Miles O'Brien—invented to bridge our two universes using the transporter system," Dax explained. "It duplicates the effect that caused the very first crossover more than a hundred years ago."

"I think Taran'atar might have used something like that

on Harkoum," Tenmei said. "Cylindrical, with a flashing red light? It fit in the palm of his hand."

"That's it exactly," Dax confirmed. "During one of our encounters with the alternate universe, the Chief had the chance to study one up close. He made scans of the device and stored them in the station's computer system. It was one of the classified files Taran'atar got into before all this started." She turned back to Nog. "Why can't you replicate it?"

Nog sighed. "It's a complex and delicately balanced piece of equipment. None of our scanners are capable of the quantum resolution necessary to re-create one that actually works. Building one from unreplicated components is the only real option, which I suppose is what Taran'atar must have done."

Dax sighed. "Okay. Do the best you can. But I also want you to construct a second working unit so that we can use it to make crossovers ourselves, if the captain decides that's necessary. Sam, I want you to work with Nog on assembling the devices. Familiarize yourself with the principles, see if you can develop a defense against it."

Bowers's brow furrowed. "You expecting an attack?"

"At this point, I have no *khest'n* clue *what* to expect," Dax said, unintentionally using one of Curzon's preferred Klingon expletives. "I just want to be prepared for any contingency."

Bowers nodded. "I'll see what I can do."

"All right, both of you get to work. You too, Julian. Dismissed." As the tac officer, the engineer, and the doctor headed for the turbolift, Dax turned to Tenmei. "Prynn, I want you to work on the *Rio Grande*."

Tenmei blinked. "But, Lieutenant, there's nothing wrong with the *Rio Grande*," the pilot said.

"I know that, Ensign," Dax said. "I remember Chief O'Brien saying the same thing seven years ago, after the ship returned from its unexpected trip to the alternate universe. You see, we know of two ways that passage between the two universes is possible. We've been discussing one of them—using Smiley's invention. The other was the fluke of somehow winding up there during a passage the *Rio Grande* made through the wormhole. Somewhere in that runabout's systems there has to be a clue to why that crossover happened. I want you to find it."

Tenmei swallowed, but then her gaze sharpened. "You can count on me, Lieutenant."

"I know I can, Prynn. Now off you go."

As Tenmei exited ops, Dax leaned forward against the situation table and sighed heavily. She glanced toward the captain's office, but Kira was still on the comm. *I'm doing what I can, Nerys. I just hope it's enough.*

Dax turned toward the sound of an arriving turbolift, and rising into ops was a sight to bring a puzzled grin to her face.

Benjamin?

Student and protégé to Curzon, commanding officer to Jadzia and Ezri, and stalwart friend to all three of Dax's most recent hosts, Ben Sisko smiled when he saw her, his Starfleet combadge looking strangely incongruous against the multicolored vest he wore over a bright yellow civilian tunic.

"My gods, who dresses you these days?" she teased as he descended the steps into the command well. He embraced her warmly as she stepped around the situation table.

"No cracks about the vest, Old Man," he told her. "I'll have you know it's my daughter's favorite."

"Rebecca isn't even four months old yet," Dax pointed out.

"And already she has impeccable taste," her friend said proudly.

Dax shook her head. "What are you still doing here, Benjamin? I thought you'd have returned to Bajor by now."

"There are still a few errands I need to take care of," Sisko said, glancing toward Kira's office. "How have things been around here?"

"They've been better," Dax admitted, and then she lowered her voice. "Have you heard about Commander Vaughn?"

Sisko nodded. "Word's gotten around."

"Well, I'm glad you're here. If you ask me, Kira really needs a friend right now."

"Most captains do, more often than they let on." Benjamin looked back toward the office. "But especially at times like this."

"I just got off the comm with the Vedek Assembly," Kira said as her office doors closed behind Sisko. "Thanks for speaking to them on my behalf."

Sisko shook his head. "I'm just relieved you aren't asking to use the Orb of Time again. I still have nightmares about the last time. Are you sure you want to do this?"

Kira nodded, making a neat stack of the padds on her desk. "The Orb of Memory may be my best shot at finding out the truth. There's too much riding on the decision I need to make for me to be wrong." She paused, then said, "I was going to leave in a few minutes. Do you want a lift back to Bajor?"

"Not just yet. There are a few people I want to see. Most likely I'll still be here when you get back."

Kira stepped around the desk. "You probably don't want to hear this, but I'm going to tell you anyway. I want to thank you again for staying close while I got back on my feet." She averted her eyes; she couldn't help herself. "After what happened . . . it's been hard for me to trust anyone, even the people I've known for years."

"That's understandable," Sisko said. "But you know you're going to have to deal with those feelings, probably a lot sooner than you want to. You've got good people here."

"So what do you do when one of them disappoints you?"

"There's no single answer to that. Each situation is unique, and you just have to work through them as best you can." Silence settled between them, and Sisko said quietly, "Scuttlebutt is that you relieved Vaughn of duty over his handling of the Taran'atar pursuit."

"That's right," Kira replied, more sharply than she intended, and when he said nothing else, she prompted him. "Is there a question you wanted to ask me?"

Sisko shrugged. "That depends."

"On what?"

Sisko smiled, his eyes shining almost mischievously. "On whether or not you're in an answering mood."

Kira sighed. "I'm not reconsidering the station's command structure, if that's what you want to know. I'd have to be quite the hypocrite to fire my exec for acting impulsively and on his own authority, wouldn't I?"

"If you're expecting me to disagree—"

"Thanks a lot." Kira leaned heavily on her desk, bowing her head in sudden weariness. "I guess this is just the Prophets' way of balancing things out. What's that human word for it? Karma?" She looked up at him. "I accused

Vaughn of making it personal, and he asked me if I'd ever done the same. Me. Suddenly all I could think about was Silaran Prin."

Sisko's eyebrow rose slightly at the name, and Kira knew well the memories she had conjured for him: Prin, a Cardassian civilian, had been one of the survivors of a bombing Kira had carried out during the occupation, blowing up a gul's residence in retaliation for the execution of fifteen Bajoran farmers. Nearly four years ago, Prin resurfaced and began assassinating the former members of Kira's resistance cell. And Kira, despite being in the final days of her surrogate pregnancy, had gone after the mad Cardassian alone, putting herself and the O'Briens' unborn baby at risk but ending his killing spree.

"You know, looking back, I honestly don't know how you ever put up with me," Kira confessed. "Seriously . . . How did you and I ever get past some of the stunts I pulled over the years?"

"What are you hoping I'll say, Nerys? That the chain of command isn't that important? You don't get off the hook that easily," Sisko said. "But what I think every captain eventually comes to understand is that there will always be some things that transcend the discipline of the service. It isn't until a captain and first officer face that kind of situation that whatever bond they have is put to the test. Because the bottom line is that you either trust your exec, or you don't. And while I won't deny that you and I hit a few bumps over the years, there was never a moment when I didn't trust you."

Sisko paused before continuing. "But we both know this isn't about you and me, or even you and Vaughn. This is about guilt."

"Guilt?" Kira asked.

"Yes, guilt. The guilt you're feeling. The misguided notion that all this was ultimately your fault, either because you were out of commission, or because Taran'atar was compromised on your watch . . . or because you think it was a mistake to trust him in the first place."

Kira closed her eyes and blew a breath out through her nose. She pushed off the desk and walked to the great window behind her chair, folding her arms as she stared out into space.

"That's it, isn't it?" Sisko asked gently. "You're angry with yourself for allowing Taran'atar to stay aboard the station."

Kira didn't answer right away, just lost herself among the stars. "I keep going over and over what happened, thinking about Julian's certainty that Taran'atar was under some kind of control. And I keep asking myself . . . what if he's wrong?"

"You think Taran'atar acted on his own?"

"No," Kira answered. "But I do wonder if he acted entirely against his will. Maybe what happened was inevitable from the start. And maybe I was a fool to think Taran'atar was ever anything more than what I always feared he'd turn out to be . . . a ticking bomb."

"Odo seemed to think otherwise," Sisko pointed out.

"I know. And that's why for the last nine months I fought every instinct I had about this." Kira made a fist and raised it to eye-level, thumping the edge of it against the window. "But not a day has passed in all that time when I didn't have my doubts about his hopes for the Jem'Hadar. Five years ago, when he tried to tame that Jem'Hadar child, I knew, *I knew* it would turn out badly. The kid had no self-control, no way to overcome his programming, no matter how much Odo tried to help him."

"Then what made you accept Taran'atar?"

Kira focused on Sisko's reflection in the smooth surface of the viewport. "Because he was older, more experienced, more in control of himself. He had no need for ketracel-white and he acted against his own kind to protect me and help save the station. I thought if any of them could overcome their hardwiring, he would." She paused, turning to face her old friend. "And I accepted him because Odo asked me to. Because Taran'atar was a living connection to the man I love, and no matter what doubts I had, I couldn't reject him." Again she shook her head. "I was a fool."

Sisko started pacing the office, his expression thoughtful. "I go into battle to reclaim my life," he murmured.

Kira frowned and turned to face him. "What?"

He stopped at the edge of the desk and folded his arms. "Do you remember the story I told you after we retook the station during the war, about the Jem'Hadar troops we faced on that planet in the dark nebula?"

"Where you crashed the Dominion ship."

Sisko nodded. "The unit we encountered was led by a Jem'Hadar third named Remata'klan. Taran'atar actually reminds me a lot of him. Remata'klan felt compelled to obey his Vorta and lead a suicide attack against us. They didn't stand a chance. I tried to persuade him to surrender, to show him that he could choose not to follow his orders instead of throwing his life away for what he called 'the order of things.' He told me it wasn't really his life, and that it never was."

"What are you saying?" Kira asked with rising anger. "The Jem'Hadar aren't responsible for their actions?"

"No," Sisko said evenly. "But I've had a lot of time to think about Remata'klan . . . and Omet'iklan, and other individual Jem'Hadar this crew has encountered over the years. I've wondered what it meant for them to be so obviously intelligent yet seemingly denied free will. And I've thought about that oath they recite before they go into battle, the one they start by declaring that they're dead."

"I go into battle to reclaim my life," Kira echoed.

Sisko nodded. "I used to think it was just a ritual, something imposed upon them by the Founders or the Vorta to keep them focused on their objectives."

"I take it you don't believe that anymore?"

"Think about it, Nerys. If the Jem'Hadar really believe their lives are not their own, then how can they ever hope to reclaim them? Unless the battle they're talking about in their oath—the one that they're really fighting—is with themselves, to overcome the Founders' programming and to find the strength of will for self-determination."

"I'm not sure I understand what you're getting at."

"I'm suggesting that maybe Odo didn't send Taran'atar here to learn peace," Sisko said. "He sent him here to win the war against himself."

"Does that distinction even matter anymore?" Kira asked bitterly, turning to gaze out the viewport again. "Either way, he failed."

"Are you sure about that?"

"He nearly killed me and Ro both."

"And yet he spared Tenmei and Vaughn. Maybe he tried to fight what was done to him. Maybe he's still fighting it." At her expression, he added, "Don't look so surprised. I may be on leave, but I'm not out of the loop. I read the after-action reports of the mission to Harkoum. Tenmei is a resourceful officer, but there's little doubt in my mind that she couldn't have survived her attempts to escape or overpower Taran'atar unless he was fighting every instinct to kill her that he possessed. The same holds true for Vaughn."

"Then why did he try to kill me?" Tried? He *had* killed her; Kira had flatlined on the operating table, revived only through Julian's efforts.

"Nerys, you look exactly like the woman who controls him. Did you ever consider that maybe he wasn't trying to kill *you*, but lashed out because on some level he *knows* he's been compromised, and he associates your face with what's been done to him?"

My face . . . Kira stared at her reflection for a long moment, her *pagh* in turmoil. Her fingertips brushed her chest, found the spot where her new heart beat steadily beneath her uniform. She imagined she could feel her regenerated flesh, her re-fused sternum. Her thoughts turned to Ro, who still hadn't regained the use of her legs after the savage blow that had shattered her spine.

Had Laren sustained those injuries simply because, in his conflicted state of mind, she had been standing in the way when Taran'atar tried to kill the woman he mistook for his real tormentor—the one who had made him her slave?

If and when Taran'atar stood before her again, what would she do? Even if Sisko was right, could they ever move beyond what had happened?

5

Feeling the sharp sting of branches whipping her face as she crashed through a thicket along the slope of the hillside, Kira knew that between the trail of torn leaves, smashed bushes, broken tree limbs, and the heavy boot-prints she left in the frosted earth, even a blind *batos* couldn't fail to track her. There was no way she was going to evade the Cardassian troops on her tail much longer.

But that's the point, isn't it? she thought. *That's why they call it a diversion.*

With any luck, Furel and Lupaza had made the most of the opportunity she'd given them. Kira didn't need to keep the Cardassians occupied forever; just long enough for her teammates to make their way back to the caves and warn the other members of Shakaar's resistance cell.

Her heart beat as if it were about to burst from her chest. Her labored breath was loud as thunder in her ears.

But she could no longer hear her pursuers, and that was a problem.

She continued to push through the forest, the thin branches making small cuts on the edge of her weaponless right hand as she ran. In her left she kept a firm grasp on the butt of her phaser. Without slowing, she swung her arm back and fired four shots the way she'd come, then quickly took cover behind a thick tree trunk and listened.

Cardassian weapons fire answered her. She heard distant shouts, followed by the far-off noise of armored troops lumbering through the forest. Kira allowed herself a weary grin, then took off again.

More enemy fire split the air, getting closer to her line of travel. Fortunately, after an entire winter of lying low in the Dahkur hills, Kira had become intimately familiar with the terrain, and she already had another good reason to change direction. There was a clearing coming up on the left, under a steep ridge. If she could get there fast enough, she could gain the higher ground before the Cardassians caught up with her. From there she could pick off a good number of them as they emerged from the forest.

Her white-knuckle grip on her phaser was threatening to become a cramp. *C'mon, Nerys, stay loose or it's all over.* She willed her hand to relax just enough to ease the ache, then spared a glance at the weapon, noting in dismay that its power cell was almost depleted. *Four shots couldn't have used up* that *much energy! Gotta be a defective cell. Great, just great . . .*

The familiar rattle made by the Cardassians' armor as they pursued her no longer seemed as distant as it had been only minutes ago.

Up ahead she saw the tree line. If she remembered correctly, it would be about twenty paces across the clearing to the ridge wall, then a climb of about five *linnipate*s up the steep slope. With a running start she might actually make it to the top before the Cardassians found her and shot her in mid-ascent. Fortunately, the leafy trees not only interfered with enemy targeting, they made much slower going for the less nimble soldiers in their stiff uniforms. It was one of the things that made the hills so effective a hiding place—hardy, year-round foliage. Toss in the freezing temperatures, and the terrain was about as disadvantageous to the Cardassians as it could get.

Kira burst through the tree line and kept running as the ridge wall came into view, her feet splashing as she dashed through a shallow stream of new meltwater that bisected the clearing. She knew even before she slipped that she was going too fast.

Three paces were as far as she got. On the fourth her left foot slid off a smooth, slick stone and twisted. Pain shot through her leg as she pitched forward. She instinctively threw out her arms but still wound up face first in the icy stream. Her chin and right cheek struck hard against some rocks just below the surface, the impact like a hammer blow. Her eyes squeezed shut against the bite of the bitterly cold water, and her head swam—

Keep moving! Get up you idiot get up now!

Half blind and freezing, Kira scrambled on all fours the rest of the way across the stream, pain flaring in her ankle as she moved. She stumbled on the rocky ground, unable to get to her feet; the icewater that had soaked into her clothes stiffened her joints and threw off her balance. She could hear indistinct shouts growing steadily louder and knew the Cardassians were almost upon her. Still, if she could just trust her phaser—

Prophets, no!

She had lost her grip on the weapon when she hit the water and had been too distracted by her injuries and her rising desperation to realize that it was no longer in her hand. With a grunt she flung herself back toward the frigid stream, crawling on her elbows toward the half-submerged pistol, not sure if it would even work anymore. She reached out and grabbed it in both hands, her numb fingers wrapping around the grip as she rolled onto her left shoulder and aimed toward the tree line—

Six Cardassians stormed the clearing in a broad arc, one trooper roughly every *linnipate*, each one with his rifle raised. No way to get them all. Maybe no way to get *any* before one of them got *her*.

Kira let out a feral scream and opened fire anyway.

The air above her erupted with phaser fire as a spray of orange beams lanced five of the Cardassians at once. The sixth roared and returned fire, aiming not at Kira, but beyond her, his shot blazing far over her head. Three more beams converged on the soldier, and he fell over dead with his compatriots.

She stared at them from the stream, breathing heavily and shivering, vaguely aware that she still held down the trigger of her weapon and that nothing issued from it. She heard someone yelling: "—go get her and get back up here, fast! We need to start moving now! Latha, make sure they're dead!"

Kira's phaser fell from her fingers, slipping beneath the surface of the water. Still groggy, she rolled onto her right shoulder and looked across the clearing. There on top of the ridge, barking orders, was Shakaar. At his side, keeping watch, was Lupaza. Furel was sliding down the slope toward her, while Latha and their medic, Gantt, were already down and running in her direction.

Kira struggled to a sitting position as Gantt got to her first and helped her out of the water. Latha ignored them both as he leapt past to check on the fallen Cardassians, the wide grooves of his thick-soled boots proof against the treacherous stones beneath the stream. She heard him kicking the Cardassian weapons away from the bodies as Gantt got her to dry ground. Furel met them halfway, throwing his long, woolly coat across Kira's shoulders and supporting her as she hobbled to the base of the ridge, where Gantt performed a quick check of her injuries.

"How is she?" Shakaar called down.

"Not as bad as she looks," Gantt said. He wiped at her chin, and she could feel embedded pebbles coming loose. His fingers came away slick with blood. There was pain where he touched her cheek. He produced a small light from his pocket and waved the beam across her pupils. "Looks like cuts and bruises for the most part. No broken bones, and she doesn't appear to have a concussion."

"What about the ankle?" Furel asked. "I thought I saw her foot go wrong when she took that spill."

Gently removing her boot, Gantt's hands probed her injured foot and lower leg. Kira winced, but only slightly.

"Rotation's good," Gantt said, then slipped the boot back on. "What do you think, Nerys? Can you stand?"

Letting go of Furel's shoulder, Kira put her weight against the injured foot. "Sore," she admitted. "But I can travel."

"You sure?" Furel said. "I can carry you—"

Kira glared at him. "Nobody's carrying me."

Latha walked by at that moment with a half-dozen

Cardassian rifles strapped to his back. "Not a bad catch, Nerys. You make good bait."

"*Phekk* you," Kira snapped.

"You wish." Latha laughed as he went up the slope.

"She's fine!" Furel called up to Shakaar.

Kira shoved past Furel and started to climb. "I'm keeping the coat," she told him.

"Good," he snapped back. "Just don't forget to feed the fleas."

Near the top of the ridge, Kira was met by Shakaar's outstretched hand. She accepted it, and he pulled her up the rest of the way. "You and your damn stunts," he said, the disapproval in his voice matching his expression.

Kira's eyes narrowed. "You're welcome," she answered, and limped past him, feeling his eyes on her as she and Lupaza took the lead on the long hike back to the caves.

The cell members back at their base greeted Kira warmly on her return. Bre'yel, a black-tressed teenager who was currently their youngest member, seemed especially pleased that she had survived. Not surprising; Bre'yel was orphaned prior to joining the underground, and tended to look up to Kira as her mentor if not her surrogate mother, despite the fact that Kira was only three years her senior. Kira told herself she put up with it only because Bre'yel seemed sensible enough not to push her attachment to the point of being a pest, though Kira had recently overheard Latha express the opinion that the only reason she tolerated Bre'yel's attentions was that the girl reminded Kira of Dakahna Vaas.

Kira didn't like to think about Vaas.

Lupaza helped her find some dry clothes: an orange thermal body stocking with rips in the knees and elbows, worn brown leggings, and a child's red wool sweater that annoyingly failed to reach her wrists or her waist. Kira laid out her damp clothes, including Furel's mangy coat, on the cave floor to dry.

Gantt saw to her cuts and abrasions with a dermal regenerator, then bandaged her ankle. He told her to spend a couple of hours next to a heating unit, preferably getting some sleep, before she returned to work. Kira gave herself fifteen minutes, sipping a cup of hot water that Bre'yel brought to her while she surveyed the activity in the cave to determine where she could do the most good. Finishing the water, Kira tied off her tangled hair and decided the first thing she needed to do was help Latha and Roku sort through their stockpile of weapons.

Everyone was packing up. The close call with the patrol had confirmed the growing belief among them that their cell was no longer safe. It was clear now that the Cardassians had been concentrating their most recent sensor sweeps within ten *kellipates* of the caves—too close for anyone's comfort. Making matters worse, their stores were running dangerously low; few medical supplies, less food, and the problem with Kira's power cell led to the unpleasant discovery that close to sixty percent of their energy weapons were similarly defective. If the Cardassians found them now, it was all over. Shakaar had decided they needed to find a new place to hide, and fast.

It was for that reason that Kira, Lupaza, and Furel had ventured out—the Cardassian security grid functioned on a network of sensor towers scattered all over Bajor, watching the skies for resistance raiders and the ground for unauthorized Bajorans crossing into restricted areas.

The trio had risked themselves to blow up one of the towers, and in doing so had succeeded in blinding the security grid to this part of Dahkur, at least temporarily. The cell now had a finite window of time in which to resupply itself and find a safer hiding place.

Kira was transferring a crate of defective power cells to their discard area when she saw Shakaar poring over a map with Furel and Lupaza. Still fuming over his remark on the ridge, she was unable to walk by without bringing it up. "It wasn't a stunt."

Shakaar kept his eyes on the map. "This isn't the time, Nerys."

"Somebody needed to lure the Cardassians away from the caves. I was the fastest. I stood the best chance of keeping them busy so Furel and Lupaza could get back and warn you."

"And we still had to go out there and save your ass, didn't we?"

"I didn't *ask* to be saved," Kira fired back, throwing the crate down onto the rubbish pile. "I was ready to give my life for this team."

"A little too ready."

Kira gaped. "What the *kosst* is that supposed to mean? Wait, you know what? Don't even answer. I made the right call under the circumstances. How you can take me to task for that, especially when my 'stunt' was the only reason your ambush succeeded—*after* we'd already managed to take down the sensor tower—is beyond me."

"You gotta admit," Lupaza told Shakaar gently, "it worked out pretty well."

Shakaar shot her the look he used when he expected people to shut up; Lupaza held up her hands and walked away. For his part, Furel kept frowning at the map, seeming oblivious to the argument. Shakaar tapped his arm. "Give us a moment, would you?"

"What?" Furel looked up at Shakaar, then at Kira, then back at Shakaar. "Oh. Sure thing. You two take your time. I'll be checking the proximity scanners if you need me. Just do me a favor and aim away from the rations if you decide to start shooting each other." That earned him two stern glances as he folded up the map, handed it to Shakaar, and got out of the line of fire.

"Look," Shakaar began, turning back to Kira. "You did good out there today, I'm not denying that. But you seem to be taking a lot of risks lately. More than usual, even for *this* outfit. This group has been together a long time, and we've lost too many good people along the way to put up with anyone's recklessness."

Kira shook her head in disbelief. "This is about Dakahna, isn't it?"

Shakaar folded his arms. "I never mentioned Dakahna. But isn't it interesting that she came to mind?"

"If you're gonna blame me for what happened to her, then just say it!"

"*Kosst* it, Nerys, *nobody* blames you for what happened to Dakahna—except you! It wasn't your fault. We were damn lucky more of us didn't die on that raid, and I don't want to lose anyone else if it can be avoided."

Kira's mind went back to the day that still haunted her nights: Four armored skimmers and ten times that number of footsoldiers had surged over the rise before the cell even realized that they'd walked into a trap—the "survey station" they'd gone out to hit was a fake—bait to draw some too-cocky resistance fighters into an ambush. It had been one of the Cardassians' earliest tests of the security grid.

Latha was the first to react, lobbing two of his home-made plasma charges toward the advancing strikeforce even as Shakaar shouted for the cell to fall back. The Cardassians broke formation as one bomb exploded in their midst, and then fell into complete disarray when the second explosive landed in the path of one of the skimmers. The underside of the guncraft erupted into flames as the charge went off, and the skimmer went spinning out of control into more than a dozen soldiers.

Kira and Dakahna had taken cover behind some rocks to return fire, but it wasn't until after Nerys had started running again that she realized Vaas was no longer with her.

Kira forced the memory down, blinking back tears. "Aren't you the one who's always saying we're in this fight for a cause more important than our lives?"

"That doesn't mean I expect us to throw those lives away," Shakaar told her.

"That's not what I was doing!"

"Are you sure?"

Kira resisted the urge to slug him, but only just. "How can you even ask me that?"

Shakaar glanced over his shoulder. Some of the others were staring at them, reacting to the raised voices. "Get back to work," he snapped. "Mobara, that skimmer had damn well better be ready for the move. If we have to leave it behind, I'm leaving you with it." As Mobara hastily put his goggles back on and turned his attention back to the skimmer's open engine compartment, Shakaar gestured Kira toward a more secluded section of the caves.

"All right, let me ask you something else," he said softly. "Where do you see yourself after the Cardassians are gone?"

"What's that got to do with—?"

"Hey, humor me. It's a simple question."

Kira scoffed. "I don't know. I'm more worried right now about kicking the Cardassians out. I don't exactly have time to think beyond that."

"*That's* my point," Shakaar said. "You're living for the fight. That's it. That's as far as your imagination takes you. You've forgotten why you joined the cause in the first place. For you the fight has become an end unto itself. You don't see yourself existing beyond it."

Kira started to turn away. "I don't have to put up with this."

"Actually, Nerys, you do," Shakaar said, his tone stopping her in her tracks. "All of us talk about what we'll do once the Cardassians are gone. Mobara sees himself working on spacecraft. Gantt wants to travel. Bre'yel wants to help orphans find new families. I want a farm of my own. Lupaza—well, she seems to change her mind every week, and Furel's just happy to do whatever Lupaza does. But the point is, every one of us is living for a time when this war will be over. Except you."

"Oh, please. You think because I don't daydream of someday tilling soil like you, there's something wrong with me? That I have a death wish?"

"Maybe not yet," said Shakaar. "But that's the direction you're headed, and I won't stand for it. Bajor has already produced more than its share of martyrs. If that's what's in your heart, you're with the wrong cell. We're fighting to live, not fighting to die."

Kira held his gaze for a long moment before responding, hardly daring to consider that what he was saying might be true. She thought about her most recent missions, the decisions she had made, the risks she had taken, the close calls she had survived only by luck or the will of the Prophets. After all the years she'd followed Shakaar in the long, hard struggle for Bajor's freedom, had she really lost sight of the reason that struggle was so important? Fighting for the end of Cardassian rule was one thing, planning for the time after it was something else entirely. Kira lived by the belief that the occupation was evil, and that evil could not be allowed to stand, to go unchallenged. But when she thought about all the things she'd done in the name of that ideal—when the image of Vaas falling to enemy fire haunted her nightmares, the sound of her voice screaming Kira's name as the Cardassians stepped up their attack, forcing Kira and the others to withdraw—she wondered how she could ever move beyond them. The truth was, she *didn't* think about the future, ever, because part of her believed she didn't deserve one. Not after so many moral compromises, so many terrible choices . . . so much death at her own hands.

How could the Prophets ever forgive that?

"That's not what's in my heart, Edon," she told Shakaar, wishing it were true.

"I hope not," he said quietly. "We need you." He turned away, suddenly looking embarrassed. "Just think about what I said, okay?"

"All right. . . . I will."

Shakaar nodded curtly but seemed to have a hard time making eye contact with her now.

Kira smirked. "And since I didn't say it before . . . Thanks for saving my ass. Again. I owe you one."

Shakaar finally met her eyes and shrugged. "I'll add it to the list."

• • •

The following morning, Kira's ankle felt much better, and Shakaar called a group meeting to hand out assignments. Lupaza felt sure she knew someone in Hathon who could discreetly procure a decent supply of power cells and volunteered to go seek him out. Furel naturally insisted that he accompany her. It fell to Gantt, Chavin, and Bre'yel to make their way into the valley, slip into Jinara township, and convince their contacts there to load them up with as much in the way of dried foodstuffs and medical supplies as they could carry back into the hills.

Shakaar tasked Kira, Klin, Ornak, and Latha to scout out a new base of operations in one of the neighboring hills. They split up to cover more territory, and because their biosignatures would be harder to detect individually than if they stayed together. Shakaar and the remaining members of the cell continued preparations for their relocation, and arranged a warm reception if the Cardassians got too close to the caves. He said he wanted everyone back to base and ready to move in seven days' time.

On her third day out, and with little to show for it, Kira was two hills east of the caves, her search bringing her just within the perimeter of the Bestri woods. Her reconnaissance had yielded nothing promising in the way of new base sites, leading her to hope that at least one of the others was having better luck.

She paused to check the Cardassian comm unit on her wrist. Weapons had not been the only equipment Latha had recovered from the corpses near the ridge; the Cardassians' communicator cuffs made excellent proximity detectors in autoscan mode, as long as their transponders were disabled. Any military communications within half a *kellipate* of her position would come through loud and clear, letting her know she needed to get moving. For the past three days, however, the unit had remained gratifyingly silent.

Satisfied that it was still cycling through the most common frequencies used by the Union's infantry, Kira decided she could afford a short break from her recon to fuel up with a few bites of dried meat from her ration pack and a gulp of water. Sitting on the ground against a large rock, she considered her situation while she chewed. These woods weren't an obvious place to look for a new hideout; the terrain lacked the dramatic unevenness and deep cracks that defined the upper hills. But if she recalled correctly, Bestri was also home to a pair of ravines, half a *kellipate* apart, that were linked by a long subterranean cave. It would be a problematic site for a base, to be sure; it might not be a place the Cardassians would think to look for them, but it was relatively easy to blunder across and readily accessible. It probably had plenty of room, but also twice the usual number of entrances to defend. The potential for flooding also couldn't be ignored. Kira held little hope that it would suit their needs but thought she should check it out anyway, just to be sure.

She brought her canteen to her lips for a final sip before setting out once more, when she suddenly got the sense that she wasn't alone. Whether it was a flicker of motion in her peripheral vision or a faint vibration in the air that she registered only subconsciously, she could never be sure. She knew only that the fine hairs on her skin were suddenly standing on end. She froze and listened, her eyes alertly panning the dense forest until she caught a glimpse of gray in the distance.

The lone Cardassian was partially obscured by the

trees but seemed to be lying flat on his stomach, as if he had just stopped in the act of crawling. Had he spotted her? She forced herself to remain still, grateful she still held her phaser but knowing that it might not make any difference; she might already be in his sights. But if she wasn't—

His arm moved.

Kira dived to the right and fired. The Cardassian screamed, but not in a way she had ever heard before. Pieces of him jerked back from his central mass and yelped as they disappeared into the brush.

What the kosst *. . . ?*

Kira stared, unable at first to wrap her mind around what she thought she was seeing. Then the scene resolved itself, and with a sick feeling in her gut she crept forward to survey her handiwork.

It was no Cardassian soldier she had slain. Lying dead at Kira's feet on the forest floor was an adult *hara* cat, its gray fur burned black where the phaser beam had struck it. The kittens it had been nursing had scattered in terror when Kira shot it, probably hiding in the underbrush somewhere nearby, waiting until they felt safe again and could return to their mother.

Prophets, what have I done . . . ?

Tears were streaming down Kira's cheeks. She wiped at them angrily, cursing herself for becoming emotional, for the sorrow she felt toward a dumb beast and its orphaned young when her people continued to be oppressed, and abused, and killed like—

Like animals.

How many Bajorans had died thus far under the occupation? The Cardassians kept a count somewhere, she was certain—some obscene ledger where every interroga-

tion victim, every combat fatality, every death from starvation, sickness, and slave labor, every murder, and every
suicide was duly noted, indexed, and cross-referenced in
exacting detail. It was a point of pride to them, after all.
But they also kept such information to themselves. Their
official public statements on occupation-related mor-
tality were few and far between. Those they did release
emphasized the Cardassian loss of life, as if the killing
fields of Bajorans they'd cultivated for the last thirty years
were irrelevant, as if they *weren't* turning her world into a
single mass grave. Kira had heard estimates well into the
millions, but who knew how high the death toll would
ultimately go?

*And me? Where's my ledger of victims? And not just Car-
dassians, oh no, but Bajorans too—collaborators, innocent by-
standers, the young and the old . . . the friends I had to leave
behind. Friends like Vaas.*

What accounting will you give the Prophets, Nerys?

Racked with sobs, Kira doubled over, pressing the
heels of her hands against her forehead and gritting her
teeth against the grief and rage that shook her body.

"*—nverge on sector blue-one-four. Weapons fire detected. All
units respond. Repeat—*"

The voice from the comcuff squawked in her ears, but
Kira didn't move. She imagined rooting herself where
she now stood, letting the Cardassians come to her, waiting as they came into view and opening fire on each of
them in turn, until one of them finally, mercifully, ended
the life she had come to despise so completely.

"*Squad leader, this is unit four in sector blue-one-six. Estimate ten metrics to reach rendezvous point. . .*"

Kira stared into the *hara* cat's dead eyes, envying its
state of peace, longing not to feel anything, wishing the

Prophets would simply call to her, would free her *pagh*, would let her rest.

"*Unit three here. I've found footprints. Bioscan shows traces of Bajoran DNA on some of the foliage . . .*"

She saw Shakaar's face, heard his voice: "*We're fighting to live.*"

"*This is unit two. I have visual contact. One Bajoran female directly south of my position. She's armed——*"

Without conscious thought, Kira raised her weapon and fired north: once, twice, and then a third time, each shot burning into the soldier who had gotten within twenty paces of her position. He fell back, dead before he hit the ground.

She ran.

"*Unit two, report! Unit two!*"

"*Unit three here, squad leader. Unit two is dead. I'm in pursuit of the target . . .*"

"*Shoot to disable, three. Repeat, shoot to disable. I want that Bajoran bitch alive . . .*"

"*This is unit five. I see unit two and am moving in to follow . . .*"

Kira leapt over a fallen tree and slid down a bare earth slope. She continued on through the dense forest, hoping her memories hadn't misled her, cursing herself for not staying higher up in the hills.

There!

The ravine opened up ahead of her and she ran toward it. If she could make it to the cave, she'd have a chance. Phaser shots burned the air around her as she neared the ravine's edge. She returned fire——

A final blast slammed into her chest, enveloping her in the numbing effect of a Cardassian disruptor on heavy stun. Her legs gave out and she hit the ground, her momentum carrying her over the edge of the ravine and sending her rolling down the slope into its muddy bottom.

Her vision blurred, then darkened. The sounds of the forest receded until only a voice remained.

"This is unit four. I got her."

The world was still dark when she came to. Her eyes adjusted to it slowly, recognizing the dim blue indoor lighting the Cardassians preferred, and she realized that she was lying on the floor of a holding cell, caged with three other Bajorans.

The place smelled like a sewer. The air was thick and hot, the stone floor slick with grime. The cell itself was large, and took up one half of a long stone room that was divided by a metal latticework partition complete with a sliding gate—the same variety that had sprung up all over Bajor in the past thirty-odd years, surrounding labor camps, ghettos, and anywhere else the Cardassians felt they needed to keep Bajorans penned. A heavy-looking metal door on the other end of the room, far beyond the lattice, stood closed.

All of the prisoners, including Kira, were wearing tattered clothing. Her own belongings were of course nowhere to be seen. She sat up unsteadily.

"Easy there," said her nearest cellmate, a man with small eyes and dark hair. He was gaunt and filthy. "They banged you up pretty good."

Understatement of the year. Her entire body felt sore, her head was pounding, and her tongue was a dry lump of muscle.

"Take this," the man said. He was holding what looked to be a damp rag in his hands. "Go on, take it. I know you're thirsty. You've been out cold since you got here."

Kira did as instructed and wrung the rag over her open mouth, letting water drip onto her parched tongue. It had a metallic taste, but it helped. "Thank you," she said, handing him back the rag. "Where am I?"

"Elemspur Detention Center," a woman said, walking over from the far end of the cell. Both her voice and the man's had a weary quality to them that Kira recognized: hunger. No, much more than that: starvation.

"Elemspur," Kira repeated. "Hedrikspool Province. How long . . . ?"

"They dumped you in here yesterday," the man told her. "Like I said, you've been out the entire time. My guess is they gave you a sedative. I'm Yeln. This is Alu." Yeln nodded toward the fourth prisoner, a pitifully thin man who sat on the floor against the bars of the cage, hands buried in his armpits while he rocked back and forth muttering nonsensically to himself. "That's Bakka."

"Kira," she told Yeln, but she was watching Bakka. "Is he all right?"

"He's been better. You from Dahkur?"

"That's right."

"Figured. I recognized the accent. Long way from Hedrikspool. Is that where they picked you up?"

Kira ignored the question, compelled to ask one of her own. "How long have you people been here?"

"Weeks," Yeln said.

"Months," said Alu. "Bakka's been here the longest, but he'd already lost count of the days when I got here. Now he couldn't tell us even if he knew."

Kira was gradually becoming more aware of her injuries. She felt her lower lip with her tongue. It was swollen and scabbed. She reached up and touched her forehead, feeling the puffed edges of a nasty laceration.

Alu knelt down next to her. "That must hurt," she said. "You'll get used to it, I'm sorry to say."

Kira peered at her and in the dim light she made out the fact that Alu's left eye was swollen shut, and much of her face was covered in bruises.

"Between the conditions in here and the excuses they come up with to beat us every few days, the pain becomes routine," Alu said.

"She's right," Yeln agreed, rolling up his sleeve to reveal a mutilated forearm of extensively scarred tissue. "Acid burns," he explained. "Bajorans are sent here for one reason: to suffer. Bakka there, they kept him awake and on his feet for days because they thought he knew something about the resistance, then beat him unconscious when he wouldn't talk. When he woke up, they started over. Only this time they cut off one of his fingers every time he dozed. They kept it up until they'd taken every digit on his left hand."

"Did he tell them anything?" Kira asked.

Yeln's eyes narrowed. "He didn't *know* anything. Bakka was a carpenter from a speck of a village in Musilla. The only thing he's guilty of is being Bajoran." Yeln sighed, shaking his head. "We're not even people to them. We're vermin. I'm sorry to tell you this is the worst place you could have landed yourself."

Kira said nothing.

From far away, a noise shook the air, a sound she recognized: the slide and snap of a heavy gate slamming shut. Somewhere in Elemspur, someone started screaming. Bakka suddenly became agitated and Alu went to his side, trying to comfort him.

Speaking softly, Yeln asked, "So what did you do to piss off the spoonheads?"

Kira looked away. "Wrong place at the wrong time."

Yeln grunted. "Yeah. Aren't we all?"

The days that followed were torment. Kira studied their cage for flaws that she could exploit, and remained watchful for any opportunities she could seize. She peppered her cellmates with questions, seeking any information that might help her to devise a plan of escape. Every avenue was a dead end. The fusionstone walls of the cell were solid and thick; Elemspur had been a monastery before the Cardassians took over, and the ancient artisans responsible for its construction had built it well. The floor-to-ceiling lattice and its gate were a duranium composite, beyond her ability to damage. The high ceiling was a metal slab studded with lighting elements and what she thought might be access panels, but they were all beyond her reach. The Cardassians, for their part, were mostly absent, taking precious little interest in their prisoners.

Bakka, Kira learned, was gravely ill. He had developed some kind of infection prior to her arrival, one the Cardassians seemed perfectly content to ignore. It was making him delirious and weak. He slipped into unconsciousness a day after she awoke and died shortly thereafter. It was two days more before the Cardassians saw fit to remove the body. Heralded by the metallic snap of locks releasing, the heavy cell door swung open to admit five Union soldiers. Three of them were armed and kept their disruptor rifles trained on the remaining prisoners, while the other two opened the gate, bagged up Bakka, and hauled him out like so much trash. There was nothing Kira could do but watch.

They were fed once during those first few days: through a slot at the bottom of the gate came meager portions of a rancid soup that made Kira vomit not long after she'd forced it down. A dripping pipe in one corner was the only source of water, which they collected in their hands or with torn sections of their grimy clothing. The pipe stood over a fetid drain that served as the room's only sanitation.

Day by day they grew weaker. Yeln and Alu both wept. Kira kept silent, sitting on the floor with her back to the wall, moving as little as possible to conserve her energy, taking refuge in prayer. But she was finding it increasingly difficult to think, to focus.

On the seventh day, the cell door unlocked again, and once more five Cardassian soldiers filed in. The one in front trailed what looked like heavy black rubber tubing that was attached to a cannon-like nozzle on a shoulder mount.

The next two guards took positions of readiness outside the lattice, weapons drawn, while a fourth unlocked the gate and rolled it aside. He touched a control on his cuff and one of the panels in the ceiling opened over the holding area. A long vertical pole extended down, stopping at about the height of a man. The guard then headed straight for Kira and forced her to stand, binding her wrists in manacles that were joined together by a square of metal with a small hole in the center. He pulled Kira to the middle of the cell and then raised her arms toward the pole, threading it through the hole in the shackles and locking them in place.

Another touch on the guard's cuff, and the pole retracted partway. Kira gasped as her bare feet rose up off the floor, her entire body weight becoming the burden of her manacled wrists.

The guard turned to await instruction from the fifth soldier to enter the room, a glinn who was consulting a padd near the outer door.

"Listen to me, I beg you," Yeln pleaded. "This is a terrible mistake! We haven't done anything!"

"Please!" Alu cried. "We're innocent!"

"*None* of you is innocent," the glinn told them. "Now be quiet or I'll have this entire cell gassed." When he was satisfied there would be no further outbursts, the glinn's eyes returned to the padd and he began to read aloud. "Kira Nerys, you have been found guilty of numerous acts of terrorism and homicide, the sentence for which is death. Trial to confirm this verdict has been waived. Sentence to be carried out following medical interrogation."

He nodded to the fourth guard, who produced a serrated knife from behind his back and cut Kira's soiled clothing from her body. The guard then moved aside as the Cardassian with the shoulder mount stepped forward, opened the nozzle, and blasted Kira with a jet of cold water. At such high velocity, the water pounded her like a mallet, forcing the air from her lungs. She was vaguely aware that Yeln was screaming, that the guard who had stripped her was beating him to make him stop, that Alu was trying to protect him.

Kira gritted her teeth against the punishing jet. But it wasn't just water; from the smell and taste she could tell it contained some kind of industrial cleaning agent. She forced herself not to breathe.

"That's enough," the glinn shouted over the roar.

The water ceased, and finally Kira took in air, gasping

as her lungs expanded. The manacles suddenly detached from the pole, dropping her to the floor. She fell to her knees and savored the rush of blood back into her hands.

Her relief was short lived. The fourth guard walked over to her again and pulled her up by her hair, then proceeded to drag her naked out of the cage. She could hear Alu weeping, but no sound came from Yeln. Kira prayed that he hadn't been beaten to death, but the blood she saw pooling near his head made her fear the worst.

While the Cardassian with the hose relocked the cage, the fourth guard forced her to stand before the glinn, who was eyeing her with disdain. "And here I thought you'd have more fight in you. I'm almost disappointed. Still, we won't be taking any chances." He smiled and showed her a hypospray. "This will make certain you're . . . co-operative for what comes next."

She stared into his eyes but didn't actually see them. Instead, she found her reflection in his dark irises, saw her sunken cheeks, her hollowed eyes, her long, dripping mane, and she knew with certainty that she would never leave Elemspur. That hope was gone. She was going to die . . . and so she had nothing left to lose.

As the glinn leaned in to press the hypo to her neck, Kira seized the moment and smashed her forehead into the glinn's nose with all her might.

Howling in agony, the glinn covered his face with his free hand, blood gushing between his fingers. Kira reached out with her manacled hands in time to snatch the sidearm from his holster and immediately fired it over her shoulder, into the face of the stunned fourth guard, who was still holding her by the hair. She felt a clump of it rip from her scalp as he fell backward, dead.

Her moment had come. Without the fourth guard at

her back, there was no longer an obstacle between her and the other soldiers. She spun around to face her soon-to-be executioners, turning her weapon on them, a final act of defiance so they would see her face as they killed her, and remember.

She felt the kiss of a hypospray on the back of her neck. Her weapon discharged, but the shot went wild, blasting harmlessly into one stone wall of the cell. Kira felt her muscles betray her and she collapsed, feeling only surprise that the glinn had recovered so quickly.

"Take her to Entek," the glinn shouted. "Now!"

Reality fades in and out. She never loses consciousness, but her perceptions are chaos. Colors swim. People and objects distort. Sounds slow to dull, incomprehensible groans, or blare painfully inside her skull. Moments of clarity come and go, and she clings to these as long as she can. She's aware of being gurneyed through dim stone corridors, of coming to rest in a room filled with machines. Cardassian machines. *Interrogation room?*

Dry gray hands affix metal objects to her forehead, her temples, the base of her skull. Someone very close, a woman, asks what will be done with her. A man replies, saying the body will likely be filed back in the Order archives. Kira turns her head, sees herself in another gurney next to her own. *Mirror?*

More voices talking, machines turning on, and suddenly her entire life flashes across the broken landscape of her conscious mind.

She plunges into darkness for a time and floats among shadows. They're arguing, shouting. Everything is a haze, but the shadows are slowly resolving into men: Cardassians, and one of them has a face she knows.

Dukat.

". . . You're bluffing," says the other Cardassian, a civilian.

"Don't be naïve," says Dukat.

"Even if I agreed to this, you cannot expect my superiors to believe my report without Kira's body."

Dukat moves toward an instrument tray, picks up an empty hypo, presses it against Kira's bare shoulder, and extracts a vial of blood. He pops the vial and holds it out to the civilian. "Make one."

The civilian hesitates, then takes the vial and departs. Dukat watches him go.

"Sir, this one's awake."

Kira tries to move, but her limbs feel like clay. The most she can manage is lolling her head toward the voice. She sees her reflection again, stirring, a guard standing over her.

"Sedate her," says Dukat. "She has a long journey ahead of her, and she's going to need her rest."

"What about the Bajoran?"

"I want her memories of the last seven days altered. She's to believe she's been in the Dahkur hills the entire time, hunted by Cardassians and unable to return to her unit. Give her back her clothes and her belongings and leave her somewhere safe. Make *certain* you aren't seen."

Then she feels Dukat's breath on her neck, but she doesn't see him in the mirror. Strange. Not even when he begins whispering in her ear as her world once again starts to fade. "You'll never know how close you came to your end, Nerys. I sincerely hope you won't waste this second chance. . . . You're so very much like Meru. And whether you know it or not . . . I'll always be watching."

• • •

Captain Kira's hands pushed against the doors of the Tear's ark. She slumped against it, shaken by the flood of memories that had been restored to her—the fear and self-loathing, the humiliation and degradation, the brutality and hopelessness.

She remembered the rest: finding herself back in the hills, thinking she'd somehow lost the Cardassians she believed had been hunting her for seven days straight. Lupaza's relief at finding her, saying the cell had almost given her up for dead as she led Kira to the group's new base.

And she remembered the long talk with Shakaar afterward, in which she admitted her despair to him, and how she'd almost lost the will to survive . . . until she recalled his words to her. They'd become her lifeline, and from that day forward, she fought for the future.

In a strange, sick way, she now knew she had Dukat to thank for that. By having her memories of Elemspur expunged, he had allowed her to hold on to that moment after the death of the *hara* cat, when she had decided to live. She was in his debt . . . and she hated him more than ever.

He knew about me. He knew I was Meru's daughter. He knew I was with the resistance. He knew it the day he walked into the security office on the station while Odo was interrogating me in the death of Vaatrik!

He knew all along, and he pretended he didn't.

"I'll always be watching."

Kira slammed her fist on the altar.

And then there was the civilian in the treatment room, a man she now recognized: Corbin Entek of the Obsidian Order. Entek who, when he kidnapped Kira six years ago to use her as a pawn against Tekeny Ghemor, had mixed his lies with just enough truth to keep her off balance. She never mentioned the incident with the *hara* cat to anyone, but of course Entek had learned of it when her memories had been imprinted onto Iliana, and he used that memory against Kira, making her doubt its authenticity just as he had made her doubt her real identity.

But now she knew the truth, at least as far as her own life was concerned. The Orb of Memory had separated fact from fiction. What had become of Iliana between that last day at Elemspur and her sudden, savage return was still largely a mystery.

She was wearing my face. She had my memories.

So what did Dukat do with her?

$\mathbf{R}$o's door chimed three times before she finally shouted, "Go away!"

There came a fourth chime; not the door this time but the familiar tone that heralded an announcement from the station's main computer. *"Medical override engaged. Privacy locks deactivating."*

Ro was livid. She looked up from her console and prepared to give Dr. Tarses an earful as the door opened. "Dammit, Simon, I don't have time for— Oh, it's you. What do you want?"

Nurse Etana Kol offered her a knowing smile as she barged in, medical kit in hand. "Now is that any way to treat your old deputy?"

Ro turned back to her padd. "You quit, remember? How do you expect to be treated?"

"Ouch," Etana said, looking around at the disarray of Ro's quarters for someplace to set down her kit. "Well, I'm glad to see that your big, bad attitude is back—even if it *is* misdirected at me. By the way, I love what you've done with the place."

"Don't try to be funny," Ro snapped. "And don't make this about me. I recommend you for your Starfleet commission, and what do you do with it? Out of nowhere, you transfer to the medical department."

"Out of nowhere?" Etana said, finally pushing the padds on the dining table to one side and laying her case flat on top of it. "Are you kidding? Laren, I was the medic for my cell during the occupation. My girlfriend is a Starfleet nurse I didn't get to see very often, even though she's stationed here. Are you *seriously* going to sit there and tell me you didn't see this coming?"

Ro didn't answer immediately, but when she did, it was with slightly less heat. "All I'm saying is that your timing could have been better."

"Not for me," Etana said. "After Bajor joined the Federation, the opportunity for Militia personnel to transfer to Starfleet made it exactly the right time. I thought you'd understand that."

"Fine, I understand it. Are we done? I'm busy here."

"Well, you're gonna need to take a break. I didn't come here just because I missed the yelling. I'm here as your physical therapist."

Ro scoffed. "Tarses gave up, did he?"

"If he'd given up, I wouldn't be here," Etana said pointedly. "Somebody took a spill down in engineering, and he was called away. But before he left, he was adamant that you can't continue to put off your rehab. You need to get back on your feet."

"I don't need my feet right now. I need some peace and quiet so I can work."

"What's that smell?" Etana asked, sniffing the air. "When was the last time you took a shower?"

"Good-bye, Kol."

Etana sighed and moved to the console. She reached across it and snatched the padd out of Ro's hand.

Ro's eyes flashed. "So you've grown a pair, is that it?"

"Let me lay this out for you, Laren," Etana said. "Doctor Tarses pulled off a minor miracle so you'd have a chance to walk again, and you're squandering it."

Ro kept her voice level. "Ensign, give that padd back to me immediately."

"Respectfully, *Lieutenant*, Doctor Tarses—"

"I don't report to Doctor Tarses!" Ro shouted, throwing herself out of the chair in an effort to reach far enough across her console so that she could snatch back her padd. Her legs wouldn't hold her, and she fell hard against the panel, wrenching her shoulder. Grimacing in pain, she barely succeeded in settling back into her wheelchair.

To her credit, Etana didn't rub the obvious in her face: that Ro's inability even to stand by now was pathetic. Instead, she kept her voice subdued. "I get it, Laren. You need to prove something. You want the universe to see that nothing's going to hold you back."

"It's not about me," Ro snarled.

"Sure it is," Etana said. "Why else would anyone willingly stay half-paralyzed if not to make some ass-brained point?"

Ro felt herself breathing hard. She braced herself against the console, fighting down the anguish that demanded release.

Etana's voice was soft, concerned. "Laren, what the *kosst* is going on with you?"

The truth of her inner turmoil forced its way from her teeth. "I liked him," she whispered.

"Who?" Etana asked.

Ro bowed her head. "Taran'atar," she confessed.

"He was always—*himself.* I don't know how else to explain it. He wasn't trying to assimilate, to become more like the rest of us. He was trying to be a new kind of Jem'Hadar—a better one—despite never having a clue about how to go about it. He just had faith that, by sending him here, Odo was giving him an opportunity to figure it out. . . . I couldn't help but admire that about him." Ro squeezed her eyes shut against the memories, as if by doing so she could shut them out. "And the thing is, I really believed that—in his own way—he felt the same about us. About me. Now someone has turned him into a weapon. People are dead . . . and I don't know how any of that can be made right again." She raised her tear-streaked face to Etana. "But I have to do *something,* Kol, and this is all I know."

For a long time, Etana didn't say anything, and Ro was afraid to imagine what she must have been thinking. But when Etana finally did speak, it was in the voice of a friend. "Look, I'll make a deal with you. Let me help you with your physical therapy—and I mean regularly, every day. You start taking better care of yourself, and I'll assist you with the investigation. I'll help with the research, I'll be your sounding board—"

"You don't have to do that."

"I know I don't, but I *want* to."

"And how are you gonna clear that with Tarses?"

Etana shrugged and offered her a lopsided grin. "I'll just tell him you're crazy, that I'm the only person who can deal with you. He'll believe that."

"Yeah, he probably will," Ro mused. "But I can't let you do this. It isn't fair to you, it isn't fair to Krissten, it's why you got out of—"

"You don't need to worry about that. Kris and I are

fine," Etana assured her. "Laren, I just want to help you. I shouldn't have to beg."

Ro lowered her eyes, sighing in resignation. "Thank you, Kol."

"All right, then," Etana said and set the padd aside. "Let's get started."

Vaughn stared into his unfinished brandy, imagining that the walls of his quarters were pressing in against him. On several occasions throughout his career, he'd been in circumstances where he'd been trapped, physically. Sometimes his confinement had been painful, sometimes terrifying, sometimes merely dull, but always he'd had the hope of escape to buoy his spirits, to keep him from sinking into complete despair.

This was different. Many hours had gone by since Sisko had paid his impromptu visit, and Vaughn's doubt had escalated with every passing second. The promise he had made, the course of action to which he had committed himself, would conceivably carry a heavy price, personally and professionally. Yet from what Sisko had told him, the alternative was unthinkable.

To make matters worse, he would be flying practically blind, on little more than faith. Even that wasn't too bad; although it was never desirable, Vaughn had been compelled to carry out missions on little or no information before. At times he'd even been forced to look fellow officers in the face and lie to them in order to save lives. But again . . . this was different.

He was still staring into his brandy an hour later when the call he'd been expecting finally came.

"Incoming transmission from U.S.S. Yolja," the station's computer announced.

"Put it though," Vaughn said.

"Vaughn, this is Kira."

"Go ahead."

"I'll come right to the point, Commander. You and I have a great deal to talk about, but unfortunately now simply isn't the time. Are you ready to return to duty?"

"Absolutely."

"Good. Lieutenant Dax will bring you up to speed. Report to ops at the start of alpha shift tomorrow morning."

"Yes, Captain. Thank you."

Kira signed off and Vaughn closed his eyes, unable to escape the fact that some lies, especially lies of omission, were simply unforgivable.

"It must have been very difficult to endure," Cenn began, addressing his four prisoners through the force-field barriers of their cells. As much as he loathed Deep Space 9 as the site of so much Bajoran suffering during the occupation, he had to admit to having developed a grudging appreciation for the design of the holding areas: three cells, each with a clear view into the other two. He'd had the two females placed in the center cell, and split up the males on either end, facing each other. Until today, Cenn had been keeping all the prisoners isolated from one another and under guard in make-shift cells mid-core. The divide-and-conquer tactic had allowed him to weed out the hired guns from the rest with relative ease. Bringing the remaining four together for the first time since their capture—now that Cenn knew what they had in common, thanks to Quark—would make them wonder how much Cenn really knew, or if they'd been singled out because one among them had talked. Cenn intended to use that uncertainty to his advantage.

"Endure?" the Lissepian asked. He was tall, gray, and

massive in frame, with small eyes that peered at Cenn from a bony, oversized head.

"The way your leader fled with her new Jem'Hadar friend," Cenn said. "Being discarded like that the moment someone better, stronger, more resourceful comes along—that has to sting . . . especially after all you'd been through together."

The Efrosian scoffed. "You don't know anything." The shimmering white hair for which her kind was well-known was cropped short. Small, intricate designs were tattooed at the outer corners of her reflective irises.

"Be silent, Fellen," the Romulan hissed. The perpetual scowl on his angular features lent him an air of menace far greater than any of the others.

"I know a few things," Cenn said, addressing the Efrosian directly. "For example, as a Bajoran, I know something of the kind of brutality Cardassians are capable of, especially to people who aren't of their species. Everyone else is inferior to them, isn't that how they think? And if you run afoul of their justice system—well, that's got to be the worst." His prisoners glanced uncomfortably at each other, and he continued. "The brutality and degradation, the denial of your dignity as a sentient being—I can't imagine anything more horrible than being held in a Cardassian prison."

The Lissepian's lips curled back, exposing large, carnivorous teeth. "It sounds terrible," he sneered. "Perhaps we should be thankful to have landed in the custody of newly-Federated Bajor."

Cenn smiled. "Oh, don't thank me yet. There're still the extradition questions that need to be sorted out. But what I'm wondering is—"

"What do you mean, 'extradition'?" the Efrosian said,

moving closer to the forcefield. The blue light of the emitters dulled her deep tan skin.

"Oh, that's right. You don't know what's been happening since word got around about your capture," Cenn said. "It seems that in addition to your suspected complicity in the murder of more than two hundred seventy Bajorans, the Cardassians are petitioning for you to be handed over to them for suspected acts of piracy, theft, illegal trafficking, not to mention a long list of other charges. Then, of course, there're the Romulans. . . ."

"What about them?" the Romulan demanded.

Cenn shrugged. "They're a bit irritated with Starfleet for violating their protectorate in Cardassian space to go after your employer's Jem'Hadar friend. Plus, neither they nor the Cardassians were happy to find out that your group was operating right under their noses all this time. It's quite an embarrassment for both of them, frankly." Cenn looked over his shoulder as if to make sure no one else was listening, then said, "Just between us, I don't think the Romulans have much of a claim over the lot of you. But it may be that just to avoid two diplomatic incidents—especially if we can't prove your involvement in the Sidau deaths—one of you will have to be remanded to Romulan authority, while the rest are turned over to the Cardassians."

"You vile piece of—" The Efrosian's enraged scream cut off abruptly as she collided with the forcefield. She stumbled back against her cell's bench, panting and cursing. "I'll kill you—you *and* your false captain. I'll kill you for Kira."

Cenn kept his face expressionless, and for the first time, the Kressari spoke, moving in quickly to calm her cellmate. "Hush, Fellen. Just breathe."

"I can't go back to a Cardassian prison, Shing, I can't!"

"Shhh," the Kressari said soothingly, stroking her shimmering white hair. "Don't worry. He won't give us to the Cardassians."

"But—"

"Remember your vow. Focus on that."

The prisoners fell silent, and Cenn considered his next move. The Efrosian was clearly the weak link, but there was a real danger of his strategy backfiring if he pushed her too far. He needed to start cracking the resolve of one of the males. "So you all took a vow to remain loyal to your leader," he said to the Romulan. "I can respect that. It says to me that you all share a belief in something bigger than yourselves. I suppose that quality is what enabled you to survive all those years on Letau and what's held you together since then. Is that where you met Iliana Ghemor?"

The Romulan looked bewildered, and again the usually quiet Kressari spoke up, cutting off her compatriot's response. "Ignore him. He's trying to divide us."

She knows, Cenn realized. *But the others don't.* Cenn stayed focused on the Romulan. "Your name is Telal, correct? You used to be an assassin for hire, wanted by the Cardassians, the Federation, the Klingons, even your own people."

"You left out the Talarians and Breen," Telal said. "Who is Iliana Ghemor?"

"I said ignore him!" the Kressari shouted.

"You don't command me, Shing-kur," answered Telal. "None of you does. I've had enough of this madness. Of *her* madness. None of this was part of the plan."

"You are a fool, Telal," the Lissepian said. "You always were."

Cenn turned to him. "Mazagalanthi, isn't it? You were a smuggler by trade, specializing in the trafficking of classified technology. Telal is a fool, is that what you said? Do you think that because he seems to have become fed up with covering for your absent leader? Then what does that make the rest of you? The one you followed lied to you, abandoned you, and some of you seem to think you still owe her your loyalty."

"She never lied! She saved us!" Fellen shouted.

"She let you believe she was Kira Nerys," Cenn said calmly.

"She *is* Kira Nerys!"

Cenn shook his head. "No. She isn't. She isn't even Bajoran." He turned to the Romulan. "Her name is Iliana Ghemor. She's a Cardassian, an ex-agent of the Obsidian Order who was altered to look and think like she was Kira Nerys. You swore your allegiance to a lie." Cenn nodded toward Shing-kur. "And she knew it all along."

Fellen was shaking her head fiercely. "You're the liar. Or the fool. Your captain is the impostor." She turned to the Kressari. "Shing, tell him . . ."

The Kressari said nothing.

"Shing-kur," rumbled Mazagalanthi. "He's telling us the truth. Isn't he?"

The Kressari sighed and seemed to withdraw into herself. She folded her coarse, tree-bark arms, clutching her elbows with each hand.

Telal looked at Cenn. "I want to make a deal."

"As do I," Mazagalanthi said.

"Shing," Fellen whispered, her voice cracking with emotion. "Shing, why?"

The Kressari looked into her eyes. "I'm sorry."

Cenn heard a click as Shing-kur pressed her thumb into the soft flesh at the crook of her elbow, and all at once, her compatriots began to convulse.

Oh, for fire's sake— Cenn slapped his combadge as the aliens collapsed almost as one. "Cenn to infirmary! Medical emergency in security holding area two! Three humanoids down!"

Shing-kur was looking at him, calmly shaking her head. "It's too late."

The summons had come while Ghemor was in Kira's office. The captain had apparently come by some persuasive information since their last meeting and now believed that Ghemor was telling the truth. She hadn't revealed what that information was, or how she'd come by it, but Ghemor had her suspicions.

Even so, Kira remained reluctant to consider an incursion into Ghemor's universe, or to allow her to return there yet. The Bajoran made a good argument against such action; her people were still trying to build a functional copy of Smiley's cursed invention, and her Ferengi engineer was actually close to setting up a comlink with Terok Nor. If they could establish contact with the rebels, Kira would at least have a better idea of what awaited them on the other side.

When security had alerted the captain to the incident in the holding cells, Kira surprised Ghemor by asking her to come along. "I want to trust you" was her answer to Ghemor's questioning look, as the lift took them from ops to the security office. "I want to believe you when you say that we share the same objectives, that your stake in this is as great as mine. If that's true, then we need to start helping each other."

The tension was palpable as the turbolift doors opened onto the Promenade. Guards were holding back curious civilians as three body bags were gurneyed out of security by the medical staff. Dr. Bashir and the interim security officer, Major Cenn, were waiting for Kira inside the office as the captain marched out of the lift toward them, Ghemor following close behind.

"Report," Kira said.

"Three dead," Bashir informed her. "Cause of death is unconfirmed, but my preliminary scans show the presence of a powerful neurotoxin in each of their brains. It was probably stored in some type of organic implant prior to release. My guess is that it was almost instantly fatal. I'll know more after I conduct the autopsies."

"Thanks, Doctor. Carry on," Kira said. Once Bashir was gone, she turned to Cenn. "What happened, Major?"

The tall Bajoran seemed hesitant at first to speak in front of Ghemor, but Kira's direct question overrode his natural caution. "It was the Kressari, sir. She had some sort of triggering device implanted in her arm. She used it to activate something in each of her associates that was obviously meant to kill them if they talked too much."

"You witnessed that?" Kira asked.

"Yes, Captain. It all happened so fast—"

"Why didn't you know about the toxins, or the kill switch? Weren't the prisoners scanned when they were processed?"

"It wasn't meant to be found," Ghemor offered, saving Cenn from further embarrassment. "The Obsidian Order perfected the art of concealing body implants from scanning devices, masking them so they appear to be part of the surrounding organism, unless you know what to look for. There's no way any of you could have known. It's likely the victims didn't know about it, either."

"You're saying your counterpart put those devices in her own lieutenants, without their knowledge?" Kira asked.

"It's what I would have done," Ghemor admitted as she crossed her arms. "What I find interesting, however, is that this Kressari was entrusted with the kill switch, but that she herself didn't die along with the others."

Kira turned back to Cenn. "What did you learn about her, Major?"

"Her name is Shing-kur. She used to be an independent bioresearch scientist living on one of the border colonies in the old Demilitarized Zone. By all accounts, she's something of a genius. Until the end of the Dominion War, she'd spent five years in the Cardassian prison on Letau. It was there that she met the people she just murdered. She knows that the other Kira is really Iliana Ghemor, but she was concealing that information from the others. In fact, they seemed to be under the impression that you're the impostor, Captain. They were all zealously devoted to their Kira—up to a point, at least. It isn't clear to me what she did to merit their loyalty, but Shing-kur— Well, if those other three were the lieutenants, then I'm betting she was Iliana Ghemor's right hand."

Not bad. "What's her condition?" Ghemor asked, finding herself admiring Cenn's black hair and high cheekbones. For a Bajoran, he wasn't that ugly.

"Withdrawn," Cenn said, pointedly ignoring her and directing his answer instead at Kira. "She's been unresponsive since she killed her friends. I have her on suicide watch, but if she has one of those implants, I'm not sure there's anything we could do to stop her from using it."

"There must be a reason she hasn't released the neurotoxin into herself yet," Ghemor suggested.

"Maybe she's just a coward," Cenn said, sounding annoyed.

"I don't think so," said Ghemor. "If she's still alive, it's because she has unfinished business." She turned to Kira. "We should speak to her. Together."

The captain's eyes narrowed. "You think it'll spook her," she guessed.

Ghemor nodded toward Cenn. "If your man is right, and her devotion to my counterpart is fanatical, then there probably isn't a better way to throw her off balance."

Kira nodded thoughfully. "All right. We'll try it."

"I'll need to borrow your tricorder," Ghemor said, addressing Cenn.

The major looked at Kira, who nodded, and Cenn warily handed Ghemor the scanning device holstered at the waist of his gray uniform.

"Thank you," Ghemor said sweetly. "I'll be sure to bring it right back."

Cenn nodded brusquely.

Ghemor reluctantly turned away and followed Kira through the door that led to the holding areas. "Were you *flirting* with him?" the captain whispered.

"Don't be ridiculous," Ghemor said. "*He* was flirting with *me*."

Shing-kur looked up at them as they approached. She sat on the bench in her cell, her posture relaxed. Her textured face made her expression difficult for Kira to read, but the Kressari's eyes darkened noticeably when they focused on her visitors.

After telling the guards to wait outside, Kira allowed the Kressari a moment to take in the sight of the captain and the alternate Iliana facing her, side-by-side. "We've come to talk," Kira said.

Shing-kur ignored her. She became fixated on Ghemor. "You're even more beautiful than I imagined."

"You're really not my type," the Cardassian answered, fiddling with the tricorder as she spoke. "Do you know who I am?"

Shing-kur's eyes blackened again, and Kira remembered that this was how Kressari smiled. "You're the other one."

"And me?" Kira asked.

White pupils swelled within the dark irises. "You're another."

Kira sighed, already growing impatient. "Why did you kill your friends, Shing-kur?"

"They were going to break their vow to her. I couldn't allow that," the Kressari said. "Besides, I wanted to spare them her pain."

"Then I'm sure they must have appreciated the agonizing death you just gave them," Ghemor scoffed.

"*Her* pain?" Kira repeated. "What pain?"

"The pain she hid from them."

"But not from you," noted Kira. "You knew her very well, didn't you?"

Shing-kur's eyes turned green. Wistful? "Better than most. Yet still not well enough to ease her suffering."

"What does she want, Shing-kur?"

"The same as any of us. The right to exist."

"She had to kill nearly three hundred Bajorans to assert that right?"

"Her worlds abandoned her. She owes them nothing."

"Whereas you," Ghemor said, "think you owe her everything."

"My life belongs to her, as does my death," Shing-kur said, keeping her eyes fixed on Kira now. "I have a message for you."

"I'm listening."

"Trakor's First Prophecy."

She said nothing more, and for a long time, Kira was silent, carefully concealing her emotions behind her stone mask of command authority. When at last she spoke, she strove to project a certainty she didn't feel. "I'll stop her."

"You won't."

Kira felt her self-control ebbing. She wanted to scream, to reach through the forcefield and grab Shing-kur by the throat and force her to admit that she was lying.

Fortunately, Ghemor preempted her thoughts of rash action. "That's it?" the Cardassian asked. "*That's* why you haven't triggered your implant?"

"What?" Shing-kur whispered as her eyes turned yellow. Surprise?

"The neurotoxin," Ghemor prompted, showing the Kressari the face of her tricorder. "I found it."

Shing-kur said nothing.

"You still can be a martyr to your cause. What's stopping you?"

Kira frowned at Ghemor. "What are you doing?"

"What does it look like I'm doing? I'm putting this wretched fanatic out of our misery. What about it, Kressari? You delivered your message. Aren't you ready to die for her yet?"

Kira grabbed her arm. "Stop it, Ghemor!" she shouted.

"Go on!" the Cardassian pressed. "What are you waiting for? Do it!"

"Shing-kur, don't listen—"

Click.

Kira held her breath at the sound and froze at the sight of Shing-kur's thumb pressed against the crook of her elbow. A moment passed, then two, but nothing happened. Shing-kur seemed astonished.

"I neglected to mention," said Ghemor, "that when I found the implant, I was also able to hack into the triggering device. It's offline."

Shing-kur's eyes went completely white. *"You—"*

"Your way out is gone," the Cardassian said, stepping to the very edge of the forcefield. "There's no escape. You no longer get to decide how this ends."

The Kressari averted her eyes. She shifted uncomfortably, looking for the first time like a trapped animal.

"Get out, Ghemor," Kira growled. "Get out of here now!"

"Fine. You deal with her." The Cardassian turned and walked out.

"How could you be against her?" Shing-kur screamed at Ghemor's back. "You of all people!"

"She's an egomaniac," Ghemor said over her shoulder. "My side has enough of those already. We don't need one from your universe."

For several minutes after Ghemor left, Kira simply stared at Shing-kur, trying to think. Ghemor's tactics, while deplorable, had given Kira the time she needed to regain some of her faltering composure, but she was still too shaken to know what she should do next.

Finally Kira whispered, "Why are you doing this? She fled. She abandoned you. She used you. All for her own twisted—"

"If she's twisted," Shing-kur snarled, "then it's because of *you*."

"Me?"

"You . . . and all the other corpses."

"Is that supposed to be a threat?"

"Call it a prediction. She's not going to rest until all the pretenders are gone."

"She's the pretender," Kira said. "You know that."

"No," said Shing-kur. "What I know—what I've come to understand—is that she's more deserving of being Kira Nerys than you, or that so-called Intendant, or any of the others out there could ever be. No one has the right to take that from her. Not even you."

Kira regarded the Kressari a moment longer before she turned and walked out. She almost—almost—felt pity. But the ghosts of Sidau consumed any such sentiment.

Ghemor was waiting for her in the surveillance room with the two security guards. After telling the officers to resume suicide watch over their prisoner, Kira sealed the door and advanced toward the Cardassian.

"You knew all along, didn't you?" Kira said. *"Didn't you?"*

Ghemor stood her ground. "Yes."

Kira tried to land a backhand blow against Ghemor's face. As she anticipated, the former Obsidian Order agent blocked the blow easily, but Kira quickly latched onto

Ghemor's wrist and twisted her around. She shoved the Cardassian hard against the wall and pinned her there.

"So what was your job?" Kira asked through her teeth. "To keep me and my people running around in circles while your counterpart fulfilled Trakor's First Prophecy —while she became the Emissary by throwing open the Temple Gates?"

"Just the opposite, actually," Ghemor said, her voice tightening against the pain Kira was inflicting. "I still want to stop her, same as you."

"But you didn't think I needed to know *this*?"

"Take a good look at yourself, Captain. You're way off your game. You're still recovering from your injuries, you're letting your emotions get the better of you, and you can't be objective when it comes to your precious Prophets. You're so damn worried about trusting me, you haven't given me much reason to trust *you*."

"I'm not the liar," Kira spat. "And I damn sure don't need you to protect me from the truth!"

"Maybe not," Ghemor said. "But from what I've seen so far, giving you the whole truth at once wouldn't have served either of us. You're too close to the problem."

Kira's thoughts went automatically to Vaughn. After a moment, she slowly eased her grip on Ghemor until she released her altogether. Kira stepped back, bracing herself for an attack, but the Cardassian simply rubbed her shoulder as she turned to face the captain.

"You should have leveled with me from the start," Kira said. "But you're always holding something back. Tell me now, once and for all, why I should trust you."

Ghemor exhaled heavily. "It's complicated."

"You're the double of a woman who was surgically altered to replace *me*, but who has instead replaced *my* double in an alternate universe. How simple do you think I expect it to be?"

Ghemor gave her a weary grin. "Fair point. All right. In order to carry out my original assignment to eliminate the Intendant, I needed to make contact with the religious authority on my continuum's Bajor."

"I thought the Bajoran religion—at least, the one I know—didn't exist in your universe."

"It would be more accurate to say it doesn't exist anymore—for the most part, anyway. Underground enclaves continue to survive, in secret, hoping someday to unshackle Bajor from the Alliance and restore their world to the way it used to be, before the Terran Empire conquered it. As you can imagine, this movement is sympathetic to the rebels on Terok Nor. Some of these religious dissidents are well placed in the secular hierarchy, and when they can, they pass along strategically useful information to the rebellion. I was sent to one of those enclaves, hoping to confirm a rumor we'd heard aboard Terok Nor that the Intendant would soon be making a rare special trip to Bajor. My objective was to put together enough intel about the visit so that I could plan her assassination." She paused, as if momentarily lost in her own memories. "What I got instead was a revelation I wasn't expecting."

Her choice of words caught Kira's attention. *And that look on her face—*

"You've . . . you've looked into an Orb, haven't you?" Kira asked.

An unsettled expression seeped into Ghemor's features. "Something like that. The enclaves do possess certain artifacts that fuel their faith. They're closely guarded secrets. My exposure to one of them is where my information comes from. It was how I learned about my counterpart in your universe, and what she was planning to do.

"You see, Captain," Ghemor went on, "unlike your world, my Bajor is still waiting for its redeemer, the one who is supposed to lead them into a new era. And according to the enclaves, the time of the Emissary is *now*."

"Benjamin Sisko," Kira realized. "The Sisko of your universe is dead. He was destined to become your Bajor's Emissary, just like mine. That's why no one from your side has found the wormhole yet."

"That's right. There's a void in my continuum that demands to be filled," Ghemor finished. "Under the right symbol—the right person—my Bajor could become the nucleus of a benign new order in my continuum. It could unify the quadrant's underclass, strengthen the rebellion against the Alliance, and bring about a revolution that could usher in a new age. But if my counterpart is the one to take up the mantle of Emissary, then there's a very real possibility that the new age will be even darker than the present one."

8

"Would somebody please explain to me what in the name of Gint I'm doing here? I have a business to run."

Nog sighed. Uncle Quark was certainly in rare form today. Just getting him to take a lift to ops had required considerable negotiating; namely, a promise from Nog to moonlight in the bar for a week, waiting tables during his off-duty hours. And free of charge, no less! At the time it had seemed like a small price to pay for his uncle's cooperation—Lieutenant Dax had been adamant about securing his involvement in their attempt to contact the alternate universe—but Quark's current belligerence toward his nephew was making Nog doubt his handling of the matter. After all, how much haggling had he really done? Judging from the look of disapproval on his uncle's face, too little.

Maybe Quark was right to be annoyed with him; Uncle had never made a secret of his concern that joining Starfleet would only lead to the erosion of Nog's cultural identity—a compromise of the traditional values in which he'd been raised, and to which Quark was firmly devoted, despite the political and economic reforms that had taken hold on Ferenginar over the last year. And the truth of it was, Nog's Starfleet duties didn't always afford him the luxury to think like a proper Ferengi.

But whether or not his uncle appreciated the circumstances, Nog knew in his lobes that this was one of those times when the dividends to the many outvalued the dividends to the few. Or the one.

"Uncle, will you please just *relax*," Nog whispered, trying to stay focused on triple-checking his modifications to the engineering console. "Sam," he called over his shoulder. "I need the tricorder we used to make the original calibrations."

Bowers, seated a few meters away at tactical, quickly reached for the specified device and yelled "Heads up!" before tossing it to Nog. Quark had to dodge to avoid being struck by the handheld scanner as his nephew snatched it out of the air.

"You gentlemen are obviously very busy," Quark said as he started back toward the turbolift. "Why don't you call me when things are a little less . . . hectic."

"As you were, Quark," came the sharp voice of Captain Kira. She was emerging from her office, followed by Lieutenant Dax and Captain Sisko.

"Captain," Quark said, "I appeal to you as a reasonable female——"

"Save it," Kira snapped. "I'm in a bad mood as it is."

"And who wouldn't be?" Uncle asked. "All the tension around here lately—it's enough to depress anyone. But there's a solution to that. I'm pleased to announce that Happy Hour at Quark's begins the moment I return to the bar, for anyone who cares to join me——"

"Give it up, Quark," Dax said. "It's oh-eight hundred!"

Uncle scowled. "Fine! I'll stay! But would someone kindly tell me *why* I'm staying?"

"I already *told* you why," Nog muttered.

"I'd like to hear from someone a little higher up in the station hierarchy, if you don't mind, *Ensign*."

"I'm a lieutenant!"

"Even so, I'd rather— Wait, really?"

"Yes!"

"Oh. When did that happen?"

Nog threw up his hands and went back to work.

Quark turned back to Kira. "As I was saying—"

Sisko had walked over to Uncle and was now laying a friendly hand on his shoulder. "Settle down, Mister Ambassador. We just want to make use of those diplomatic services you keep advertising on the Bajoran comnet."

"Diplomacy?" Quark said, sounding skeptical. "With *whom*?"

There was a hum, and an arriving turbolift deposited Doctor Bashir into ops. "Is everything ready?" he asked.

"Almost," Nog said.

"What exactly are you doing, anyway?" Uncle asked him.

Dax sighed. "Quark, your nephew has figured out a way to make contact with the alternate universe."

"Really?" Quark said, eyeing Nog with a new appreciation. "You know, that could be *extremely* lucrative."

"When he does," Dax went on, "we want you, Nog, Julian, and Benjamin to speak for the station."

"Actually, Captain Sisko will be doing the talking," Kira stressed.

"Right," Dax agreed. "But we want you three to be present as well."

"Captain Sisko just said I'm here in a diplomatic capacity," Quark said.

"Yes," Kira said in a warning tone, "and part of diplomacy is knowing when to keep your mouth shut."

"Wait a second—the four of us, specifically?" Quark asked with growing suspicion, and Nog could see his mind working. "Oh, don't tell me. . . . You want the *dead* people, don't you?"

"You're not the 'dead people,'" Dax said irritably. "Your counterparts are the dead ones."

Quark stared at her for a prolonged moment. "Goodbye."

Ezri blocked his path to the turbolift and spoke quickly. "We don't know how they're going to react to our transmission. We need to convince them as quickly as possible that we're who we say we are. We want to put them at their ease."

"Of course you do. Why else would you parade corpses in front of them?"

"We don't want them to think someone is trying to deceive them, Quark. If they see Captain Kira, they might think—"

"What about *you*?" Quark asked pointedly. "You're not dead, but if they see a second Ezri in a Starfleet uniform, don't you think they'll figure out who they're talking to?"

"But we can't count on my counterpart being on their station when we make contact. If she isn't, it'll give them reason to doubt, and we don't have time to waste convincing them."

"Exactly when did *I* die?" Bashir asked.

"Apparently just over a year ago," Kira informed him.

"When Ezri suggested this approach, I asked our visitor for a fatality update."

"This has to be the sickest thing I've ever heard," Quark said. He looked at Dax. "And I'm very disappointed to learn that you were the one to think of it. Also slightly aroused. But mainly I'm disappointed."

Dax rolled her eyes. "I'll carry on somehow. Don't go anywhere." She patted his shoulder and descended the steps from the captain's office to take her usual place at the situation table.

Another hum heralded the arrival of a second turbolift, this one carrying the Cardassian woman and, to Nog's great relief, Commander Vaughn. "Reporting for duty as ordered, Captain," the first officer said.

Kira nodded to him. "Good to have you back, Commander."

Vaughn returned the nod and joined Lieutenant Dax in the center of ops. Some of the tension in the room dissipated as the reality settled in that the strife between the captain and her X.O. might finally be past.

"Where would you like me, Captain?" Ghemor asked.

Kira beckoned her over. As the Cardassian crossed operations, Nog couldn't help but notice how her gaze lingered on Sisko.

"Nog, how's it coming?" Dax asked.

"We're ready here," Nog said, finishing his last pass with the tricorder. "We should take our positions. Ensign Selzner."

"Sir?" said the communications officer.

"When I give the word, please load the program I left standing by on channel D."

"Yes, Lieutenant."

Bashir, Sisko, and Quark had already gathered on the platform just outside the captain's office, facing the ops center's main holoframe. Nog moved to stand next to his uncle, while Kira and Ghemor joined Vaughn and Dax at the situation table, out of camera range, at least for now. Feeling his captain's eyes on him, Nog took a deep breath, made a silent plea to the Great River, and gave the order: "Initiate."

There seemed to be a collective intake of breath as everyone in ops turned their attention toward the screen, and Nog realized he probably should have mentioned that there would be nothing out of the ordinary to mark this historic bridging of parallel universes. At first, there was only a prolonged and quite unremarkable curtain of static cascading within the oval imaging area of the holoframe. By the third minute, Quark was beginning to fidget. "Is it supposed to be taking this long?"

"Sshhh!" Nog hissed, mainly because he didn't have an answer. As far as he knew, nobody had ever done this before; there were no precedents against which to judge how well it was working.

Nog's eyes widened with hope when he saw a humanoid upper body beginning to take shape within the static, but his spirits promptly fell when the static intensified again. "Selzner, can you clean that up?"

"Trying, sir . . ."

The silhouette returned, more defined this time. There was a squawk on the audio, fragmented and faint: " . . . *lo?* . . . *entify . . . rself . . .*"

"Did you hear that?" Nog asked excitedly.

Only Uncle Quark nodded; the voice was obviously still too unintelligible for non-Ferengi ears, but Nog's confidence soared. This was going to work!

"It's a female," Quark said, confirming Nog's own impression.

Slowly the image resolved. Not completely; streams of static threatened constantly to break up the signal, but it cleared up enough for everyone watching to know that they were seeing an exact duplicate of the ops situation table. The figure who stood behind it, staring back at them openmouthed, was also familiar.

Quark shot a look to Dax that said *I told you so,* but the lieutenant was too transfixed by the sight of herself in the holoframe. Longer hair, dark civilian clothes, and a pair of Klingon disruptors strapped to either hip, the alternate Ezri stared back at the contact team, her blue-shadowed eyes narrowing as she focused on Quark, who was giving her an awkward smile.

"Oh, no . . . not you."

Never taking his eyes off the screen, Nog turned his head slightly toward his uncle and spoke out the corner of his mouth. "She doesn't look too happy to see you."

In Bashir's estimation, their opening conversation with the alternates went fairly well.

Ezri's idea to assemble a contact team with, as Quark had astutely noted, "the dead people" achieved its desired effect. Helped along by a few persuasive words from Captain Sisko, the alternate Ezri—Ezri *Tigan,* Bashir reminded himself, recalling that this Trill was unjoined—quickly, albeit reluctantly, accepted who it really was that was speaking to her.

As more rebels from Terok Nor appeared at Tigan's side, Bashir was struck with mixed emotions. He was relieved to see Smiley still alive and well, albeit visibly careworn with the burdens of leading his rebellion against the Alliance. The doctor even smiled when the alternate O'Brien introduced his first officer, Keiko Ishikawa. Bashir studied the pair's body language carefully as they stood side-by-side, suspecting their relationship extended well beyond the professional. It lifted Bashir's spirits to think that it might.

Soul mates in any universe, he mused, carefully reining in the impulse to cast a wistful glance at Ezri Dax.

Reassuring as he found it to see Miles and Keiko together and serving the cause of freedom, Bashir wasn't quite sure how to feel about Smiley's next two lieutenants, Michael Eddington and Luther Sloan, who seemed to regard the doctor across the dimensional gulf with the same uncertainty. Sisko had once told him that Bashir's counterpart had been something of a brute; a hot-tempered fighter with quite a vicious streak. Julian was forced to concede that if he himself could turn out so differently on the other side, then surely these men, both of whose faces conjured unpleasant memories of treachery, manipulation, and subterfuge, might be equally unlike the Sloan and Eddington he had known.

It wasn't until Captain Kira and Operative Ghemor joined the conversation that they finally got down to business. Bashir found it interesting that the rebels hadn't known of Ghemor's crossover until this moment; the Cardassian had never returned from her mission to Bajor, weeks prior, and there had evidently been some speculation that she'd been captured or killed. She quickly offered the rebels scraps of personal information about several of them to prove her identity, and then went on to explain the dire and convoluted circumstances that had led to her disappearance.

"Iliana, I'm not sure how much of this I can believe,"

Smiley told her. *"You're telling me that the Intendant may already be dead, but not really because your own counterpart may have taken her place in order to fulfill some Bajoran religious prediction?"*

"I realize it's a lot to take in," Ghemor said, "and I'm sorry that it's taken me this long to report back. But you have to understand that I was trying to combat an outside threat not just to the rebellion, but to the entire balance of power in our universe. If this woman succeeds in doing what she intends, Bajor will follow her like some kind of messiah. She could even start a damn holy war within the Alliance."

"You make that sound like a bad thing," Tigan remarked.

"It would be," Ishikawa said. *"A war like that would devastate the region. People like us would be its first victims."*

"The faithful versus the infidels," Eddington agreed. *"With a madwoman calling the shots."*

"You see now why we felt the need to warn you," Kira said. "General O'Brien, I also have a stake in seeing this woman stopped. She's proved herself a threat on our side as well as yours. My people and I stand ready to assist you."

"I appreciate the offer, Captain," Smiley said. *"And I accept. You can start by explaining exactly where . . . What the bloody hell—?"*

Bashir could hear alerts going off on Terok Nor, automated tones that sounded identical to the tripping of DS9's long-range proximity sensors. The rebels sprang into action: Tigan and Sloan immediately rushed off camera, presumably to their stations, while the others read incoming data off the situation table.

"We've got multiple warp signatures on approach vectors," Keiko reported. *"Looks like Klingons. ETA, two minutes."*

"Raise shields," Smiley ordered. *"Charge all weapons and prepare for planetary bombardment. I want a torpedo lock on Ashalla in the next thirty seconds."*

Bashir's mouth dropped open. Did he really just hear Smiley order preparations to attack the Bajoran capital?

The doctor looked at Kira and saw that the captain was as shocked as he was. "General, what are you doing?"

"What I warned them I'd do, Captain."

"You can't attack Bajor," Kira said. "Millions of innocent lives—"

"Captain . . . ow do you think we've managed . . . hold Terok Nor all this time?" Smiley asked. *"It's by . . . nvincing the Alliance tha . . . ushed me too far, Bajor wou . . . fer the . . . nsequen . . ."* A new curtain of static was falling over the comlink.

"Nog, he's breaking up!" Kira shouted. "Do something!"

The engineer was already back at his station. "I'm trying! Something's interfering with the signal lock, overriding the link. . . . Wait, I think I've got it back . . ."

Bashir looked at the holoframe. The signal was clearing, but not in the way any of them had hoped.

A face identical to Kira's filled the screen, a thin smile spreading across it, her forehead adorned with the silver headpiece of the Intendant. *"Well, hello . . . Captain. What an unexpected surprise. And how clever of you to have devised a way to communicate with Terok Nor. You've no idea how pleased I am to see you alive."*

Kira glared at Iliana. "I sincerely doubt that."

"Oh, believe me, I wasn't happy to learn what Taran'atar had done to you. That was a task I'd reserved for myself. It's actually reassuring to know I get to come back for you . . . once I'm done here, of course."

"You won't succeed," Kira vowed.

"Of course I will. Haven't you heard? I walk with the Prophets." She brought her hand into view and gave Kira a taunting little wave. Around her palm was an ornate gold band with a green jewel in the center—the same one Bashir had seen in Sidau village eight years ago. Then the comlink abruptly ended, leaving only static.

Kira turned to Nog. "Can you get Terok Nor back?"

Nog shook his head as he wrestled his console. "I can't get through. It's like there's an expanding wall between us and the alternate universe, blocking my attempts to reestablish contact."

"A shield?"

"I don't know, maybe. Or it could be a scattering field. Whatever it is, the effect is spreading."

"Can we beam across?"

"Not a chance." Nog studied his instruments. "Not to Terok Nor, anyway. But maybe . . ."

"What?"

Nog looked up at her. "If I'm reading this right, the field hasn't overtaken their Bajor yet. I may be able to beam over two people now, if we act fast."

"Two," Quark scoffed. "What good would that do?"

"More than sending nobody would," Dax said. "I volunteer, Captain."

"Your attitude is commendable, Lieutenant, but last I checked, I'm the only member of this crew who can pass for the Intendant, and we may need to take advantage of that." Kira looked at Ghemor and spoke quickly. "That enclave you told me about—where?"

"Vekobet," Ghemor said, "in Kendra Valley. I can guide you."

Kira nodded and the two of them started toward the transporter stage.

"No," Vaughn said suddenly, stepping forward. "Captain, take me instead. You don't need a guide. You need someone who has your back."

Kira hesitated. Bashir wondered what was going through her mind as she met Vaughn's gaze. Finally she said, "All right, Commander. You're with me."

Ghemor started to protest. "Captain—"

"I'm sorry, Ghemor, but he's right. Nog, I don't want to alarm the locals by beaming directly into Vekobet. Can you put us down somewhere isolated?"

"I think so. I have to use what we know about our own Kendra Valley for reference, and hope that the site I pick will be a close match for the other side."

"A rocky hilltop might do the trick," Bashir suggested. "Or some other natural formation that has stood the test of time."

"Akorem's Rock," Sisko said suddenly. "It's a bare slab of granite jutting out of a hill a couple of hours' walk from Vekobet. The locals tell me it's been unchanged for centuries."

Nog nodded. "I've got it. The interference is getting stronger. We've got only a few more seconds."

Vaughn handed Kira a phaser and the two of them mounted the transporter stage. Kira nodded to Dax. "Take care of our station, Ezri. Mister Nog, energize."

Sisko watched as the curtain of light enveloped his friends, and for long seconds he stared into the empty air they left behind. He was vaguely aware that ops had erupted into a frantic flurry of activity, with Dax issuing a yellow alert and ordering Bowers to implement whatever safeguards he'd come up with to protect the station from transdimensional incursions, then tasking Nog with trying to reestablish his comlink and transporter lock with the other side. Bashir and Quark were heading for a turbolift, the Ferengi ambassador shaking his head at the turn of events, muttering something under his breath.

And there in the corner of his eye was Ghemor, watching Sisko intently, as if she somehow knew that something secret had transpired here. Had she seen the look Vaughn had given him before the transporter effect had taken the commander? How much did she suspect?

"Benjamin?" Dax said. "You okay?"

Sisko shook himself. "It's time for me to go," he told her.

Dax blinked. "All right. I can have Ensign Lankford take you back to Bajor in a runabout—"

"That's not necessary," Sisko said. "You have enough to deal with without giving up a runabout and a pilot for a milk run. I'll get passage aboard the afternoon ferry."

"You're sure?"

"Absolutely," Sisko said.

"Well . . . thanks for all your help."

Sisko waved away her gratitude. He certainly didn't feel he deserved it. "You've got good instincts, Old Man. Trust them."

"I will," Dax said. "Thanks again."

Sisko continued to feel Ghemor's eyes on his back as he headed for the turbolift, wondering if she truly understood what he had done.

9

EIGHTEEN HOURS EARLIER

Despite the urgency of purpose with which Sisko strode through the habitat ring, he found he couldn't help thinking back on his conversation with Kira that morning. When he'd left her office, Nerys still seemed to be grappling with what Sisko had said regarding Taran'atar. He didn't envy the decisions she would need to make in the days ahead, but he'd done what he could; he had tried to offer her a glimmer of hope. The rest was up to her.

Reaching his destination, Sisko heard the faint sounds of music wafting through the door. When his finger touched the chime, the music stopped. He wished there was another way to accomplish his task, but it had been made clear to him during his encounter with the Orb of Souls: for now, he could only influence; others would need to act.

The door slid open, and Vaughn faced him across the threshold, out of uniform, his red division shirt open at the neck. "Captain. This is a surprise. Is everything all right?"

"I'm sorry to disturb you, Commander. May I come in?"

"Of course." Vaughn stepped aside, allowing Sisko to enter. Ben noticed a stringed musical instrument resting on a large padded chair, the arm of which also held Vaughn's discarded jacket. "Please sit down." Vaughn indicated the couch opposite the chair. "Can I offer you a drink?"

"Whatever you're having is fine," Sisko said, moving toward the sitting area. He picked up the instrument, delighted by the look and feel of it.

"Here you go," Vaughn said, returning with an open bottle of Saurian brandy in one hand and two half-filled tumblers in the other. He held out the glasses to Sisko, who took one of them as he gently set the instrument aside. Vaughn placed the bent-neck bottle on the coffee table between them as the two men sat down, and then raised his glass. "*Ad astra.*"

With a smile, Sisko echoed the old academy toast as they clinked glasses and drank. The brandy burned smoothly as it went down. Sisko's gaze returned to the instrument. "Acoustic guitar?"

Vaughn nodded. "I find it relaxing."

"Hand-crafted or replicated?"

"Replicated, unfortunately. It's not an instrument you hear much of these days, and the real ones are hard to find. Most of them are in private collections." Vaughn took another sip of brandy. "What's your instrument?"

"Piano," Sisko said. "My father has one, back on Earth. I grew up with it. How long have you played?"

"A little over twenty-six years. I took it up not long after Prynn was born. Whenever I could make it home,

I'd play for her. Nothing serious, just a few songs she seemed to enjoy."

The image of Vaughn playing melodies for his daughter made Sisko smile. "How is Prynn?"

"She's recovered, thank you for asking. No lasting injuries."

"I'm glad to hear it. I read her report on what she went through. You should be proud of her."

"I am, sir. Thank you."

Silence settled between them. Vaughn had to know that Sisko hadn't come to his quarters merely for drinks and small talk, but he apparently sensed Ben's reluctance and wasn't going to press the issue until his guest felt ready. It was a courtesy Sisko appreciated.

Sisko set down his unfinished brandy and leaned forward, folding his hands in his lap. "Elias, you know that I'm still on temporary leave from Starfleet, so what I'm about to say can't be viewed as an order. Nevertheless, I've become aware of an aspect to our current situation that needs to be dealt with, and I'm here to ask you to see the matter through."

"I'd be more than happy to help you any way I can, Captain, but I guess you haven't heard the news," Vaughn said. "I've been relieved of duty."

"I'm aware of the situation. But your captain is going to need you soon, whether she realizes it or not. This thing with the alternate universe is coming to a head, and however it plays out between you two, eventually Kira's going to decide that making another crossover is unavoidable. When that happens, you need to be ready to act."

Vaughn blinked, clearly unsure about what to make of what he was being told.

"Obviously, this isn't an official assignment," Sisko went on. "It's off the record, extremely sensitive, and risky . . . and it requires a leap of faith on your part. You should therefore consider it completely voluntary."

"What's the op?"

"In a nutshell, I need you to locate my counterpart and convince him to find the wormhole so he can fulfill the prophecy of the Emissary for that continuum."

To his credit, Vaughn managed not to choke on his brandy. "My understanding was that your counterpart died years ago."

"Some . . . intelligence has come my way to suggest he faked his death in order to escape the responsibility of leading the Terran rebellion, and that he's been in hiding on the alternate Bajor ever since."

"I see," Vaughn said. "I don't suppose I could have access to this intel?"

"It . . . isn't that kind of intelligence," Sisko told him.

"I guess that's where the leap of faith comes in." Vaughn set down his glass. "All right. In that case, can I assume that the successful completion of this mission will neutralize Iliana Ghemor as a threat?"

"No. But it may minimize the damage she does."

Vaughn's face became etched with concern. "But if your counterpart fulfills his destiny, the Bajor of that continuum is likely to be profoundly affected."

"Yes."

"It sounds like I'm going to be effecting a fundamental change in the development of that universe."

"That's where the 'off the record' part comes in," Sisko said. "It turns out that I was supposed to have accomplished this some time ago. The increased . . . permeability between the two universes in recent years was supposed to facilitate my influencing the other Sisko, help him to discover who he really is, so that he could begin the process of healing his Bajor and preparing it to face its future. But because I never considered our cross-overs within the context of my own evolving under-standing of my role as Emissary, a madwoman now has an opportunity to pull the whole structure down."

"Captain—Ben—if that's the case, surely this task is meant for you."

"Not anymore," Sisko said. "Reaching out to my counterpart now, after all the changes I've gone through as Emissary—confronting him with a living example of the sort of future that awaits him—would only drive him farther underground. I need a proxy, someone who understands what it is to be Touched by the Prophets but is still in the early stages of working through what it all means. That's why it needs to be you."

"And Kira?"

Sisko hesitated, knowing this would be the hardest part. "You can't tell her, Elias. Please don't ask me why."

Vaughn stared at him for a long moment, as uncertain and conflicted as Kira had been about Taran'atar, and Sisko again felt the frustration of afflicting his friends with such doubt, of wishing he'd been able to tell them everything.

Finally Vaughn gave Ben the answer he needed. "I'll do it."

Sisko rose to his feet and shook the commander's hand, grateful for Elias's faith, knowing that he was re-paying it with betrayal.

END OF SIDE ONE

SIDE TWO

STAR TREK
DEEP SPACE NINE®

FEARFUL SYMMETRY

OLIVIA WOODS

Based upon STAR TREK®
created by Gene Roddenberry,
and STAR TREK: DEEP SPACE NINE
created by Rick Berman and Michael Piller

POCKET BOOKS

New York   London   Toronto   Sydney   Letau

For Lola

"You are really enjoying all this, aren't you? Hm? All your sick little games?"

"I must admit, I do get a certain . . . perverse pleasure out of it."

• • •

"You've got to laugh at a universe that allows such radical shifts in fortune."

1

" . . . *that* despite cowardly attacks by insurgents, Union forces continue to make progress in their efforts to restore stability to Bajor. Three more terrorist cells were routed yesterday in the southern province of Musilla; and, thanks to intelligence provided by the Obsidian Order, a plot to transport chemical explosives onto space station Terok Nor has been thwarted. The six conspirators connected to the plot have been arrested, found guilty, and are currently awaiting trial to confirm sentencing.

"In related news, Cardassia will formally welcome home one of its heroes as Gul Trekal Darhe'el is honored at a formal reception in the capital this evening. Darhe'el, who served on Bajor with distinction for more than a quarter-century, is retiring from military service in order to spend more time with family. When asked what he believed his legacy would be, the longtime proponent of labor initiatives on Cardassian subject worlds said he hoped the example he tried to set on Bajor would inspire others in the struggle to end the unrest as quickly as possible.

"According to the official announcement, tonight's recep-

tion will also honor Gul Morad Pirak, who leaves next month to join the heroic military effort on Bajor; and Legate Tekeny Ghemor, newly promoted to Central Command . . ."

Ordinarily, hearing her father's name over the comnet feed from the Information Service would have given Iliana Ghemor a momentary thrill, even if it meant having to endure the tiresome updates from Bajor. But on this occasion, preoccupied as she was with figuring out the proper way to don the absurdly elaborate dress her mother had chosen for her to wear to the reception, the announcement had served instead merely to remind Iliana of her bleak expectations for the evening ahead. With an irritated jab of her finger, she cut the feed and resumed trying to decipher the bizarre complexities of her gown.

The house intercom chimed. *"Iliana, are you dressed yet?"* Mother.

"Another moment," she called back, pulling her arms through the sleeves of the dress and gasping as the autofasteners did their work along her spine. She didn't particularly care for gowns, preferring the easy comfort of her usual tunics and trousers, or the liberating feel of a painting smock . . . or just about anything *other* than the flowing jade frippery in which she had draped herself. Standing before the full-length mirror situated next to her vanity, she was both startled and bemused by the sight of the feminine features she routinely tried to conceal. The dress was definitely pinching her waist, accentuating her hips, and its off-the-shoulder cut and plunging neckline played up the ridges of her neck as well as the pectoral scoop between her breasts.

The things I do for family.

She had stubbornly refused to make any modifications

to her hair; she took considerable pride in her long black tresses and rejected the current fashion that required women to arrange their manes into absurd geometric shapes.

Reaching for the tray of pigments on her vanity, she added a final touch of blue to her forehead dimple, and then, telling herself it was only an afterthought, applied the color to her pectoral scoop as well. *What a sight you are,* she mentally told her reflection. *I'm not even sure I recognize you anymore.*

There was wry amusement behind the thought . . . coupled with a twinge of ruefulness. The hypocrisy of her current circumstances weighed heavily on her; the very thought of participating in a political event orchestrated to celebrate the military and strengthen its public image felt like a betrayal of her true self, and tantamount to a personal endorsement of the troubling direction in which Cardassia seemed inexorably determined to slide.

Iliana glanced at her dresser across the room, recalling the item it held, reminding herself that she could put those feelings aside for one evening.

She turned back to the mirror and studied herself a moment longer, frowning, thinking she'd forgotten something. She nearly jumped when she focused past her reflection and saw that someone was staring at her from the bedroom door.

Iliana spun around. "Mother, you startled me! What's the matter?"

Kaleen Ghemor strode toward her daughter, her full, brown-glazed lips spreading into a smile. "I was just wondering where the years have gone. It seems only recently that you were a determined baby trying to stand, struggling to find your balance. Now I see you as a grown woman." Kaleen shrugged. "I suppose it just takes getting used to." As her mother moved, her midnight blue gown seemed to bleed into the air, as if it were made partly of smoke.

"Is that what you're wearing tonight?" Iliana asked in amazement. "It's beautiful!"

"Isn't it?" With a playful flourish, Kaleen turned so Iliana could see her from all sides. Parts of her mother's dress appeared to coil around her before settling back into ordinary fabric. "Holographic diodes woven into the gown produce the effect," Kaleen explained. "I bristled at the expense at first, but your father persuaded me to buy it anyway, reminding me how important it is that we all make a good impression tonight."

Kill me now. "Do I really have to go?" She regretted the question even as it escaped her mouth.

Kaleen's smile fell. "Let's not have this conversation again, please. Your father is the newest appointee to Central Command. That's no small thing. I have a duty to him, and you have a duty to us both, to show his peers the love and devotion we share as a family. Especially with so many powerful men and women on hand who will be assessing us as potential allies. Or adversaries."

"They won't be assessing *me,*" Iliana pouted, looking out the window. Beyond the high walls of the estate, she saw, the sky was turning purple with the approach of night.

"Oh, but they will," Kaleen said, grasping Iliana's chin and forcing her to pay attention. "Make no mistake about that. Whether you choose to believe it or not, Iliana, your presence and your conduct matter in this. They speak to how we've raised you, and to what sort of example your father will set for Cardassia. Those things matter as much as anything he has done during his career." Kaleen released her chin and started fussing with the top of Iliana's dress. "I know how you feel about the military, but this night isn't about you. Your father's star is rising, and it's important that we do nothing to embarrass him."

With an air of mischief, Iliana said, "I suppose having a radical-minded malcontent for a daughter *could* be a liability to his public image."

"It's a forgivable offense, particularly in an artist," Kaleen allowed, "but only up to a point. You're not a child anymore. You're a young woman, and it's past time you took your responsibilities seriously. Do you understand me, Iliana?"

"Yes, Mother." Then, once again failing to suppress her impulses, she added, "I imagine your own career will benefit greatly from Father's promotion."

"Indirectly, perhaps," Kaleen replied evenly, refusing to be baited. She reached for the pigment brush and gently touched Iliana's neck ridges. "The truth is, I'm quite content as a university inquisitor, because I know that's how I can best serve our homeland. I have no further ambitions, other than to support my husband in his new position, and to secure my daughter's future. There. Have a look."

Iliana sighed inwardly as she turned to face the mirror again, easily grasping the subtext of her mother's words, which could have come straight out of *The Never Ending Sacrifice* (a painfully wretched book as far as Iliana was concerned, despite its popular reputation as a literary classic; she had never been able to finish it). All respectable Cardassians devoted their lives to selflessly serving the State in some capacity, but children of the ruling elite were expected to pursue leadership careers, regardless of any personal desires they might have to the contrary. Years ago when she came of age, Iliana had narrowly avoided being sent to one of the regimented institutes that groomed privileged young people for those roles, her impassioned pleas for the chance to independently explore her art winning the day. But she knew her parents' patience was not without limits. Now well past the age of emergence, Iliana was recognized as an adult and therefore long overdue to settle on a path that would reflect well on her family. Cardassia valued its artists, but only so long as they remained politically correct.

Those pressures notwithstanding, Iliana had been clinging doggedly to an ever-dwindling hope that she might eventually attend school in the northern township of Pra Menkar, a remote academic community sufficiently removed from the pervasive conventionality of Cardassia's cities to permit the unrestricted pursuit of art for its own sake, rather than as a tool for "proper" political expression. That desire had become a source of tension and heartache within her family, of defiance and self-doubt, of angry words and challenges to authority— both her parents' and the State's. The contrariness her father and mother had once been willing to overlook as nothing worse than youthful spiritedness was tolerated less and less as Iliana grew older. Nonconformity, after all, was too often just another word for sedition.

But it's my dream. That should count for something, shouldn't it? More than anything, Iliana wanted her parents to be proud of her, but she harbored a growing fear that they might never be.

"Well, what do you think?" her mother asked, peering over her shoulder.

Iliana noted the new hints of blue on both sides of

her neck. The stranger in the mirror was now complete. She had to admire Kaleen's subtle touch.

"It's quite a difference," Iliana said.

Kaleen's face brightened suddenly. "I almost forgot— Do you remember Ataan Rhukal? The boy you used to play with?"

Ataan? There was a name she hadn't heard in a while. A little older than Iliana, he had been her constant companion and closest friend through most of her childhood. She remembered playing hunter-prey with him on the grounds outside her parents' house. She beat him every time, no matter which role she took. He'd also had a crooked smile that she vaguely remembered thinking was adorable.

"What in the world made you think of him?" Iliana asked.

"His mother still teaches political doctrine at the university. I spoke to her recently, and she mentioned that he just completed his studies at the Dekaris Institue. He's already a glinn. In fact—"

Iliana rolled her eyes. "Another fine addition to our glorious military, I'm sure."

"Iliana . . ."

"I'm sorry, I'm sorry," she said quickly, unable to keep herself from laughing. "That was my last sarcastic comment for the evening, I promise."

Her mother shook her head. "You're absolutely impossible, do you know that?"

Iliana put a hand to her abdomen as she tried to even out her breathing. "No, this dress is impossible. I'm simply incorrigible."

"Aren't you two ready yet?"

The bellow startled her. Tekeny Ghemor, clad in full

military regalia and sporting the symbols of his new rank, stood in the open threshold of her bedroom door. Kaleen stepped to one side, allowing him to take in the sight of his only daughter. "Oh, my," he said breathlessly. "Iliana . . . you look radiant."

Iliana's heart skipped a beat, absurdly pleased. Tekeny's approval always did that to her. In that moment, she even forgot how much she hated the dress. "I'm glad you think so, Father."

Tekeny tilted his head to one side. "Iliana, I know how you feel about these state affairs. . . ."

Iliana shrugged. "I'll get over it."

Tekeny glanced at Kaleen, and from the corner of her eye, Iliana saw her mother give him a slight, reassuring nod. "Very well, then," her father said. "Let's be off. We're running late as it is." Tekeny started to turn.

"Father, wait." Iliana moved to her dresser, opened the top drawer, and took out the cloth-wrapped bundle she'd placed there that morning. She might think the military was leading Cardassia down the wrong path, but this was her father, and whatever their disagreements, that still meant something. "I know how important it is to you that I be a true and dutiful daughter of Cardassia tonight, and I have every intention of honoring that obligation. But before I do that, I want to be just *your* daughter, if only for a short while longer." She presented Tekeny with the bundle. "I made this for you. It's just my way of saying I love you."

Moved by her little speech, Tekeny cradled the bundle in one arm and embraced her with the other. "I love you too, Iliana." They released each other and her father removed the cloth covering from her gift, his eyes glistening as he looked upon it for the first time.

The bone carving had taken her weeks to fashion, its fused layers of stylized wings curving and overlapping as they rose from its circular base. She hadn't known precisely what she would make when she first set to work on crafting a tribute for her father, save that it would be an abstract. But as she began scratching away at the flattened fragments of *taspar* bone, the wings and their symbolism slowly began to take shape; a fitting gesture, she hoped, to honor the most important man in her life on his rise to Central Command. "It's called *Ascension,*" she told him.

Tekeny didn't speak at first, and when he finally found his voice, it cracked with emotion. "I don't know what to say. It's . . . it's beautiful. Truly, Iliana. Thank you. Kaleen, have you seen this? The detail is extraordinary."

Iliana's mother smiled as she joined them. She regarded the carving almost reverently as Tekeny handed it to her. "It's lovely," Kaleen said, and glanced at her husband. "It seems you were right for a change," she teased him, and Tekeny laughed, nodding.

Iliana's eyes shifted back and forth between them. "Right about what?"

Tekeny let out a long breath. "I guess there's no better time to tell you. Your mother and I have been talking . . . and we both agree that perhaps Cardassia needs another artist right now more than it needs another jurist, or another soldier."

Iliana blinked, hardly daring to believe what she was hearing. "Does that mean I can go to Pra Menkar?"

Kaleen placed a hand on her daughter's bare shoulder. "If that's really what you want . . . yes."

"Oh, thank you, thank you!" Iliana cried, overcome by the moment and throwing her arms around both her parents. To know she had her their support in choosing her own path, to pursue her dream—

"I'll make you both proud of me," she whispered. "This I vow."

Against the blue-white glare of Cardassia's day, the massive cobalt pyramid of the State Museum of Natural History was an unmistakable fixture of the capital's crooked skyline, rising from the center of Torr Sector in all its stark grandeur. At night, however, its seemingly simple beauty took on new dimensions as focused spotlights, strategically aimed along its base of ornately carved granite buttresses, revealed details that were lost in the blinding light of Cardassia's harsh sun.

All other things being equal, Iliana would still have preferred a visit to the Tiluvus Gallery, a small, nondescript building that was almost lost among the drab and oppressive warehouses that crowded the Munda'ar Sector, unless you knew to look for it. Privately funded and perpetually in debt, Tiluvus wallowed in obscurity despite boasting works from, in Iliana's estimation, some of the most talented and overlooked artists of the last fifty years. Beautiful as this place was, she thought it unsubtle; too obvious in its intent to awe. The fact that it seemed to function as more mausoleum than museum only compounded her distaste. It promoted itself as a center of scientific and historical inquiry. To Iliana, it was merely a monument to extinction.

It was therefore with a sense of mounting unease that Iliana followed her parents up the grand steps of the building, joining the flow of polished uniforms and formal civilian attire that funneled through the towering main doors, discovering as she passed through them that everything was exactly as she feared it would be, only more so. From the first moment, the opulence of her surroundings and the self-indulgences of the guests assaulted her: The museum's majestic main gallery—its high vaulted ceiling painted with the constellations of Cardassia's southern hemisphere—was crowded with so many partygoers that the inlaid blue marble floor was almost invisible. And there, surrounded by the reconstructed skeletons of gigantic, long-dead animals, the upper echelons of Cardassian society mingled, sipping the finest *kanar* from flutes of exquisite crystal and sampling the delicacies of the Union off gold-press latinum trays that rested on evenly spaced pedestals throughout the hall. A live performance by a shellwind quintet, playing classical music at one end of the hall, veiled the reception in a fairly convincing illusion of civility, but Iliana knew better than to be taken in by the pretense. For many of those in attendance, these affairs were simply battlefields on which the combatants fought for personal prestige, or to strike a blow against a rival, or to advance a political agenda. It had all the makings of a grand opera.

No, she decided, that wasn't quite right. It was more like a waltz, one in which the participants stepped with calculated precision across the crowded floor, sometimes moving deliberately in ways to provoke another dancer into a disastrous misstep.

Steeling herself, Iliana dutifully followed her parents as they navigated the gallery, waiting patiently whenever they paused so Tekeny could accept congratulations from someone. If Iliana knew the well-wisher, she properly offered a polite comment or two; if introductions were necessary, she would likewise endure the inevitable shallow compliments, her smile locked firmly in place.

Within minutes, she felt frayed enough to shed her skin.

"There they are," she heard Tekeny say warily. Iliana followed his gaze and saw what appeared to be a number of high-ranking military officers gathered in a circle near the middle of the room, immersed in what sounded like a contentious debate.

"Dukat's there, isn't he?" her mother asked, smiling at a passerby.

"I'm afraid so," Tekeny said, nodding to someone else.

"Wonderful," Kaleen said through her teeth. "I trust you'll remember what I told you."

"I can handle Dukat, Kaleen."

"I hope so."

Iliana was about to ask her parents who Dukat was, but as they passed a long glass case containing the mummified remains of a pre-Hebitian warlord, Kaleen spied a small clutch of her associates from the judiciary gathered near a marble column at the edge of the gallery. Iliana took note of the subtle, knowing glances that passed between them and her mother, whereupon Kaleen whispered something in her father's ear. Tekeny nodded and the two of them briefly touched palms before her mother turned to her. "Mind your father, Iliana," she said. "See to it he doesn't get himself into any trouble."

"Just go, will you?" Tekeny said. "We'll be fine."

Never taking her eyes off Iliana, Kaleen squeezed her arm. "Try to enjoy yourself. And be watchful."

Iliana nodded. "You too."

Kaleen gazed at her a moment longer before she turned and moved off to perform her social duty. Following in her father's footsteps, Iliana resigned herself to doing hers.

• • •

". . . and we cannot forget what's at stake," said Gul Trepar, the sharp-featured commander of the Fourth Order, his taut, dry skin flaking at the ridges as if the skull beneath was trying to burst free. "Fueled by that perverse religion of theirs, the Bajorans are fostering nothing less than a culture of terrorism that has been allowed to endure far too long. Imagine if such indiscriminate hatred were to infect other asset worlds. It has to be contained now, quickly and with finality, before it spreads." Trepar's left eye twitched from time to time as he spoke—a side-effect, Iliana suspected, of suppressing the urge to scratch his face. She found it thoroughly ruined her appetite for the succulents that were attractively arranged on the tiered pedestal standing inside the circle of her father's peers.

"I agree that there must be zero tolerance for violence," drawled Gul Dukat, his speech slow and stretched, as if he thought it made the words more interesting. She had instantly understood her mother's apparent disdain for the man; self-absorption radiated from him like an aura, making his oratory as difficult to stomach as Trepar's face. "But I still believe we can best achieve our goals on Bajor by taking a more subtle approach—buying off more Bajorans who would be in a position to influence their people, rewarding those who are accepting of the annexation, offering demonstrations of Cardassian magnanimity. It's all about perception."

"My thoughts exactly," asserted Gul Pirak, one of the evening's honorees, a man whose soft, sagging features stood out from the more finely-chiseled faces around him. He had the look, Iliana thought, of a bureaucrat, not a soldier. "I salute your astuteness, Dukat. We've spent far too much time and energy trying to break Bajor's spirit when we should be looking for ways to remold it in our image. We must alter the message, show the Bajorans that the annexation isn't about exploiting them or subjugating them, but about Cardassia raising them up."

"Oh, please," muttered Trekal Darhe'el as the broad-shouldered gul threw back his head and consumed the last of his *kanar*. Darhe'el had heavy eyelids that added a strange menace to his gaze; he seemed to impale anyone he looked at. He was also drinking quite a bit more than anyone else in the circle, and he struck Iliana as surprisingly bitter for a celebrated hero of the Union.

The remark had evidently not escaped Pirak's notice. "I'm sorry, Darhe'el, the evening's lovely music drowned out your last comment. Would you care to repeat it?"

For a moment, Iliana thought Darhe'el wouldn't take the bait, but then he turned his hateful gaze with deliberate slowness on Pirak. "If you really believe you can combat a virulent insurgency with propaganda about the Bajorans' bright and glorious future as valued subjects of the Union, you're an even bigger fool than I'd imagined. The Bajorans may be loathsome, superstitious vermin, but they aren't stupid. They understand the true nature of our relationship all too well, I assure you. And the only way we're going to maintain our hold on their planet in the long term is by being merciless. They must be made to see that they have just two choices: accept their fate, or die."

"It's been my experience," Dukat said, "that violence works best when employed as a precision instrument, not a bludgeon."

"Such an approach might benefit the current prefect of Bajor," Trepar scoffed, "but it sets a dangerous precedent."

So Dukat is the prefect of Bajor, Iliana thought. *No wonder he seems so self-important.*

To his credit, Dukat didn't respond in kind to Trepar's blatant antagonism. As far as Iliana could tell, that was Trepar's primary reason for being there; he seemed to have something personal against Dukat, and was determined to provoke him, or at a minimum, to embarrass him.

Trepar pressed on and told the gathering, "I agree with our esteemed Gul Darhe'el, and I submit that any sign of hesitation on our part, any show of mercy, would be seen as a lack of Cardassian resolve—weakness to be exploited. We should never underestimate the Bajorans' fanaticism . . . or their capacity for viciousness. They're too easily inflamed and emboldened by a sick religion that gives them the arrogance to believe gods are on their side."

"Their religion is no longer a concern," Dukat countered. "I have put severe restrictions on their freedom to practice it. And without their so-called Orbs, their faith has weakened."

"Wasn't the ship carrying one of those . . . artifacts lost in the vicinity of the plasma storms some years ago?" Trepar asked pointedly.

"The *Kamal,* yes," Dukat admitted. "No trace of it has ever been found. We believe it was destroyed with all hands, along with the Orb it carried. But the other seven Orbs were captured long before that."

From where she stood, Iliana noticed a man, a civilian with distinctly large dark eyes and prominent facial ridges, drawing closer to the circle . . . and clearly he was trying to do so without drawing too much attention to himself. It was obviously working; no one besides Iliana seemed to notice him.

"There have been rumors of a ninth Orb," Legate Kell said casually. A stocky man with iron gray hair, Kell was the ranking officer present, and it seemed to Iliana that he was subtly encouraging the debate among his subordinates, as if by setting them against each other he could gauge their strengths and weaknesses. He was, Iliana thought, not unlike a keeper of riding hounds who occasionally tossed scraps of meat into their midst in order to see what lengths each beast would go to in order to feed, and which ones would go hungry.

"You may rest assured, we found them all," Dukat insisted. "Locating and confiscating Bajoran religious artifacts has been one of my highest priorities, and my men have been most thorough. If there were indeed a ninth Orb, I'd have found it by now."

"Are you certain?" Trepar asked with a sneer. "Perhaps your appetite for Bajoran women has affected your vision."

Dukat regarded his opponent coldly for a moment before speaking over his shoulder. "Do you hear the way he speaks to me, Akellen?"

"What?" Another partygoer, standing behind Dukat and facing the opposite direction, turned at the mention of his name. Iliana recognized the newcomer's distinctive insectile brown uniform as the one currently being worn by the forces assigned to defend the border that Cardassia shared with the Federation. He also bore an uncanny resemblance to Dukat himself. Perhaps that explained the atypical facial hair Akellen cultivated on both sides of his chin, which, along with the different uniform, would make it fairly easy to tell the two men apart at a glance. Apparently having a grand time, the brown-uniformed gul seemed positively jovial as he put an arm around

Dukat's shoulders. "Forgive me, Cousin, I was commiserating with the museum curator. What seems to be the matter?"

Dukat gestured with his glass. "Our colleague Trepar here has been casting aspersions upon my integrity."

"Really? Skrain, I'm shocked." Dukat's cousin seemed genuinely amazed. "Who knew you had any integrity?"

The circle erupted into laughter—all except Trepar, who regarded Dukat with contempt as Akellen rejoined the curator and drifted away again.

Interesting, Iliana thought. *Dukat deflects a slanderous public accusation by opening himself to good-natured ridicule. Shrewdly played.*

"And you, Ghemor?" Kell said suddenly, addressing Tekeny. "How would you handle the Bajoran annexation?"

Her father looked down at his *kanar* as he considered the question. As the last one to arrive, Tekeny listened more than he spoke, taking in what was being said, and by whom, and usually keeping his own counsel unless asked a direct question. "I daresay I would begin by reconsidering the need for the continued occupation of Bajor at all."

"What an interesting notion, Legate," said the large-eyed civilian who was now gently shouldering his way into the circle, between Pirak and Dukat. "Please elaborate."

Tekeny reacted as if the intrusion were entirely expected. "Gladly, Mister Entek. After all, we would not want your report to Enabran Tain to be anything less than complete, would we?" Ignoring the narrowing of Entek's eyes, her father continued. "I simply think it would serve us well to examine the need to maintain a planetary annexation when the gains clearly do not exceed the costs."

Darhe'el chuckled mirthlessly as he reached for another bottle of *kanar* on the serving pedestal, but said nothing as he refilled his flute.

"With respect, Legate," Dukat said to Tekeny, "that is a shortsighted view. A planet's resources take time to deplete, after all, especially on a world as bountiful as Bajor. To ignore the long-term benefits—"

"We have had control of Bajor now for over thirty years, extracting its uridium and other resources virtually nonstop," her father said. "We have never gained the acceptance of the native population, and all our attempts to beat it into submission have failed. Public support here at home for our continued involvement with Bajor is in decline, and some have even argued that, rather than being a force for stability, the occupation is actually feeding the insurgency. In my view the price of holding the planet far exceeds any benefit. The cost in Cardassian lives alone should give pause to anyone in this room. Factor in Bajoran lives—"

"The Bajorans," Darhe'el interrupted firmly, casting an appreciative glance at his refilled glass, "don't count. They're the labor force, just another resource, nothing more, to be used and discarded as we see fit." His eyes met Tekeny's. "And I personally have exacted payment for every Cardassian life lost under my command, a hundredfold."

"Your mathematics are most impressive, Darhe'el," her father said. "I'm sure it served you quite well at Gallitep."

Darhe'el glared at Tekeny. "Take care, Legate."

"Or what?" Tekeny asked. "Will you repay me a hundredfold?"

Iliana dug her fingernails into her palms. She wanted desperately to drag Tekeny away from these men, for her father to stop joining in this ridiculous posturing. Instead, she kept her expression neutral, remaining silent and rooted where she was, standing behind her father and to his right, just outside the circle of swaggering guls and legates.

Kell, she saw, watched the confrontation unfold with interest. *He's enjoying this.*

"Whatever you think you know about Gallitep is nothing compared to the reality," Darhe'el told Tekeny.

"Of that I have no doubt whatsoever," her father replied.

"Gallitep," Darhe'el continued, gathering heat as he spoke, "was a shining example of how Bajor *should* be handled: productive, efficient, and unforgiving. Those qualities were precisely the reason its mines there were so thoroughly emptied. And if my personnel had not subsequently been halved . . . and if I had been able to finish what I started in exterminating the workforce and razing the camp to the ground, the terrorists who overran the facility would never have succeeded, and forty-seven Cardassian soldiers would still be alive. But you . . . you and Dukat and this . . . goodwill ambassador here," he went on, gesturing at Pirak with his glass, "you seem to think there's some kind of compromise to be made, that the rabble on Bajor can be allowed to go unpunished for challenging Cardassia's manifest destiny. You may have forgotten the lessons we both learned at Kiessa, *Legate,* but I have not. And while you have not set foot on Bajor in twenty-five years, I have served there that entire time—too long to see our leaders toss aside the world I have spent my life taming."

Kell finally decided to intercede, cutting off whatever Tekeny was about to say. "And that is precisely why we are all here today, Darhe'el: to honor your long years of service to the Union, to welcome you back to Cardassia, and to wish Pirak here good fortune on his assignment to Bajor." The legate raised his glass. "To the sons of Cardassia, those who return home victorious, and those who go abroad seeking victory."

Most of the gathered officers followed Kell's lead and raised their flutes in kind, but Darhe'el was already setting down his unfinished *kanar*. "If you will all excuse me, I see nothing here worth celebrating." Without further comment Darhe'el turned away, the crowd of partygoers before him dividing as he marched to the exit. Trepar followed in his wake, calling after him, but Darhe'el refused to slow down.

"Good riddance, I say," Pirak muttered, prompting a stern glance from Kell.

"And yet, he has a point," Dukat said, watching Tekeny intently. "The lessons of the past should not be brushed aside so easily. For some of us, the famine and poverty that once imperiled our world before we annexed Bajor is still a livid scar. We have invested too many years and too much blood in Bajor simply to abandon it."

"I have not forgotten those difficult times, Dukat," Tekeny countered. "But I will not use them to justify policies that no longer serve our people's best interests."

"A strong and prosperous Cardassia is in our people's best interest," answered Dukat, as if daring Tekeny to contradict him.

"And by your estimation, with how much more blood should we be willing to pay for that prosperity?" Tekeny asked.

Dukat opened his mouth to reply, then seemed to re-consider his answer. "I think perhaps we are not really so far apart, Legate," he said at length. "Both of us want an end to wasteful death and destruction, after all. But as operational commander of the annexation, I do have a rather unique understanding of the Bajoran people, and I daresay that my singular perspective on what is happen-ing in the B'hava'el system ought to carry some weight in the deliberations of Central Command. It's for pre-cisely this reason that I have submitted recommendations for several targeted changes to our foreign policy, partic-ularly as it pertains to Bajor."

"I'm aware of your recommendations, Gul. They will receive due consideration at our next joint strategy ses-sion with the Detapa Council."

"The Detapa Council?"

"Yes. As I noted earlier, with the violence on Bajor continuing to escalate, public support of the annexation is eroding. In response, the civilian leadership has peti-tioned for a more active role in shaping Bajoran policy. My first official act as legate will be to meet with them on that very subject."

Pirak's mouth dropped open slightly at this revelation. Dukat, for his part, seemed unfazed, but Iliana perceived a subtle tensing of the muscles in his neck. "I see," he said neutrally. "I'll await the outcome of those meetings with interest." Then he grinned broadly and held up his flute. "And since Legate Kell made no mention of you in his toast, permit me the honor of wishing you success in your new position. All Cardassia celebrates your rise to Central Command."

"S-seconded," stammered Pirak, his jowls quivering as he spoke.

Once again, glasses were raised. But as Dukat's head tipped back, his eyes found Iliana's. With the departure of Darhe'el and Trepar, the circle had thinned enough that she was now clearly visible to the remaining officers. "And who is this lovely creature?" he asked, his smile taking on a strange quality. It made her feel vulnerable, exposed, ashamed even, as if she were an object of perverse curiosity, or worse. And from that moment, she hated him.

She felt her father's reassuring hand come to rest on her shoulder. "This is my daughter, Iliana," he said. "Iliana . . . Legate Danig Kell, Gul Morad Pirak, Mister Corbin Entek, and Gul Skrain Dukat." His voice had a slight edge to it as he said Dukat's name, one that she found strangely comforting.

Dukat, however, seemed untroubled by her father's show of protectiveness. He continued smiling at her, bowing slightly as he said, "It's a pleasure to meet you, Iliana. You must be very proud of your father."

Iliana knew that to ignore an invitation to praise Tekeny in front of his peers would be scandalous. She was not, however, required to prolong this uncomfortable encounter longer than necessary. "He's a great man," she said simply.

"Who will no doubt bring as much honor to his family as his leadership will bring to Cardassia," Dukat agreed. "Your mother Kaleen serves the State with great distinction also, as I recall. To have two such esteemed parents must be a source of great inspiration. I wonder, will you follow in your father's footsteps to the military, or will you join your mother in the judiciary?"

"I have my own ideas about how best to serve Cardassia."

From the periphery of her vision, Iliana noted that Mr. Entek's large eyes turned slightly in her direction.

"Lovely *and* fiercely independent," Dukat drawled, delight seeming to ooze from every elongated syllable. He raised his glass to her. "I salute the future of the empire."

Iliana's eyes narrowed. *Is he mocking me?*

"Run along now, Iliana," Tekeny said. "I'll call for you when it's time to go."

Thank you. Iliana gave her father a quick nod and immediately turned away from the circle, fleeing into the milling crowd of guests. It was some time before the feeling of eyes on her back went away.

Anxious to put some distance between herself and the company her father kept, Iliana briefly considered seeking out her mother, but quickly realized that Kaleen's circle of peers was likely to be as insufferable as Tekeny's. In the end, she found relief from the reception's suffocating atmosphere in the cool, breezy air of a sparsely occupied outdoor balcony, east of the museum's main hall. The balcony looked out onto a sprawling, well-tended garden under a canopy of towering trees. Guests seemed to be drawn to the grounds in pairs, descending curving granite stairs on either side of the balcony and fading into silhouettes as they followed the white stone paths that veined the garden. Innumerable lights strung through the canopy gave the place a surreal illumination, the bright pinpoints artfully merging with the stars of the black sky above. To Iliana, it was like finding an oasis after crossing a dark desert.

Most surprising of all, though, was what she found on the balcony itself. Bracketing the balustrade, near the top of each stairway, stood a bone carving—two of the largest and most extraordinary works Iliana had ever seen. Unlike the tapering curves or sharp-edged tiles that dominated so much of Cardassian design, these forms were far more abstract: flowing in a way that made Iliana think of rushing water, their unbroken fluidity in harmony with their stillness, power and violence merged with serenity.

Even more amazing, these weren't fusions, but whole pieces, each one evidently hewn from a single enormous bone like those found among the skeletons inside. So few animals on Cardassia were larger than men, save a few remaining species of deep sea leviathans, that most bone carvings were either very small, or they were amalgams of pieces from more common animals, like the one she'd made for Tekeny. These two on the balcony had been fashioned from very old bones, and judging from their color and texture, they were sculpted centuries ago. The realization made her wistful.

So much ancient art had been lost during the great arming of Cardassia, decades before Iliana was born, when the military had confiscated the treasures of her world's past and sold them to pay for the current age of imperialism, or destroyed them for their subversive content. It always saddened her to think about the works that she would never see: paintings and sculptures that were now part of private offworld collections; ancient books that were outlawed; artifacts of exquisite beauty crafted from rare minerals and precious metals, recycled for their value as raw materials for the military's war machines. This pair of enormous carvings had somehow survived all that. It struck Iliana that perhaps more of Cardassia's true soul was still out there somewhere, just waiting to be rediscovered.

"Um . . . excuse me?" someone said. Iliana considered

pretending that she hadn't heard the voice, in part because the intrusion at this moment was unwelcome, but also because she'd already noticed the cautious approach of the uniformed soldier who had spoken, and decided she'd had her fill of such men for one night. Iliana had no desire to be engaged in more calculated conversation. Then she considered the possibility that the man might have been sent by her father, and ignoring him would therefore be ill-advised.

"Yes?" she said as as she turned to face him, and noticed immediately that he was quite young.

The soldier smiled rather crookedly. "Iliana?"

She blinked, recognizing him. "Ataan!" she said. No longer the boy he'd been all those years ago, he'd grown tall, his broad shoulders and wide neck flattered by his uniform. *Mother! She had to have known he'd be here. Why else would she have mentioned him back at the house? But why hadn't she simply told me so?*

Then again, maybe she would have, if I hadn't derailed the conversation with my usual charming commentary.

"I can't believe it's you," he said. He opened his arms to give her a hug, and after only a moment's hesitation, she met him halfway. "How have you been?" he asked.

"I'm well," she told him, feeling a strange electric thrill from the embrace. She quickly stepped back. "Dekaris seems to have agreed with you. You're all grown up."

Ataan's crooked smile returned. "So are you."

Her ridges flushed as she suddenly remembered the dress. "Your family. Um, they're well?"

"My parents are both fine. My brother Ghel was just promoted to dalin. He's first officer on the *Aldara*." Ataan nodded toward the main hall. "Your family is obviously prospering."

"It's been quite a night. Is that why you're here?"

"Indirectly. I'm a member of Gul Pirak's security staff. I'll be joining him on his assignment to Bajor next month."

Bajor again. There seemed to be no escaping it. "I met Gul Pirak a short while ago," she said.

"What did you think?"

Iliana bit back the first answer that came to her and shrugged. "I'm afraid one gul is like another to me."

Ataan wagged a finger at her. "Dekaris would have cured you of that improper notion."

"Just as well that I didn't attend, then. I'm rather fond of my improper notions."

Ataan shook his head. "Same old Iliana. Tell me, do you still draw?"

He remembers! She had discovered her talent for illustration when they both were still children. Ataan had seemed so in awe of her talent, and she still recalled how good his admiration had felt. "I do. I also paint now. And sculpt. As a matter of fact, my parents have just given me their blessing to complete my studies at a special university in Pra Menkar."

"That's wonderful news! Congratulations." And the way he said it, she could tell he wasn't simply being polite. He was genuinely happy for her. "I still can't get over seeing you now. You look amazing."

Iliana grinned involuntarily, embarrassed and flattered. She gestured at his uniform. "So do you."

An awkward silence settled between them, broken by a commotion from inside the museum; a throng of boisterous guests was making its way toward the balcony. Ataan cocked his head toward the garden. "I don't suppose you'd care to take a stroll?"

She didn't even consider refusing the invitation. "I'd be delighted."

He offered her his elbow, and together they began their descent.

Finding the paths nearest the museum too well trafficked for their taste, Iliana and Ataan cut across a meadow toward a more sparsely populated quarter of the garden. The sound of running water drew them deeper still, to an artificial stream that Iliana assumed must be part of the park's necessarily extravagant irrigation system, vital to keeping the arid heat of the surrounding capital at bay. A stone bridge spanned the water flow, and it was there that they stopped, standing against the railing as they talked.

Their conversation began with a flood of shared memories; reminiscences of childhood that cascaded out and bubbled over with laughter: everything from the pranks they pulled on Ataan's far too serious elder brother, to the trouble they'd get into digging up onyx beetles and letting them loose inside her parents' house.

Eventually they moved on to Ataan's experiences at Dekaris, which suited Iliana just fine, as it saved her from having to discuss how she had spent the years since they'd last seen each other. Not that she was in any way ashamed of her artistic pursuits; she was simply having too good a time listening to Ataan, getting used to his deepened voice, watching the way his face would light up when he spoke of his schooling, learning about his plans for the future. Unfortunately, those topics inevitably led them back to the last place she wanted to go.

"The Bajor assignment is an incredible opportunity,"

Ataan was saying as he took in the scenery. "Still, I'm going to miss home."

"How long will you be gone?" Iliana asked.

"My rotation is five years," he said.

"Oh."

"After that, I may receive orders to stay on Bajor, or I could be reassigned elsewhere. You know the military."

More than I care to, that's certain.

"I'm looking forward to playing whatever small part I'll have in helping to quell the violence," Ataan went on. "It's considered quite a privilege to be selected for such a posting. Once Gul Pirak received his orders, he was allowed to handpick his staff from among the recent Dekaris graduates."

"You must be very proud."

"It's an honor to serve," Ataan said automatically. Iliana thought the response predictable, but once again held her tongue. Her face must have betrayed her disappointment, because Ataan's eyes abruptly narrowed. "What is it?" he asked.

"I'm sorry. It's nothing." Iliana wished she felt comfortable simply speaking her mind, but she didn't want to risk offending her old friend and thereby ruining their brief reunion. She tried shrugging off the thought. "Another improper notion, I'm afraid."

"For the daughter of a legate, you seem to have a lot of them."

"I know," Iliana said, shaking her head. She spread her hands. "What can I say? I'm an anomaly."

The crooked smile returned. "You know . . . I rather like anomalies."

Iliana rolled her eyes. "Oh, do you, now?"

"Absolutely. I could spend the rest of my life poring over one."

"I'll bet you could."

Ataan laughed. "What about you?"

"What about me?"

"Well . . . what have you been doing since we last saw each other?"

"The usual," she said. "Promoting dissent, plotting revolution, overthrowing the government."

"Ah, and how's that coming along?"

"We take over Central Command at midnight. You should come. There'll be a party afterward. Maybe a game of hunter-prey."

He laughed again. "Hunter-prey! Do you know, I haven't thought about that since . . ." He shook his head. "I'm surprised you brought that up, considering how often I used to beat you."

Iliana blinked. "Excuse me?"

"Oh, come on," Ataan said. "Please tell me you haven't forgotten how I won practically every game we played."

A short laugh burst from her throat. "You most certainly did not."

"I most certainly did."

Her eyes narrowed. "You're joking, right? Or have they started altering memories at Dekaris? *You* beat *me*?"

"Well, admittedly, only when you weren't cheating."

"How *dare* you!"

"How dare *you*!" Ataan bellowed.

Iliana's ridges flushed again. Her heart beat faster. She started to feel light-headed. Thrilling sensations to be sure, but confusing; Ataan's sudden display of belligerence was a parade of masculine signals her body seemed to recognize before her brain did, triggering the involuntary physical responses common to most Cardassian women.

She stared into his eyes, captivated by the power of his voice and overwhelmed by the intensity of his emotions, which seemed to mirror her own. *This is happening too fast,* she warned herself. *Keep your head, girl, and your heart, or you'll likely lose both before this night is done.*

Iliana scoffed and made a point of turning away from him. She was much better off avoiding eye contact with Ataan; it would help her to control the conversation. But no words came to her, and in the silence that followed, Ataan walked around her slowly. She felt him stop behind her, his body very close. She gazed out over the stream. Reflecting the lights in the trees above, the water below was a dark swath broken by glittering streamers. She felt his breath on the right ridge of her neck, and she closed her eyes.

"Iliana."

Her eyes snapped open at the sound of her mother's voice. She spun around to see Kaleen standing at the foot of the bridge, her arms crossed.

"Mother!"

"Lady Ghemor," Ataan said, inclining his head. "It's good to see you."

"Hello, Ataan," Kaleen said, scrutinizing him as though he were a newly discovered insect. "Oh, I beg your pardon—it's *Glinn Rhukal* now, isn't it?"

Ataan smiled. "I could never insist on such formality from one who used to bathe me, my lady."

"Hmm, yes," Kaleen said, her mood seeming to soften. "Well, that's what happens when you spend your youth in my garden, digging up onyx beetles." She looked at

Iliana. "I confess I had hoped you two would encounter each other at the reception . . . though I rather expected you to remain inside the museum with the other guests."

"Mother, I—"

"We'll talk about it later, Iliana. Come along now, it's time for us to go. Your father is waiting. Pleasant evening to you, Ataan."

"To you as well, my lady. Please offer my congratulations to Legate Ghemor."

"You can do that yourself at dinner."

"Dinner?"

Iliana's eyes widened.

"At our home, tomorrow evening," Kaleen explained. "Be there at sunset. Unless, of course, your duties will prevent it . . . ?"

Ataan grinned. "I'll look forward to it, my lady."

"As will we." Kaleen nodded to him and steered Iliana back toward the museum.

When Iliana felt certain that Ataan was out of earshot, she said, "Mother, it wasn't my intention—"

"You forget that I was once young too, Iliana," Kaleen said. "Unfortunately, a sense of propriety is not genetic. It needs to be learned."

"I understand."

"I hope you do."

After a moment, Iliana asked, "You're not going to tell Father, are you?"

"I have no intention of withholding this from him," Kaleen said sternly. "But I think he'll handle it better after he's had the chance to get reacquainted with Ataan, and has seen for himself what a fine, honorable young man he's become. Don't you agree?"

"Absolutely," Iliana said. Then, more quietly, she added, "Thank you, Mother."

Kaleen glanced at her, sighed, and looked away again, shaking her head. "You're welcome."

The museum came into view as they rounded a bend in the path, and Iliana realized that she and Attan had traveled much farther than she had thought. "How did you know where to find me?"

"I didn't," her mother said. "But while I was looking for you, I encountered an acquaintance of your father's, Mister Entek. He was kind enough to mention that he saw you here."

Ilana blinked. "Entek?"

"Yes. . . . Is something the matter?"

Iliana's eyes panned from side to side, futilely searching the dark grounds. But all she found were shadows.

"Iliana?"

"No," she said after a moment. "I guess not. . . ."

2

They moved as one. Skin against skin, their bodies entwined, fingers gently roaming as their breathing gradually fell in step and their hearts began to beat in unison, faster and faster toward a shared ecstasy that came in steady, surging waves. Iliana held on to the feeling, prolonged it, gasping as it reached its zenith and overwhelmed her . . . then released it, her breath escaping with an audible sigh as she floated back to the world.

Afternoon light warmed her eyelids as her head fell upon her pillow. She felt Ataan settle against her, their hearts and lungs slowly resuming their natural, separate rhythms.

When the breeze from her dormitory window caressed her skin, dissipating its heat and stimulating the nerves toward wakefulness, her eyes opened to night. The darkness was broken only by the glow of Letau, Cardassia's innermost moon, throwing soft blue rays into her room. She no longer felt Ataan against her.

Shifting, Iliana saw him sitting up in her bed, his handsome face tinged orange from the glow of a padd in his hand. He looked at her. "I'm sorry, did I wake you?" he whispered.

She shook her head slightly, not yet ready to raise it from the pillow. "What time is it?"

"Almost midnight. Are you hungry?"

In fact, she was famished, but her sudden distress pushed out any thought of food. "Midnight? Why'd you let me sleep? You have to leave in the morning!"

He shrugged. "Once I board the transport, my time is my own. I can sleep during the voyage. Now you're rested, and we can both be awake for our remaining hours together."

Remaining hours. It sounded like waiting to die. This past month with Ataan had seemed surreal, dreamlike. They'd spent every possible moment together, including her enrollment and relocation to Pra Menkar University. Ataan's duties had been thankfully light during that time; he'd even been around to help her get settled into the dormitory ... and subsequently shared a number of nights in her bed. Now on this, the eve of his departure for Bajor, it felt as if an essential part of her life was ending.

She pushed the unpleasant thought away, tried to focus on something else. Her eyes found the device in Ataan's hand and she tried to lose herself in its pinpoint lights.

Ataan followed her gaze and, mistaking her interest in the padd for curiosity, explained, "Cultural briefing on Bajor. Gul Pirak insisted we brush up on the customs and recent history of the planet in preparation for our mission. He's convinced we need to bond with the locals if we're going to make any progress against the terrorists."

Iliana nodded but said nothing in reply, hoping Ataan would take the hint and change the subject.

Instead, he continued, "He has high hopes about the assignment. He wants to show the Bajorans that we'd be much stronger working together than we are by remaining at odds."

She remembered Pirak's enthusiasm for the "more subtle approach" toward Bajor that Gul Dukat had espoused. Their apparent interest in, as he put it, "altering the message" Cardassia was sending Bajor had struck her as an encouraging sign. And while she remained skeptical, she hoped it would work, if only for Ataan's sake.

"I was even thinking about learning to speak Bajoran," he went on. "Translators are well and good, of course, but I think the Bajorans would respond well to Cardassians who took the time to learn their language. What do you think?"

A direct question. So much for her hope in a change of subject. "I think it's a good idea," Iliana said. "You should mention it to Pirak. Maybe he'll make it a requirement for everyone under his command."

Ataan laughed. "And have me end up a victim of friendly fire? No, thank you."

Her eyes narrowed. "Oh, I see. Pirak wants to reach out to the Bajorans, but you don't think his men share that goal."

"I didn't say that."

"Didn't you?"

"All I meant was that having to learn a new language isn't likely to be a popular directive, especially if it became common knowledge that I suggested it."

"Even if it helps you to accomplish your commanding officer's objective?"

"Look, it isn't that simple. The troops—"

"The troops, ah yes," Iliana interrupted. "You know, maybe that's the problem. Sending soldiers to do the work of diplomats."

Ataan frowned. "The job of diplomats is to negotiate," he said emphatically. "You don't negotiate with terrorists."

"I didn't realize all Bajorans were terrorists."

"Stop twisting what I say! Even if diplomacy was the answer, it isn't an option until the planet is made secure by the military."

Iliana bit back the flood of angry responses on her tongue and closed her eyes. "Can we just talk about something else? Please?"

"What's the matter with you?"

"Nothing!"

"Iliana—"

"I just get so sick of hearing about the turmoil on Bajor!" She abruptly got up from the bed and recovered her discarded undergarments, muttering as she clothed herself. "Bad enough that the comnet is full of it; or that the military can't even agree on what should be done about it, do *we* really need to be discussing it too? In my own bed?"

Ataan stared at her. "Iliana . . . Cardassians are dying there every day. You can't expect—"

"Expect? What I've come to expect is everything I hear day after day after day: violence and threats of violence, skirmishes and terrorist attacks, political rhetoric and fear mongering . . . all over a world that obviously doesn't want us there. And *this* is the world you're going to."

"Not a staunch supporter of our foreign policy, I take it."

She glared at him. "Don't mock me."

A hurt look enveloped his face. "I would never do that," he said. "I really am interested in what you think."

She could tell that he meant it. He was searching her eyes—for what, she didn't know, until she realized that when it came to his career, she seldom offered anything of substance in exchange for the trust and openness that always seemed to come so easily from him. For Iliana, it went against a lifetime of conditioning; a culture that prized conformity wasn't one that encouraged the open expression of a dissenting view.

Now as she stared back at him, she considered all the self-doubt and private heartache she carried with her: the indoctrination she had struggled with privately for years; the first tentative attempts to defy her mother and father and to assert her own identity; the eventual realization that she truly rejected her upbringing and her parents' blind devotion to the State; and most of all . . . the certainty she felt, in spite of the intense pride and profound love she had for her homeworld, that there was something terribly wrong with Cardassia.

"I think we're making a lot of mistakes," she said.

Ataan frowned. "With Bajor?"

"With many things. But yes, with Bajor in particular. Whatever our original motives were in going there, or the way we justify our continued presence, I think this annexation has confronted our people with issues we were unprepared to deal with, questions we haven't found answers to, and it's challenging the way we see ourselves."

"What do you mean?" Ataan asked.

Iliana lowered her eyes, wrapping her arms around herself. She had never expressed her thoughts this way before, and it made her feel exposed, vulnerable. "I think the Bajorans frighten us," she said. "Bajor's refusal to accept Cardassia's attempts to change it isn't just a defiance of our power. It's a repudiation of the changes we willingly made in ourselves when we let the military be responsible for our survival . . . when we gave up anything that reminded us of just how weak we'd become. Even after thirty years of conflict, the Bajorans hold steadfast to their spirituality, their rich ancient past, and their quaint way of life. They're proof that the qualities we abandoned can be stronger than the ones we kept—that maybe we made the wrong choices for ourselves. And I think that idea is simply too intolerable for us to face."

She looked up at him. "I love Cardassia, Ataan. I really do. I'm proud of our civilization. But when I think about everything we've given up to get where we are right now, I have to wonder, is Bajor really the more troubled world?"

"Was that a rhetorical question?" Ataan asked, keeping his tone light.

Iliana frowned. "No, it wasn't." She sat down on the edge of the bed, watching his face, waiting for his response. Silence settled between them. She knew she was probably ruining everything they'd built together this past month, but maybe that wasn't such a terrible thing; it would make their separation easier. *If nothing else, he can make up a polite excuse and call for an early beam-out. A clean break.*

Ataan took a deep breath. Then he surprised her.

"I think you're right," he said at last, and gave her a moment to let the admission sink in. "I think maybe Bajor has driven us all a little mad. We've become obsessed with it for exactly the reasons you give, and that fixation is slowly killing us. Like a fatal addiction." Attan's eyes fell on the padd that was still in his hand. "I don't think there's any question that the annexation has catalyzed a deepening schism here at home. It's as if those on all sides of the argument believe that how the Bajoran question is ultimately answered will define Cardassia, for better or worse, now and in the future. We're up to our necks in a quagmire." He looked up at her once more. "But what's the alternative? To let Bajoran extremism win? That would hurt them as well as us. We can't simply sit back and not take a stand against terrorism. However some of us may feel about Cardassia's present direction, imagine how much worse we would be not to oppose evil when confronted by it, Iliana. We can't hide from that responsibility . . . no matter how much we may wish we could."

The room fell silent. Iliana had never likened Ataan to the doctrine-minded automatons that in her estimation made up most of the military—not really—so his sentiments shouldn't have surprised her. Yet somehow she was completely unprepared for the surge of emotion she felt as Ataan expressed himself; the strength of his character and his personal ethics made her wonder for the first time about the good the military could do, if only there were more men like him in it. He made her hopeful about the future, something she couldn't remember feeling since she was a child.

But he's going to Bajor.

She harbored no ill will toward the Bajorans, a troubled people who obviously needed Cardassia's help as much as Cardassia needed theirs. She simply wished the conflict there could be resolved soon and without further bloodshed.

And without Ataan.

"Iliana, what's wrong?"

She gazed out the window at the small blue orb of Letau. "It's been too short a month. I wish we had more time."

He touched her bare shoulder, stroking it with the back of his fingers. "So do I. But you know I'll send you a recording as often as I'm able, and I hope you'll do likewise."

She rolled her eyes. "Of course I will. But it's not the same."

"I know. But it may make our separation a little easier. And when my rotation is over, we'll be together again."

"Not if your tour is extended, or if you're reassigned to a ship or some other forsaken rock far from Cardassia."

"Wherever I am, I'll always come home to you, Iliana. This I vow."

Iliana turned and met his steady gaze again. "What are we really talking about? Marriage?"

"Too soon?" he asked sincerely.

She considered the question. "Before that night at the museum, I'd have dismissed such an idea as absurd. But the way we've reconnected so quickly and completely . . . I can no longer imagine a life in which you aren't a part."

Ataan's mouth spread into a smile. "Nor I you."

They touched palms, then drew closer, falling together against the bed, the beating of their hearts once again becoming one.

The day after Ataan departed Cardassia was the day Entek made his opening move.

Resolved to begin the process of getting used to Ataan's absence, Iliana ventured out with her artpadd to the gardens on the outskirts of town, seeking inspiration.

Pra Menkar was that rarest of Cardassian communities: a hill town, sprawling across a sunlit slope far above the cracked desert to the north. With the higher elevation came cooler temperatures and breezier air, conditions most Cardassians found unpleasant, but the inhabitants of Pra Menkar had no such sensitivities. They simply dressed warmer as necessary, and soaked up heat on indoor basking slabs when relaxing at home. Even the university students could take advantage of such luxuries: each dormitory had communal basking rooms in which to take refuge from the evening chill. For Iliana, getting acclimated to the cooler conditions was just part of the fun of life away from home.

But though the Cardassians of Pra Menkar tolerated its atypical clime only with effort, it was ideally suited for other forms of life: a variety of flora and even a few species of small fauna that wouldn't last a day on the hot, dry plains actually flourished here. The Peripheral Gardens that ringed the community exploded during the growing season with the kind of life that existed in less than one tenth of a percent of the planet's land area. Iliana had fallen in love with the gardens on her first visit, utterly taken with their strangeness, the orgy of smells, sights, and textures that had once been outside her experience. It validated her belief that a much wider world existed on Cardassia than the one she'd been raised in; one needed only the courage and the strength of will to look for it.

As she navigated the paths that wound through the colorful beds of exotic plants, she gradually became aware of the sound of children playing. She followed the noises around a bend until she saw two small girls and a boy chasing one another in the midst of a grassy field. The oldest couldn't have been more than four, and their laughter as they played stirred something inside her that felt paradoxically sad and hopeful at the same time. Iliana recalled herself at that age, with Ataan, and she imagined someday seeing her own children—*their* children—in a place like this.

She found a sitting-stone under a shade tree that afforded her a good view of the toddlers, roughly equidistant between the elderly couple who were watching over them . . . and a serpentine stone bench on which sat a man she recognized.

Resting the artpadd on her folded legs, Iliana began her usual exercises of allowing her fingers to roam freely over the illustration surface, letting them find their way tracing abstract designs until she felt sufficiently in tune with her environment to translate what she saw into representations on the padd. The elders took notice of her early on, eyeing her with suspicion. But they came no nearer, and after a few moments their attention returned to their young charges. She suspected that on some level, the couple had initially perceived her interest in the children as some kind of threat, but that they quickly got over their natural protectiveness. Iliana was pleased with herself; sitting under the large tree with her legs folded beneath her had allowed her to appear as small and harmless as possible, and that preemptive strategy had put the couple sufficiently at their ease that they didn't feel compelled to gather up the children and leave.

In the periphery of her vision, she took stock of the lone man on the bench. He was facing away from the children, his right profile turned toward Iliana. Wearing a neat gray casual suit, he fidgeted in a way that suggested he was easily distracted by his surroundings, sometimes drawn to the scurrying of a small lizard among the flowerbeds, or the rustling of leaves in the infrequent breeze. The performance was so convincing, she almost doubted what she knew to be true: that just as she was studying him out of the corner of her eye, so too was he studying her in precisely the same way.

Four unsatisfying sketches later, she decided she'd had enough. Tucking her artpadd under her arm, Iliana slowly and deliberately walked to the bench, sat down in the vacant nook of its S-curve, and started sketching again. At no time did she or the man look directly at each other.

"Is there something you want of me, Mister Entek?" she asked, her fingers re-creating the tree line in the distance before her.

"As a matter of fact, there is," Entek answered without hesitation. "But let me first say how flattered I am that you recognized me."

"Don't be," Iliana told him. "I simply have a good memory. But if you're going to spy on someone, you should try harder to avoid being seen while doing so."

Entek smiled. "Thank you for the suggestion. But I feel I should tell you that today, here in these gardens, and that evening at the museum have not been the only times you've been under surveillance. In fact, it would be fair to say that I have been watching you nonstop since the reception."

Iliana froze, just for a second, unsure whether or not she should believe him. "Why?"

"For a number of reasons, but primarily because I've been intrigued by your exceptional powers of observation."

Iliana shrugged. "I notice things. It's a useful skill for an artist."

"And for an agent," Entek said.

"Is that what all this is about? Recruiting me for the Obsidian Order?"

"You couldn't guess that?"

In fact, she had. When at the reception her father had mentioned Enabran Tain, who was the Order's head, he had made it abundantly clear that Entek was an operative for the Union's intelligence arm. "I'm just a little disappointed it wasn't something less obvious," she told him.

"Ah," said Entek. "You expect me to speak in riddles, project an air of mystery, say things that have multiple layers of meaning so that my listeners can trip over themselves attempting to untangle the truth from the lies. We have agents like that. They're rather annoying."

"So are you, Mister Entek," Iliana said, already growing weary of the conversation. "And unfortunately for you, you've come a long way for nothing. So allow me to save you any further trouble on my account. The answer is no. Good day." Iliana packed up her artpadd and started to walk away.

"You should reconsider," Entek called to her. Against her better judgment, Iliana stopped and turned around, looking into his face for the first time, and he into hers. "I've gotten to know you quite intimately during the last month," he claimed, "and I'm convinced you would be an extraordinary operative."

"You don't know me at all," Iliana said.

Entek held her gaze. "Iliana Ghemor: only child of Legate Tekeny Ghemor of the Central Command and First Tier Inquisitor Kaleen Ghemor (née Dakal) of the Central University. A child of privilege, exceedingly spoiled, and raised in the comfort and security that comes from being a daughter of the ruling class. Despite the love and respect you have for your father—not to mention a more recent premarital relationship—you have a distaste for the military, but no real understanding of its workings or its offworld campaigns, to say nothing of Cardassian foreign policy. You consider yourself an idealist, concerned primarily with art and music and abstract learning, but these pursuits are primarily to fill the void of real purpose in your life. They have, however, allowed you to get away with a certain youthful rebelliousness; making empty calls for social change over the dinner table and in the sleepchamber, where it is tolerated. But you seldom voice such opinions outside those contexts, where your ignorance of the issues would be too easily revealed, and where your pretense of being a radical would likely attract the wrong sort of attention. Essentially, you give the appearance of dissent without actually practicing it in your everyday life, lest doing so cost you the comfortable existence you've grown accustomed to.

"You have an exceptionally well developed eidetic memory and are acutely observant of your immediate environment, especially people. You're intelligent and mildly athletic. No notable health problems.

"You've just been betrothed to your childhood companion and lover of one month, Glinn Ataan Rhukal, presently beginning a five-year tour of duty on Bajor as a member of the personal staff of Gul Morad Pirak. You worry that your relationship will not survive the separation, but you believe the depth of your mutual feelings will ultimately prove stronger than the time you are forced to spend apart. You enjoy the feel of his breath on your neck ridges, especially the right side. Oh, and you hate fish juice for breakfast, preferring a light tea made from marine plants."

Iliana felt her ridges flushing, her body heat rising

with indignation, but she refused to give Entek the satisfaction of seeing it. Instead, she offered up a slow, mocking applause. "Well done. Tell me, do you enjoy dissecting people's lives?"

"I take no joy in it at all. It's merely a tool—one I would prefer to use with discretion, but which I'm quite willing to employ openly if a task requires it."

"What task could you have that would possibly make my humiliation necessary?"

"You," Entek answered simply. "I need you to understand how serious my choosing to make direct contact with you is, Iliana."

"Excuse me, I believe I made contact with you—"

Entek shrugged. "Believe that if you must, but I can truthfully say that none of the subjects under my surveillance has ever detected me unless that was exactly what I intended."

"And you think I'm impressed by that?" Iliana asked. "Flattered? Honored?"

"I think you're curious."

She folded her arms. "And what would lead you to think that?"

Again, Entek smiled. "We're still talking, are we not?"

Iliana frowned. "Not anymore." Without another word, she turned away and started walking.

"You're misguided, you know."

Iliana almost laughed, and once again she stopped and turned to face him. "Am I really?"

"You think your pursuit of the arts is something noble and pure and an end unto itself. But I'm here to tell you that you need set no such limits. You can be much more than you think you are. There are nobler and purer forms of expression."

Iliana did laugh this time. "Service to the Order?"

"And by extension, to all of Cardassia."

"You just got through calling me a shallow hypocrite," she countered. "If that's what you really believe, why would you want someone like me in the Order? It sounds rather as if you have ample reason to arrest me, not recruit me."

"That option was considered at some length," Entek assured her. "People have disappeared for far less, after all."

"But not I?"

"You have far too much potential, Iliana. You're confused and wayward, true, but not in any way that's irreparable. The clay of your life has not yet been fired. It's still malleable, changeable. As with most young people, much of who you are now is in flux. Left to your own devices, the useless aspects of your evolving identity will be transformed or discarded as you are molded by experience into your true and final form. But the Order can give those changes direction, focus, help you to achieve clarity of self and certainty of purpose sooner than you might otherwise."

"In other words, you hope to program me."

"Not at all. Forcing you to be something you are not would be disastrous. Like any proper institute of learning, we merely cultivate whatever is already there. It would have been better for both of us if you'd been identified at an early age and risen through the levels at Bamarren or Surjada, but adult recruitment is not unprecedented, and has on occasion yielded very talented operatives.

"Despite our profile of you, Iliana, I know your concerns about Cardassia are genuine. I'm merely offering you an opportunity to be part of the solution. Being chosen to fulfill one's duty to the State through such service is no minor thing. The Union has a need for sentinels like those in the Order to stand against the enemies of Cardassia."

Iliana shook her head, unimpressed. "First you try flattery, then humiliation, now you appeal to my sense of patriotism. How soon should I expect you to threaten my loved ones?"

Entek made a show of thinking about it. "Not for some time, I hope. With any luck, one of my other tactics will work. Eventually."

"Don't count on it."

"Mm. Very well, then." Entek rose to leave.

Iliana blinked. "That's it?"

Entek stopped and smiled. "I'm sorry, have I disappointed you again?"

"For someone who claims to have spent the last month observing me closely, you're giving up rather easily."

"Who said anything about giving up?"

"Aren't you? Are we going to go through this all over again a week from now, or do you think I'm going to wake up tomorrow and decide, 'Entek was right. Where do I enlist?'"

Entek took a step toward her, leaned in, and said very quietly, "I don't expect it to happen that quickly, no. But I've done what I came to do, Iliana. I've made you an offer. Eventually, yes, I think you'll come to realize that the universe you live in isn't one in which that touching idealism you cling to can survive. And when you understand that, and remember our conversation, I'll be waiting." Entek turned and walked away.

Iliana stared after him, furious. "It'll be a long wait," she shouted.

"If that's what it takes," Entek called, but didn't look back.

3

My Betrothed Iliana,

    My first day on this new world wasn't at all what I'd expected. We docked at Terok Nor on schedule but were forced to delay beaming down to the planet. During the days leading up to our arrival there were a number of bombings in the district to which we've been assigned, and Gul Dukat's troops were still securing the area. Ironic, given the things Pirak hopes to accomplish as the new regional administrator. What was supposed to have been a mere hour's delay eventually stretched into a day, much to everyone's irritation. That said, the prefect was a gracious host, and made the inconvenience of our remaining aboard his station as pleasant an experience as possible.

    Dukat's man on the planet met us when we finally transported down, a dour dalin named Sigol Rusot. He seemed impatient to be off world as quickly as possible, as if he resented having to prepare for our arrival. He clearly has no love for the Bajorans; a group of them had

*gathered when we first arrived, and Rusot dealt severely
with a pair of youths who, in his view, had ventured too
close. Gul Pirak was incensed by the unprovoked brutality, and had harsh words for the dalin before banishing
him and his men back to Terok Nor. Rusot departed, but
with a last look directed at us that clearly bordered on
contempt.*

*You'll appreciate this: apparently our base of operations
on the planet once belonged to a wealthy Bajoran icon
painter who in later years transformed his ancestral home
into a school for artistically gifted young people. It's unclear
to me what became of him, but he left behind a sprawling compound consisting of a single extravagant man-
sion where he lived and taught his students, and several
smaller satellite buildings that served as dormitories. Gul
Pirak, his family, and his senior staff—myself included—
moved into the main house. My security force is taking
up residence in the surrounding structures, which form an
excellent defense perimeter. The bulk of our troops, however, have been deployed throughout the region, relieving
personnel rotating offworld, or where security has thinned
precipitously because of casualties suffered in terrorist attacks or skirmishes with the insurgents.*

*I'm still preoccupied by this morning's incident with
Rusot and the Bajorans. I admit that even now, hours
later, it mystifies me; the locals we saw seemed haggard,
even docile, and posed no threat I could detect. For all
anyone really knew, they were just being friendly. Maybe
Rusot was simply taking no chances, given the recent rash
of attacks he'd been sent to quell. Maybe he wanted to
send a message to any terrorists who might be watching.
Maybe he's simply a brute. Whatever the reason, it's obvious we have a long road ahead if we're going to show the*

Bajorans a Cardassian face that's different from the one they're used to.

From my heart to yours,
Ataan

My Betrothed Iliana,

Today was a revelation. I had the privilege of accompanying Gul Pirak on an aerial tour of our district this afternoon. Our guide was a Bajoran named Oluvas Del, a small, middle-aged man with dark, deeply wrinkled skin and callused hands. He was the Bajoran liaison for the previous regional administrator, and judging by his accommodating manner, I think he hopes to serve in that capacity for Gul Pirak.

Bajor is simply amazing. Our compound is situated just outside the city of Hathon in Dahkur Province. This region is one of the planet's main centers of agriculture, and it's easy to see why. Words fail to adequately describe my astonishment at the flora here—forests and farmlands that stretch to the horizon, flower beds thriving in the midday sun. You can scarcely walk ten paces without encountering a fruit tree! Can you imagine?

The city covers a hill that's surrounded on all sides by farming communities. These lands currently blur together in a disorderly sprawl, but soon they'll be more easily defined as we rezone the farms and reprioritize the crops grown on them. Central Command wants this district developed for maximum output, part of a larger initiative to make Dahkur Bajor's primary supplier of food to the homeworld, now that Rakantha Province is no longer able to meet our needs.

That's where we come in. Our mandate is to supervise the labor force and maintain security. Harvests are sent to the city for processing and transfer to Terok Nor, then shipped to Cardassia Prime. It might sound simple, but it's a logistical and security nightmare, especially while under the constant threat of terrorist attacks, which have until now been responsible for export losses upwards of thirty percent. A shocking figure, I know. It still astonishes me that the extremists here would rather see the harvests destroyed than be used by us to stave off our food shortages back home. They don't see—or don't care—that they're punishing their own people by forcing us to make up the losses from the portion of the harvests the Bajorans normally reserve for themselves. This world is so blessed—there's more than enough for everyone, Cardassians and Bajorans alike—and yet the radicals among them, living in the midst of plenty, refuse to recognize Cardassia's need, its desperation, to share the abundance that Bajor provides.

I can only hope we're able to save these people from themselves.

From my heart to yours,
Ataan

My Betrothed Iliana,

Thanks for sending those holos. Everyone here is very impressed with your work. The Lady Pirak is convinced that your paintings will be on exhibit in the capital before long, and that I'll need to ascend the ranks quickly if I'm to have any hope of keeping up with your inevitable success. (As if I didn't already feel enough pressure!) One of the gul's servants, a kindly fellow named Silaran Prin, was especially taken with the images; he keeps asking if you'll be sending more.

I've gotten to know the locals a bit. For the most part

they seem quaint and hard-working, if a bit quieter than I expected. At times I've tried to engage some of them in casual conversation, but with only limited success. Other times . . . I have to admit to being surprised and unsettled by some of the Bajorans I've encountered. There are a fair number of them who simply stare at us when we pass. On several occasions these encounters have even erupted into verbal confrontations, and these always sadden me; I don't have the option to ignore seditious behavior, certainly not in front of witnesses, and I truly wish these Bajorans wouldn't invite the punishments I'm required to mete out.

The children are inquisitive, and always look forward to the treats my men and I have taken to carrying when our duties take us to the nearby townships. Recently they reciprocated by introducing me to a local confection: jumja. The vendors claim it's a delicacy they've perfected over many generations. I believe them; it actually is quite good. But I'll tell you honestly, Iliana: it's utterly revolting to behold. Essentially, it's a wooden stick with a glob of dense tree sap on one end. A more objectionable-looking thing I cannot imagine. I'll try to send you some.

I'm pleased to report that with the help of a tip from Oluvas Del, my men and I recently foiled a terrorist plot to set off a string of explosions in the processing facility where harvests are prepped for transport. By my estimate we saved one hundred thirty-five tons of food and perhaps as many as seventy Cardassians and Bajorans from injury or worse. The would-be bombers and their accomplices were apprehended, tried, and executed. After three months, I feel as if we're finally making a difference here.

Reports of our early success in stabilizing Hathon have been well received by Gul Dukat, and the prefect has authorized us to continue our goodwill strategy. Gul Pirak recently directed Oluvas to summon the district's community leaders to a secure meeting hall in the city, for a two-day conference to promote the benefits of peaceful coexistence, cooperation, allegiance, and vigilance. The gul spoke eloquently about the greatness of the Cardassian Union and the benefits Bajor would enjoy as part of it, once the violence had ceased. He stressed to the gathered Bajorans that as leaders of this region, they bore a responsibility to aid his efforts to keep Hathon safe and secure for everyone.

The Bajorans, for their part, spoke very little during the conference. I've noticed that about these people: they seem shy and withdrawn around us. It makes them difficult to read, to gauge their thoughts and emotions. Still, I think we've made a good start.

From my heart to yours,
Ataan

My Betrothed Iliana,

That rock project you mentioned sounds fascinating. I admit I had difficulty picturing it at first, but once you described using the landscape as your medium, I started to imagine the possibilities. I'll look forward to seeing the results.

There was another attack in Hathon today. That makes five for this district in the last two weeks, and thirty-six since Gul Pirak addressed the community leaders four months ago. This time it was a skimmer rigged with explosives, crashing into the mining operation west of the city. Four of our soldiers were killed, three others wounded. The Bajoran casualties were even higher: eighteen laborers dead, and at least thirty others maimed or severely injured.

Gul Pirak attended a conference on Terok Nor last week with the other occupation commanders to discuss new strategies for dealing with the insurgency. One outcome of the meeting was the decision to establish a weapons depot here in Hathon that will provide support for counterinsurgency efforts throughout this part of Dahkur. Gul Pirak is to be in charge of the facility, and yes, it's another security headache for me. But at least we'll have easy access to a wide range of armaments.

Central Command continues to remain adamant that replenishing lost manpower on Bajor is one thing, but increasing troop strength is out of the question; our ongoing border troubles with the Federation simply make it impossible.

Other news from Cardassia has been equally troubling. We've known for some time that with the violence on Bajor continuing to escalate, public support of the annexation has been eroding. Now, apparently, the Detapa Council is petitioning Central Command to be allowed to conduct its own study of the matter, after which it will submit recommendations for ways to "resolve" the crisis. Gul Pirak could only shake his head at the idea. Of course, if this proposal is genuine, the study and subsequent analysis of the findings would likely take years, but I will admit to being concerned over the prospect of someday following military policy crafted by the civilian leadership.

I wish I understood why our progress here has been so fleeting. For now, all I can really do is step up patrols, continue bringing in Bajorans for questioning, and try not to let the crimes of a few unravel everything we're trying to do here.

From my heart to yours,
Ataan

My Betrothed Iliana,

I have sad news. Some weeks back, you may recall, I mentioned that Oluvas Del had gone missing. We now know what happened to him. It pains me to tell you this, but a few days ago, his half-naked body was discovered in a wooded area not far from the compound. He'd been strangled, the word "collaborator" scrawled across his chest. Silaran Prin found the body. The poor man was so distraught, he needed to be sedated.

I'd grown to like Oluvas over the last year and a half, and his death has come as a huge blow to me. He was one of the few Bajorans I'd met who seemed to appreciate the possibilities for Bajor, if only we could put an end to the terrorism. When I heard what had been done to him, I was filled with such anger, Iliana, I wanted to kill the next Bajoran I saw. I didn't, of course. I did my duty: I rounded up a number of the locals for questioning, made several arrests, and now justice for Oluvas, at least, has been served. Gul Pirak commended me on the speed with which I handled the matter.

Intellectually, I've always known that Bajorans won't hesitate to kill their own kind if they believe it will advance their cause, and this incident isn't the first evidence of that savage propensity. But I don't think I ever really understood it, not the way I do now. Not after what they did to Oluvas.

I heard one of my men, Gil Suru, express the opinion that the Bajorans are animals; and when an animal steps out of line, the only safe option is to shoot it. I must confess to you, Iliana . . . I'm finding it increasingly hard to disagree.

From my heart to yours,
Ataan

My Betrothed Iliana,

It's been relatively peaceful for a change. I'd like to be able to tell you it's because the Bajorans have come to their senses, but the truth is we've had to exert much tighter controls over the population of this region. It's exhausting and aggravating work, but it seems to be paying off. There hasn't been a single bombing, skirmish, or even a thrown rock, in over a week.

Gul Pirak sees this sudden calm as validation of his approach, and the beginning of a new chapter in the annexation. I'm not as sure. I hope he's right. He's invited several of the Cardassian regional administrators throughout Dahkur to come to Hathon so they can see our "good work," and perhaps model their own districts on it. They arrive tomorrow. I'm in charge of security, of course.

As an extra touch, he's issued a directive to all the local townships: In honor of the occasion, the Bajorans will display the Galor Banner outside their homes in a show of allegiance. It should be quite a sight to behold.

I'm glad to know your schooling continues to go so well. You always sound so excited when you talk about it, I regret not being able to share this part of your life.

I miss you.

> From my heart to yours,
> Ataan

My Betrothed Iliana,

I thought that after two years, nothing that happens here could surprise me anymore. But I was wrong.

These people are insane. Their need to challenge the annexation at every opportunity and provoke us flies in the face of reason. They're all stiff-necked fools who'd pre-

fer to die than show the slightest acceptance of Cardassian rule, and they proved that today.

The visit by Dahkur's other regional administrators began well enough; there was a reception at Gul Pirak's home, followed by a tour of the local townships in the gul's personal skimmer. There were few Bajorans on the streets, but those we saw were subdued and inoffensive. Cardassian banners could be seen everywhere . . . until we reached Ivassi township, where fifteen farmers had apparently conspired to defy Gul Pirak's directive.

The gul was furious. He felt humiliated in front of his peers, and by a group of farmers! I was ordered to round them up and make an example of them. Attendance by everyone in the township was mandatory—men, women, and children, all standing by and watching as I gave the order. The farmers were shot at midday, not three hours ago, for nothing except a pathetic display of passive resistance.

What's the matter with these people? How can they not understand that they're forcing us to make the annexation worse for them with every act of defiance? What else needs to happen before this madness finally stops?

From my heart to yours,
Ataan

My Betrothed Iliana,

It's quiet again. Things seem to have settled down in the wake of the last week's unpleasantness with the fifteen farmers. Perhaps that's simply what the Bajorans need from time to time: a stern reminder that willful defiance simply won't be tolerated.

I want you to know I've been giving serious consideration to your father's offer to be transferred home early so that I can join his staff at Central Command. It's certainly tempting, and not just because of the boost it would give my career. To be with you again, back on Cardassia . . . for us to be able to marry and start a family three years sooner than either of us had hoped . . . believe me, Iliana, I want all these things. I miss you so very much.

But much still needs to be done here. Please understand: it's more than devotion to duty; I feel a moral obligation to keep doing my part to help fix this broken world, despite how futile that effort seems at times. The things I'm fighting for—our manifest destiny, the security of our future children, our very survival—I couldn't call myself Cardassian if I turned my back now and allowed such a savage, backward people to threaten all of it. I hope you will understand, and know that when I do return to you, it'll be when my rotation is done and I can hold my head high knowing that I did everything I could to make Bajor a better place . . . for all of us.

From my heart to yours,
Ataan

Try as she might to find it, her true face eluded her.

Almost from the day her teachers had discovered her aptitude for clay, Iliana had labored to fashion a bust of herself, a special project given her by one particularly sadistic professor whose opinion was that Iliana needed to challenge herself more. In truth, she did prefer abstract forms to realistic sculptures, though she felt she was more than capable of handling both. But for some reason, even after months of struggling with it, of numerous abortive efforts and failed experimentation with one approach after another, her fingers still couldn't seem to call forth her own likeness from the soft, black material. Either her eyes would look too vacant, or her mouth too sad. Correct one of those, and her cheekbones seemed too pronounced. Deemphasize her cheekbones, and her nose seemed too upturned. Fix her nose, and the ridges looked wrong, giving her a comically puzzled expression. Working from a holo would make it easier, of course, but it was strictly prohibited; the professor had wanted the bust to be an expression of Iliana's self-image. The problem was, the face that stared back at her from the porous stone pedestal in the corner of her dormitory room was no one she recognized.

The door chimed. With a scowl, Iliana sheathed the bust in a plastic sheet that would keep the clay from hardening, then rose from her squatting position on the floor. *I told Nemra I needed to be alone today.* Her classmate and neighbor was sweet, but exhaustingly needy. Of late she had been making it difficult for Iliana to schedule time just for herself.

"Yes?" Iliana called as she crossed the small room, carefully navigating the clutter that had built up over the two years she'd been at Pra Menkar. She reached the door and touched the keypad next to it. "What is it now, Nem—?" She froze as the portal slid into the adjoining wall, revealing her father standing in the corridor.

"Hello, Iliana," Tekeny said warmly. "May I come in?"

"Father! Of course. It's so good to see you!" Caught completely off guard by the visit, Iliana threw her arms around him before she remembered the clay-stained smock she wore. Tekeny's uniform was now covered in black streaks. "Oh, I'm so sorry! Let me take care of that." Iliana tore off her smock, ran to the 'fresher to wash the clay off her hands, then grabbed a washcloth from a stack of clean laundry on her bed and soaked it before returning to her father. "This will come right off, I promise."

"Iliana, it's all right," Tekeny said. "Really . . ."

"Please sit down," Iliana said, guiding him toward the single chair in her room even as she continued to dab at his breastplate. "Sorry about the mess; I wasn't expecting visitors today. Why didn't you let me know you were coming?"

"Iliana . . ."

"Is Mother here with you?"

"She's home. I came alone because I needed to speak with you."

That's when she knew. Her hands froze against his chest. Iliana looked into his eyes, saw the sadness there, and she understood the nature of Tekeny's visit.

"Ataan's dead," she whispered—a statement, not a question.

Tekeny's voice was soft as he took her shoulders. "Word came from Bajor this morning."

Iliana stared dully into the middle distance. She felt strangely detached, as if she were observing herself from outside her body. *Shock,* she realized.

"Iliana?" her father prompted.

She turned away, absently realizing she hadn't received a letter from Ataan in six days. That alone should have told her something was wrong. "How did it happen?" she asked aloud.

"It was a bomb," Tekeny said. "Preliminary indications are that terrorists somehow breached the compound's security perimeter and planted a plasma charge outside Gul Pirak's window as he slept. The entire east wing of the house was destroyed. There were many injuries, but Pirak and his family were all killed, along with seven members of his staff, including Ataan. I'm so sorry."

And just like that, her life as she knew it ended.

Tekeny stayed with her for most of the day, trying to console her. She appreciated his efforts, but the truth was, she neither wanted nor required his condolences. At first she thought she would need his strength, his reassuring presence . . . but the crippling grief she kept expecting to overtake her never came. It troubled her to think that she was incapable of feeling the loss, until she realized she *was* feeling it. It simply wasn't the feeling she'd expected.

She finally told her father she wished to be alone, but Tekeny was reluctant to leave her; his plan had been to take her back to the capital so she could be with her family while she mourned. She thanked him for that, but told him what she really needed right now was time to be with herself, to think. In the end, he honored her wish, but departed only after he had extracted her promise to return home in three days' time.

She already knew it was a promise she would both keep and break.

That first night, she sat alone in her room, in the dark, sitting on the floor against the side of her bed, staring at nothing. Nem had come calling several times, but Iliana ignored her. Her room took on a strange quality; it was suddenly too small for her. It was a child's room, filled with the trappings of a child's life. As the night wore on, she realized she despised everything about it, and its occupant. Surrounded by the clutter of her paintings and sketches, her carvings and sculptures, she reflected on how utterly pointless it all seemed now. Vain self-indulgence, that's all it was. Vacuous expressions of a vacuous mind.

Her clay bust was a dark silhouette beside her. Iliana reached out and unsheathed it. Her fingertips followed its contours, seeking something familiar. But it was all wrong. There was nothing real about it. No truth. No meaning. No life.

Her fingers curled into claws, ripping into the clay, gouging out an eye, a cheek, the ridge behind the jaw. She tore into it until any trace of a face was gone.

Calm and resolute, she gathered up her belongings—all of them. She emptied her room of everything that was not university property: clothes, bedding, datarods, art supplies, toiletries, gifts from Ataan, every sketch and every art project she had undertaken during her two years in Pra Menkar. She put it all in a tight pile in the campus courtyard and then, to the dismay of the few onlookers who were awakened by her predawn activities, she set fire to it, scattering every reminder of her wasted life on the wind.

She returned to the capital that very day, but not to her parents' house. She went directly to Tarlak sector, the administrative hub of the city and headquarters to the agencies that oversaw the governance, the military might, and the security of the Union: the civilian Detapa Council, Central Command, and the Obsidian Order.

As Iliana crossed the Imperial Plaza toward her destination, she saw Corbin Entek watching her approach from the other side. He did not seem surprised to see her.

4

Iliana paced her quarters like a trapped animal. It was an apt description, given her circumstances. One day after returning to the capital and reestablishing contact with Entek, she'd gone home to break the news of her decision to join the Obsidian Order to her parents, packed a small bag of personal items, and returned to Tarlak sector, where Entek was once again waiting for her. He led her into the secret bowels of the Assembly building where the Order was headquartered, and immediately took her to a private room that was locked from the outside. After eight days, her "training" had consisted solely of filling out a seemingly innocuous questionnaire and two sessions discussing her childhood with a psychologist. Meals were brought to her by silent functionaries who refused even to make eye contact with her. The rest of the time she was alone, sequestered in a room smaller than her dormitory at Pra Menkar and even more sparsely furnished: The refresher was a small open booth at the foot of her bed, which was pushed up against the wall opposite the door. A chair and a bare table with a built-in reader stood off to the side. She spent most of her time reading the books that were loaded into the table's database: several historical texts; the collected writings of Tret Akleen; and the inevitable copy of *The Never Ending Sacrifice*.

She knew that she needed to impress upon Entek and his masters the sincerity of her desire to follow where they would lead her, even if it meant waiting interminably on their pleasure.

By the eighth day, however, she was at her wit's end. She was pacing restlessly and fighting the impulse to smash something when Entek finally came to see her. He entered the room and pointed a small device toward the door, which closed automatically. "Hello, Iliana," he began. "How are you today?"

"Bored," she answered honestly.

He smiled. "Yes, I'd imagine so. But I'm afraid this isn't going exactly as any of us expected."

"What does that mean?"

"It means you may be in this room for quite a while," Entek told her. "There's some disagreement about your fitness to join the Order, and the consensus is that we'll need more time to make the correct determination. Therefore I'll see what I can do to arrange a wider variety of reading mat—"

"I've been here eight *days,* Entek. Exactly how long must I continue to wait?"

"Until you're ready to be honest with me."

"Honest?" she repeated. "About what?"

Entek sighed and pulled the room's single chair out to the center of the floor and straddled it, facing her. "Why are you really here, Iliana?"

Iliana stared at him. "You can't be serious," she said, unable to keep the anguish out of her voice. "How can you stand there and pretend not to know what I've endured, what drove me to this decision?"

"Oh, I know all about your young glinn's violent demise, and you have my heartfelt sympathies. But what I want to know is in what way precisely has that event motivated you? Are you here because you've truly had a patriotic epiphany? Is it a desire for revenge? Or do you feel some misguided guilt for what happened to Ataan, and see joining the Order as a way of punishing yourself?"

She laughed bitterly, shaking her head. "This is unbelievable. I come to do my part to serve the State, and all we do is waste time!"

Entek tilted his head as he watched her. "You pretend to know patience, but you really don't, do you? The hurt is still too raw, creating a need deep inside you that demands instant gratification. Perhaps I was mistaken about you." He stood up and started to leave.

"Wait!"

Entek stopped.

"Ataan is dead," Iliana said. "He's dead, and I've come to you. What difference does it make why I'm here? We both know this is the right choice, the one you predicted I'd make, two years ago. If what you need is to hear me say you were right, very well: You were right, Entek."

"This is not about which of us was right, Iliana," Entek said.

"Then what do you *want* from me?"

"To know what *you* want," he replied.

"I . . ." Iliana choked on the words. "I need to atone."

"For what?"

"For my sloth. For my blindness. For my arrogance." Tears streamed from her eyes for the first time since her father had come to see her at Pra Menkar. She knew now the fool she'd been; a naïve child, sheltered by her parents, living a fantasy life in which she imagined herself unassailable by the events of the world outside. Surrounded by those who devoted their lives to serving the State in its defense, she had ignored their example, even scorned it, thinking herself above the struggles that were defining the universe around her. She had been a detached witness to the troubles of her world, a mere spectator, and that was unforgivable.

Ataan had understood that it wasn't enough to recognize what was wrong, or to simply imagine a just and brighter future. One had to act. To fight for it. Because the universe surely would never give it up without a struggle.

Without sacrifice.

"Don't you see?" she whispered. "I need to atone for all of it, for letting others pay the price of keeping Cardassia safe while I did nothing." She wiped the tears from her face, composed herself, and met his gaze. "You once promised me an opportunity to be part of the solution, Entek. To help me fulfill my true potential. Well, here I am, and I need a teacher. Is it to be you, or not?"

Entek regarded her in silence for a time. Then he said, "Corbin."

"What?"

"Call me Corbin."

Iliana swallowed. "Will you help me, Corbin?"

Entek's response was to raise his remote device to the door again. It unlocked and opened. He walked out into the corridor, and for a moment she believed he would once again leave her alone in her tiny quarters to wallow in her uselessness. Instead, he stopped and looked back.

"Follow me," he said.

The Obsidian Order, Day 22

"These raw emotions that drive you," Entek said as he led Iliana down a wide blue corridor, "shame, guilt, anger—they empower you, but you must never allow them to dictate your actions, to shape your thinking, to cloud your judgment. Once you let that happen, you're lost, and you may never find your way back."

"How can I prevent it?" Iliana asked. After weeks of grueling tests and orientation, Entek was giving her a tour of the uppermost levels of the Order, where the trainees lived and worked.

"Through selflessness," he said. "We must put the needs of Cardassia before our own. Always. Only then are we truly as great as our potential. Too many of our people forget that this was the prime ideal on which Tret Akleen founded the Union. Even our much-vaunted military is riddled with opportunists who believe that serving the State and serving one's personal ambition are not mutually exclusive."

Iliana's thoughts traveled back to that fateful night at the natural history museum. "You mean, like Gul Dukat?"

"You recognized that about him right away, didn't you?"

"He wasn't terribly subtle about it. But what makes Dukat worse than any of the other guls or legates who are managing Cardassia's foreign affairs?"

"Dukat wants what is best for Dukat, especially if it means preserving his ostensibly benign dictatorship on Terok Nor," Entek told her. "He's also well connected, politically, and he can be a formidable adversary. His enemies are as powerful and numerous as his friends, but their greatest mistake has always been underestimating him."

"The way you talk about him . . . you almost make him sound like a security risk."

"He's a dangerous man, to be sure," Entek acknowledged, "especially to those who, in his mind, have wronged him. He has no love for the Order . . . not since the unfortunate demise of his father many years ago. And if there's anything he's learned from the Bajorans, it's how to hold a grudge.

"Still," Entek went on, returning to his original point, "even such a man as Dukat understands that service to the State is a calling that demands sacrifice—and the will to endure whatever that service requires. You must always act without joy, without remorse, without anger, and without pity."

"But . . ."

"Yes?"

"I'm not a Vulcan, Corbin," Iliana said. "I can't simply turn off—"

"You won't need to. Vulcans are no more lacking in emotions than you are, Iliana. They simply don't allow themselves to be mastered by them. It's just one of many disciplines I'll be teaching you."

Iliana nodded, but was becoming distracted; her footsteps seemed strangely loud as she and Entek navigated the busy passageway.

"Is something wrong?" Entek asked.

"It's just . . . It's so quiet. No one here makes any sound when they move. Another discipline?"

Entek nodded. "A most useful one. Let me show you something." He led her toward an elevator, and a short time later, they were outside the Assembly building.

The Imperial Plaza flowed around her. She was a grain of sand in a stream of similar particles racing past in every direction: a constant flow of Cardassians moving from one aspect of their day to the next.

"Note the expressions on their faces," Entek told her, strolling at her side. "How would you describe them?"

"They look dazed" was the first thing Iliana said. Entek looked at her the way he did when he was waiting for her to realize her mistake. She considered the people around her, then amended her answer. "I meant to say, they look focused, but not on where they are, or what they're doing."

"And what do you deduce from that?"

Iliana studied a tall man moving toward her. Brown suit, black shoulder bag. He stared straight ahead, his lips silently forming words. *Replaying a conversation he recently had, or rehearsing a conversation he intends to have?* He turned his body slightly to avoid bumping into Iliana as he passed, but never once made eye contact. Other passersby seemed similarly preoccupied.

"They're not really aware of their present circumstances," Iliana concluded, "except to the extent they need to be in order to get safely from Point A to Point B. They're more focused on their destination than on their journey."

Entek nodded. "There are perhaps two thousand Cardassians moving through this intersection at any given time, yet they are in large part invisible to one another. Oh, they're aware of the people around them, but only in the abstract. The details are lost. Unless something atypical happens, later they'll remember nothing else about the experience. This is the essence of moving unseen, of hiding in plain sight."

"The ability to merge with one's surroundings," Iliana realized. "To mask one's presence by being forgettable." She was no stranger to the idea; she'd put it into practice herself on more than one occasion.

"Exactly," said Entek, sounding pleased. "The way in which we interact physically with our environment is as important as how we interact with it emotionally. We must be as ghosts to those around us."

"I don't believe in ghosts," Iliana told him.

"But my dear Iliana," Entek said, "you are defined by one."

The Obsidian Order, Day 69

"I don't understand her decision," she heard Kaleen saying. *"No, that's not true. I do understand it. The death of Ataan is something she hasn't been able to process properly, and she thinks that this somehow constitutes a positive response to it. But it's unhealthy. You don't deal with your grief by destroying yourself."*

"Come, Kaleen, that isn't what she's doing." Tekeny sounded exasperated.

"Isn't she? Our daughter in the Obsidian Order? How can you sit there and tell me this doesn't concern you?"

"I grant you it's out of character, but surely this is a posi-

tive step for her. We've both despaired for years of her ever taking her civic obligations seriously. Losing a loved one is always a life-changing event. And while I wish she could have been spared this hurt, perhaps it's exactly what she needed to give her a proper sense of duty and responsibility."

"Then why didn't she come to us? We're both well-placed in our respective careers. Why the Obsidian Order? Why not a different service?"

"My contacts in the Order tell me she's been identified as a promising candidate, with talents uniquely suited to state security. Perhaps we should consider ourselves fortunate; she can hardly come to harm working as an intelligence analyst."

"You may be satisfied by Entek's assurances," Kaleen said. "I am not. I don't trust him. I don't trust any of them."

"Kaleen, please! Mind what you say!"

"I will not! My heart is breaking, don't you understand that?" Her words poured out in sobs. "I'm angry, and worried, and utterly disappointed, and it's tearing me apart, Tekeny."

Iliana pulled the chip out of her ear and slammed it down on the table. She buried her face in her hands. The cold gray room seemed to press in against her from all sides.

"Is something the matter?" Entek asked, watching her from across the table.

She lowered her hands and glared at him. "Why did you make me listen to that?"

Entek's gaze on her was fixed and steady. "To make a point. The Obsidian Order has no room for sentimentality. No one is above suspicion. No one is beneath our notice. No one is beyond our reach."

Iliana looked away. "I don't want to do this anymore."

"That's exactly why you'll continue," Entek said. "It's not enough to keep your senses alert and aware at all

times; you must be able to process input free of personal
sentiment. Now put the chip back in your ear."

"Who listens to *your* parents, Corbin?"

Entek's metal chair scraped the floor as he pushed
back and stood up. He stepped around the table and
swung, the back of his hand striking her face so hard that
she was knocked to the floor.

Iliana looked up at him, ignoring the swelling she felt
on her cheek. *Now that was interesting.*

"Get up," Entek said calmly, "and put the chip back in
your ear. Now."

The Obsidian Order, Day 181

Trapped in a world without light, her hands became her
eyes. Memories cultivated in her fingertips from days of
repetition guided her movements as Iliana sifted through
a seemingly endless arrangement of decoy parts for the
specific components she needed.

*Main circuit plate. Superconducting emitter crystal. Rodin-
ium collar. Waveguide amplifier. . . .*

Some parts belonged to other systems; some were
fractionally off in size; some were made from the wrong
materials; some even carried the telltale scent of burnout.
She discarded these as quickly as she found them, shrink-
ing her options.

*Spiral wave accelerator. Energy flow regulator. Emission unit
housing. Control interface. . . .*

Once all the necessary components were isolated, assembling them in their proper sequence was child's play.

*Targeting sensor. Memory solid. Isotolinium ampoule. Micro-
forcefield inductors. Power cell casing. . . .*

The days preceding these exercises had been filled with the study of technical manuals, computer modeling, and performance analyses. Entek never complimented her on the speed with which she processed raw data, or her ability to retain it. But they both knew she was progressing far more quickly than expected.

Coolant module. Safety lock. Handgrip.

As the last component snapped into place, she held out the completed device before her and called out into the darkness, "Done!"

The lights in the tech lab came up at once. Her eyes adjusted quickly to the partial illumination and saw that she was aiming her newly assembled disruptor pistol directly at Entek, who stood on the other side of the room next to a weapons tech who was holding a padd. Both of them wore night-vision lenses that had enabled them to watch her every move during the exercise.

The tech checked his padd and delivered his verdict to Entek: "A new record."

Her mentor nodded curtly. "Well done, Iliana. You've beaten your previous personal best. However, next time—"

"You misunderstand, sir," the tech interjected. "I meant that Trainee Ghemor set a new record for the organization, not merely for herself."

Entek said nothing, but that silence spoke volumes. He met Iliana's gaze down the length of her gun.

"Zap," she said.

The Obsidian Order, Day 242

They circled each other atop the forcefield grid that made up the floor of the combat room. Entek was stripped to the waist, wearing only a dark green pair of loose-fitting pants that afforded him considerable freedom of movement. Iliana was dressed to match, except that she'd added a white breastband, for modesty's sake.

They both held duranium composite quarterstaffs, the ends of which were tipped with emitters designed to deliver a dual-effect electrical charge: direct bodily contact with a tip would be painful at best; at worst, a prolonged strike would render a victim unconscious. An indirect attack—stabbing the meter-wide forcefield hexagons on which they stood—would send a signal to the combat room's computer, which would respond by deactivating the hex that had been struck and opening a drop to a net above the room's true floor, six meters below. As the exercise progressed, their battlefield would gradually diminish, requiring the combatants to remain alert and agile in order to score a hit, or avoid one, as the grid disappeared bit by bit beneath them.

Iliana hefted her weapon, testing its balance as she studied Entek's body language, trying to anticipate his most likely moves. She swept her staff back and forth, then began to twirl it, her well-practiced moves transforming it into a blur.

Entek kept his left side toward her, holding his staff at an angle in his right hand. He was far too relaxed, as if he considered victory over her a given. He was probably right.

She decided to make him work for it.

She lunged forward and their staffs met in a sequence of precise thrusts and parries, each strike producing a sharp metallic report that rang through the combat room. Iliana advanced, seeking contact with Entek's bare gray chest. He deflected her staff easily.

"You need to do better than that," Entek admonished her.

"And just how often do operatives really fight people with sticks?" she fired back, keeping her own staff between them.

His expression darkened and he suddenly advanced, swatting her weapon aside, forcing its tip down against one of the hexes. The panel vanished almost immediately, leaving a gaping hole on Iliana's left. She backed off.

"Contrary to what Central Command might have us believe, battles are seldom won by overwhelming force," Entek told her. "The Obsidian Order utilizes distractions and deceptions. These are key weapons in the war we wage to keep Cardassia safe."

They started circling each other again. "A war against whom?" she asked. "The Bajorans?"

Entek scoffed. "Bajor is merely a catalyst."

"Of what?"

"Of questions Cardassians should not ask."

Iliana moved in and swept her staff upward in an attempt to catch her teacher under the jaw. Entek brought his weapon down to block, and Iliana responded by swinging her staff in the opposite direction, turning her attack into a downward diagonal arc with considerably more power. But again he blocked, and their weapons crossed, pushing against each other.

"Meaning what?" she demanded to know as she tried to hold her ground. "For Cardassia to be safe, the people must be complacent?"

"Not complacent. Resolute. Doubt and uncertainty are the mother and father of dissent, sedition . . . treason. We must be ever vigilant against such corruption, and against those who would foment it." He pressed down against her, forcing her back. Entek was bigger, stronger, more experienced; her only hope lay in whatever guile she could muster. She shifted the angle of her staff until it pointed down, then thrust the tip toward Entek's feet. Her mentor leapt back just as the floor panel disappeared.

Iliana kept circling, giving herself a moment to catch her breath. "So our inability as a society to reach a consensus on Bajor . . ."

". . . is perhaps the single greatest political and social crisis we've faced since the formation of the modern Union," he told her. "As others have noted . . . how we answer the Bajoran question will define Cardassia forever."

Iliana stumbled as her last night with Ataan came back to haunt her. They'd both said things that called the cultural psychology of Cardassia into question. Apparently she'd been right to feel exposed. She recovered quickly, keeping her eyes on Entek.

"Rather than allow Bajor to define Cardassia," she grated, "shouldn't we instead be redefining Bajor?"

"You ask that with such passion," he taunted, backing toward one corner of the room.

What is he doing? "And you say 'passion' with such scorn," Iliana retorted. "What about patriotism? Duty to the State? To one's ideology? What about delivering justice upon one's enemies? Aren't those passionate causes?"

"Passion is for zealots," he told her, and then he broke into a sprint, moving in an arc toward the room's opposite corner and tapping hexes out of existence as he went, seemingly at random. Iliana moved to intercept him, but was forced to leap when Entek responded by tapping out a panel that lay directly in front of her. He jumped as she did, and she succeeded in tagging his leg as they passed each other in mid-air . . . but Entek simultaneously executed a backward thrust that struck the base of her spine. The charge coursed through her, temporarily numbing her extremities. It took all her concentration to land on her feet and not let go of the staff. She spun around to see that Entek was watching her intently, clearly no worse for the wear.

"The safety of the State is not a cause," he said, walking back along the path of holes he'd created and casually knocking out the hexes between them until he'd created a continuous arcing chasm between him and Iliana, completely bisecting the room. "It is survival. It's a line we draw in the battlefield, a wall we fortify against the enemies of Cardassia."

Taking one end of her staff in both hands, she raised it high over her head and leapt again, clearing the break in the grid and coming down swinging. Entek, of course, sidestepped her easily, tapping out the hex he thought she would land on—exactly as she expected. She brought down the staff in front of her horizontally and let it fall flat across the new hole, braced by the intact hexes on either side. Iliana channeled her momentum into a somersault that swept her clear of the hole. She landed in a crouch and swept her staff across the back of Entek's knees, knocking him flat on his back. She was standing over him and poised to strike before he could recover.

"And when your enemy crosses that line?" she asked, one foot holding down his staff.

He looked up from the grid, regarding her with an expression bordering on amusement. "Then you make certain it's on your terms, not theirs." He moved his hand suddenly and with surprising speed, as if to make a grab for her weapon. She thrust her staff down, realizing too late it had been a feint, that he was already rolling out of the way, and that she would strike the hex that had been under him. The panel vanished and she lost her balance, pitching forward—

Instinct took over and she let go of her staff, pressing her hands flat against the intact hexes adjacent to the gap. Thus braced, she could only watch as her weapon plummeted through the new hole, passing through the safety net far below and discharging sparks as it struck the metal bottom of the combat room. Any second now, she expected Entek to tap out the panels she clung to, sending her tumbling after her staff.

It wasn't until she felt his weapon between her shoulder blades—experienced the excruciation of its prolonged contact with her skin and felt blackness threatening to close in—that she realized how much she still had to learn about her mentor.

Teeth clenched against the pain, Iliana pushed with her feet and flung herself forward. She cleared the gap and scrambed forward on all fours, trying to build enough momentum to run upright without pausing to stand. Robbed of her weapon, her only hope now was to somehow disarm Entek. She knew she had zero chance of doing so, and as he caught up to her and jolted her left leg behind the knee, she ceased trying to evade him. Iliana sagged against the grid and lay still, panting as she rolled onto her back to face her mentor. He stood over her, the glowing tip of his staff waving back and forth before her eyes.

Then, suddenly, she started to laugh.

This drew a perplexed look from Entek, and seeing his expression only made her laugh harder.

"That's the first time you've laughed in all the months you've been here," he said.

"I think . . . I think I'm actually starting to enjoy my-self," she panted between giggles. "Is that bad?"

"Not at all," Entek said quietly. "You have a beauti-ful laugh." He seemed to regret the comment even as he made it. "May I ask what was so funny?"

She laughed again. "I couldn't—I couldn't tell if . . . if you were going to jolt me again or knock out the force-field panel underneath me. I kept . . . I kept thinking . . . 'Make up your damn mind, already!'"

Entek's face softened. He altered his stance, turning the staff aside and offering her his free hand. She smiled at him and reached up . . . but instead of letting him help her to her feet, she pulled him down toward her. "Iliana, what are you doing?"

She broke eye contact and shrugged as he settled on one knee next to her. "I've been thinking on what you said."

"What I said . . . ?"

"About how dangerous our personal feelings can be," she told him, placing his hand against her hammering heart while she ran her fingers along his arms, "and how easily they can be exploited." She looked at him, making a sincere effort to appear apologetic. "I've decided you're right."

She watched his eyes as realization came too late—a comical look of disbelief as her hand pushed his weapon arm down, forcing the tip of the staff against the hex on which he knelt. It was an expression he continued to wear as his face disappeared through the newly made gap in the grid right beside her.

She rolled over and looked down the hole. "Distrac-tions and deceptions," she quoted to him. "I'll be sure to remember that."

Streams of code flew across her field of vision too fast for her to read. She ignored most of it, concentrating instead on isolating the few telltale characters within the seeming chaos that would enable her to build a decryption key. When the modified comcuff on the sleeve of her jacket had been fed enough of them, the datastream on the shatterframe monitor would resolve itself into manageable intelligence that she would be able to download, alter, destroy, or use on the spot depending on the mission objective.

So far she had found four.

"Think fast," Entek had said the first time she'd performed this exercise. *"The more complex the code, the more telltales you'll need."*

She found a fifth.

"The more telltales you need, the more time it will take. But more time is not an option."

A sixth.

"You need to train yourself to do more in the least amount of time, knowing that if you're too slow, or if you make the slightest mistake, it could cost lives."

Seven.

That first time, she had needed only four elements to decrypt the files. Her time expired before she'd found the third. Entek told her that in the field, such a failure would have doomed an operative, or a team of them, who were counting on her to override a defense grid protecting an enemy stronghold before they were detected. He'd punished her by having the furniture in her quarters removed, forcing her to sleep on its cold, heatless floor for a month, even after she'd beaten the test.

Nine.

In subsequent tests, the difficulty had increased incrementally, but she never again failed. Until today, however, no system she encountered had needed more than seven telltales to break.

Eleven.

Entek stood behind her, watching silently as she entered the twelfth telltale. The chaotic flow of alien alphanumerics on the monitor coalesced into the directory of a Romulan database. Seconds remained on her time limit.

Iliana held back a sigh of relief and looked up at her teacher for some reaction, but Entek offered up nothing except the calculating gleam that shone from his eyes as he gazed at the screen.

The Obsidian Order, Day 353

"You're thinking about him again," Entek said as she pulled him up off the exercise mat where they'd been sparring all afternoon.

"Excuse me?" Iliana said, feigning confusion.

"Please don't pretend otherwise." Entek relieved her of her practice staff and restored it, along with his own, to its place on the gymnasium's weapon wall. "I can always tell when you're thinking about Ataan. You get sloppy."

She frowned, carefully masking her surprise that he was able to read her so accurately. "I just wiped the room with you, Corbin."

"Barely," Entek said. "You got the job done, but your technique lacked subtlety."

Iliana sighed and walked to the edge of the mat, keeping her back to him as she reached for her water bulb. "Perhaps I'm simply not in a subtle mood today."

"Or perhaps you're distracted," he accused. "So unless you'd like me to double the frequency and duration of these sessions, you'll keep your mind on your work from now on."

She rolled her eyes. "Fine."

After a moment's silence, Entek said, "There is one thing I don't understand, though."

"And what's that?" she asked, taking a gulp. She sensed him walking toward her.

"You never talk about him. It's clear enough that you think about him, but you never give voice to your thoughts. Why? Is it because you fear the grief . . . or the anger?"

"Anger?"

"With Ataan. For getting himself killed because he failed to appreciate how implacable his enemy was."

Iliana didn't answer at first. Her initial thought was that Entek was trying to goad her into attacking him, to test her self-control. But she'd learned over the months to recognize his tactics for getting a rise out of her, and she sensed that this time his curiosity was genuine.

Now she wondered if on some level she really did believe that Ataan's death was as much his own fault as that of the Bajorans who had bombed the compound. She thought back on his letters, the things he described, and couldn't help thinking how naïve, how foolish, his attitude toward the Bajorans now seemed.

"I won't make that mistake," she said quietly.

Entek was at her back now, his voice soft in her ear. "I know you won't."

She felt his breath on her neck.

Slowly and deliberately, Iliana turned to face him, and she could see that her glare caught him off guard. She impaled him with that look, the way she remembered Gul Darhe'el doing it to Pirak that night at the reception, and it seemed to her that Entek shrank ever so slightly against her gaze.

She spoke slowly, keeping her voice level. "Don't you make any mistakes either, Corbin. Keep *your* mind on the work, unless you want an implacable enemy of your own."

Entek blinked.

"Now get out of my way," she said quietly.

To his credit, Entek recovered quickly. He looked down on her from his greater height as if he were still evaluating her, then offered her a thin smile. She'd come to hate those smiles. Entek smiled without joy. Only condescension.

He inclined his head and turned just enough to allow her to shoulder past him. She marched out, knowing the first thing she would do was hit the showers so she could wash his stink from her scales.

The Obsidian Order, Day 414

"Welcome back," Entek said as she walked into the room. "I trust you enjoyed your time off."

More than a year into her training, Iliana had finally earned a three-day furlough, which she'd spent with her parents at their home in Paldar sector.

Upon returning to the Order, she'd been told that Entek was waiting for her in one of the smaller trainee conference rooms, a drab gray chamber with only a table and a pair of chairs, which were typically used for inter-rogation exercises—how to carry them out, and how to withstand them. Iliana reported to the specified room at once, still carrying her overnight bag. She found Entek seated facing the door, a wide flat box resting on the table before him.

"I did, thank you," Iliana answered. She nodded toward the box. "What's this?"

"A gift," said Entek. "Just something I thought you should have."

"Oh?" She was wary, of course, but curious. "May I …?"

"In a moment. First tell me of your parents."

"They're both well."

"How did they receive you after all this time?"

Iliana's brow furrowed. "Is there something specific you want to know?"

"Just your impressions. And please, sit down."

Iliana sighed and did as she was told. "They seemed pleased to see me. They continue to flourish in their ca-reers. My father's hair has started to show signs of gray."

"I see," Entek said. "No talk of how you spent the last year?"

"My parents knew better than to ask about my train-ing. Tekeny and I had a spirited debate on foreign policy. I tried to engage Kaleen in a discussion of the law as it's applied on Cardassia's offworld holdings, but she didn't seem interested. She seemed …"

"Yes?" Entek prompted when she hesitated too long.

"My mother seemed sadder than I remember," Iliana confessed. "More melancholy."

Entek nodded. "That's understandable. The Lady Ghemor believes she has lost her only child."

Iliana scoffed. "That's ridiculous."

"To you, perhaps," said Entek, "but try seeing it from her point of view. This is not a life she imagined or wanted for you. It pains her to see you so different now from the girl she remembers."

"In time she'll come to appreciate who I've become."

"No doubt you're right."

Iliana folded her arms. "And since when are you so interested in my relationship with my parents?"

"I merely wished to be sure that you followed the proper protocols during your furlough."

"Don't lie to me. We both know you had the means to stay abreast of exactly what went on in my parents' house during every moment of the three days I was there." Iliana eyed the box between them suspiciously. "What is this, Corbin?"

He pushed the box toward her. She lifted the lid. Inside was an artpadd. A familiar one.

She stood up at once, backing away from the table. "You had no right—"

"Right?" Entek said. "I have every right. More than that, I have an obligation."

"Is that how you justify violating my privacy? This was between me and my mother!"

He gave her a curious look. "Please tell me you aren't that naïve."

She stared at him, too shocked to answer. "Is this a game to you?"

Entek leaned back. "More of a puzzle, actually. One I've been trying to solve for some time."

"A puzzle," she repeated, her indignation growing by the second. "Me?"

Entek gestured with both hands at the artpadd. "Your mother made a gift of this to you your first night back. You rejected it—discarded it. Why?"

"I no longer draw," she said simply.

"Why not?"

"Why do you care?"

"Indulge me."

"Because it serves no purpose except to remind me of the years I wasted before joining the Order."

"Iliana, it was a gift from your mother."

In one quick, violent motion, Iliana swept her hands across the table, flinging the open box across the room. The artpadd flew free and shattered against the blank gray wall. "I'm not a child in need of new toys!" she shouted.

Entek frowned. "Are you really so ashamed of the person you were? Is there nothing of her left in you?"

Iliana shook her head in disbelief. "Why are you so interested in the person I used to be, Corbin? By your own estimation, she was immature, spoiled, and shallow."

Entek shrugged. "But it was she who first caught my attention."

"So that you could one day remold her in your image," Iliana reminded him. "So that she could shed those qualities that kept her from reaching her full potential. Isn't that right?"

Entek said nothing. Iliana turned and walked toward the door, her boots crunching the broken fragments of the artpadd.

"Be assured, Corbin: you did your job well. The clay has been fired, and I've finally become what I need to be."

The Obsidian Order, Day 777

Weaponless, Iliana crept through the simulated ruins of a simulated Bajoran city, the late evening rain blurring her vision and chilling her to the marrow. Cardassians were ill-suited to such inclement weather, even in a holosuite, but she refused to let it affect her focus. She stuck to the shadows and listened, sifting through the white noise for very specific sounds. Her patience paid off: there was a low muddy splash in the distance, bearing left, around the corner of the burned-out building against which she huddled. Then another splash, louder this time, accompanied by a gravelly scrape. Someone was definitely moving in her direction.

She stayed put and felt the dark wet ground around her, careful to avoid making noise as her fingers searched the rubble for a weapon. She came across something cold and metallic—a length of pipe. Not as good as a phaser, perhaps, but it would do. It would have to; she had been warned that the holosuite safeties were off.

She picked up the pipe silently, gripped it in both hands, and waited. The footsteps were much closer now, and seconds later a silhouette detached itself from the shadows of the building, clear and stark against the rain that was glittering off the diffused light of four ascendant moons behind the storm clouds.

When the hologram—now recognizable as an armed Bajoran female—was almost on top of her, Iliana made her move. She sprang up from her hiding place and swung the pipe with all her might at the figure's rifle, breaking it on impact along with the bones of her enemy's right hand. The hologram cried out and stumbled back. Iliana pressed her advantage and advanced, swinging the pipe again in a downward arc that would have easily crushed a real Bajoran's skull, or at least knocked her senseless.

With a clang, the pipe halted in its descent, deflected by a large curved knife the Bajoran held in her left hand. The hologram pushed, using gravity against Iliana to force the pipe down. A swift kick to Iliana's midsection blew the wind from her, and she was knocked onto her back, the pipe slipping from her hand.

Careless, she chided herself. *That's going to cost you.*

The Bajoran lunged, plunging the knife between two of the neckbones on Iliana's right side, pinning her to the ground. Iliana clenched her teeth against the pain and looked into her enemy's face as they struggled. She saw hatred there, a look of murder behind the stringy wet hair. Iliana looked deeper still, and saw her own cold, determined stare reflected in the Bajoran's eyes.

Then she found her enemy's crippled hand, and squeezed.

The screams pierced the night as Iliana ground the broken bones together. She prolonged the torture, then let go, allowing the Bajoran to push off and crawl away, splashing through puddles as she held her maimed hand protectively against her chest.

Iliana quickly assessed her injury. Blood was flowing, not pulsing. The blade had somehow missed the tendons and the major vein beneath her neckbones, She grabbed the hilt of the knife and with one swift yank she pulled it free.

She rose to her feet and saw the Bajoran struggling to stand, preparing to run. Iliana waited, blood and cold rain combining and running in rivulets down her arm, over her hand, and down the slick surface of the blade. When her target had straightened up enough, Iliana flung the knife. It bit deep into the back of the Bajoran's neck. The hologram toppled face first into a puddle like a falling tree.

Iliana sagged to her knees, panting and staring at the rough wet ground as the rain continued to pelt her, stinging her wound, soaking her clothes, weighing her down. Sharp bits of rubble stabbed her where she knelt.

"Computer, end program and unseal," Entek's voice echoed over the rain.

She heard the holosuite entrance roll open. The debris digging into her knees vanished, replaced by a smooth gray floor that was lined with a grid of holographic diodes and stained with her blood. Cold night rain gave way to normal room lighting and warm, dry air.

Someone rushed in and waved a medical scanner over her. Another set of footsteps approached more slowly. "Well?" Entek asked.

The medic's report was brief and to the point. "Nothing too serious, provided she doesn't wait too long to go to the infirmary for treatment. Can you stand, Operative Ghemor?"

Iliana was on her feet before the medic finished saying her name. She was about to turn toward the exit when she saw something that stopped her cold.

The Bajoran's body had not vanished with the rest of the simulation. Nor had the knife protruding from the back of her adversary's neck. Blood was pooling beneath the black hair.

"She was real," Iliana said tonelessly.

"I thought it was time you faced an opponent who was serious about killing you," Entek explained. "It was the only way I could be sure you were ready to go out into the field."

She looked at him sharply. "An assignment?"

"As of this moment, yes."

"When?"

"Soon. There are a number of . . . preparations we need to make first."

"Tell me."

"Patience," counseled Entek. He offered her a smile. "It can wait until you stop bleeding to death."

Iliana was vaguely aware that her entire right side was now drenched in blood. She stared at the Bajoran's body. "Who was she?"

"A recently captured terrorist," Entek said. "Quite a ferocious one, too. Her name was Dakahna Vaas. The information we were able to extract from her led to the creation of your assignment. After that, her only further use was to see what sort of challenge she would present you with. You should feel proud, Iliana. You did well."

Iliana turned away, letting the medic steer her toward the exit. She thought about the irony of Entek telling her how to feel, now that she'd finally reached a place where she no longer felt anything.

5

The Bajoran on the shatterframe screen gazed back at Iliana with a dull, vacant expression, brown eyes staring out from a gaunt, pale face. *She looks numb,* Iliana thought. *Or is that merely a pretense, to make her appear as harmless as possible?* Guessing the latter, Iliana's attention kept going back to the Bajoran's unruly mane, the copper color so utterly alien that she couldn't help but stare.

"Her name is Kira Nerys," Entek said, standing next to her. "She's a member of the Shakaar terrorist group in the Bajoran insurgency."

"What's the assignment? Am I to kill her?"

Entek smiled thinly, and Iliana privately chastised herself for her display of impatience. There was a time when such a lapse would have merited a backhanded blow across the face, but Entek seemed to have grown more forgiving over the last two years.

"We have that particular task already delegated," he

said. "Yours will be to infiltrate the terrorists as a sleeper agent, posing as one of them. This one."

Iliana frowned. "For how long?"

"No longer than necessary," Entek answered. "A year, perhaps. Two at most. The plan is to have you embedded long enough to acquire intelligence that will allow us to break the insurgency more quickly, and with minimum collateral damage."

"You told me the Bajoran insurgency was structured in independent cells, mostly isolated from each other."

Entek nodded. "True. And it has proven to be a frustratingly effective low-tech defense against even our most sophisticated methods of interrogation and surveillance." Iliana thought there was an almost grudging respect in her mentor's voice. "But having a sleeper agent operating in their very midst will allow us to amass unprecedented data on their methods, their resources, their limitations, their accomplices . . . and it will put you in the ideal position from which to orchestrate a trap involving as many resistance cells as possible, once you're activated."

Iliana's eyes returned to the face on the screen. "I assume you intend to have me undergo some very radical cosmetic surgery in order to resemble this Bajoran."

"Not as radical as you may think."

"What exactly does that mean? We look nothing alike."

Entek held up a finger. "Not quite true. Some years ago, the Order's head of research, Doctor Mindur Timot, made a fascinating discovery that has revolutioned our deep-cover operations. Apparently there are a number of recurring morphologies common to many of the known cardassoid species. Why this is, no one is certain. Some have suggested that it speaks to common, albeit distant, genetic ancestry, however repugnant that notion may seem. Whatever the real reason, once the anomaly was detected, it quickly became clear how we might use it to our advantage."

"Impersonation," Iliana said.

Entek nodded. "The Order now maintains a database of alien individuals possessing morphologies that are a close match for those of living Cardassians, and we take advantage of those matches whenever the right opportunity presents itself." He gestured toward the Bajoran on the screen. "This is one such opportunity." Entek's face then took on the faraway look that often came to him when he was reliving a memory. "It would amaze you to know how many matches we've found for Gul Danar, across how many species. Human, Klingon, Romulan—it's quite remarkable, really. Unfortunate that he has consistently refused such service, but then, the work does require a degree of subtlety most guls are lacking in."

Iliana ignored the digression. "You're saying *I* look like *that*?"

Entek refocused on her. "Essentially, yes." He keyed a sequence into a remote padd he held, and the image of the Bajoran slid to one side to make room for a similar holo of Iliana. Then a red grid was superimposed over both images, highlighting specific areas on each face and seeming to follow the skeletal structures beneath their very different skins. The highlighted areas appeared identical. "On a fundamental level, you and Kira are almost a perfect match, not just in facial morphology, but in age, height, weight. Your voice is pitched slightly higher, but that adjustment will be as easy to make as the external ones. We're quite fortunate."

Fortunate, Iliana thought. *Yes, I suppose we are.*

"There's something else," Entek said, turning away from

the screen and taking a seat at the conference table. From the tone of his voice and the way he broke eye contact, she guessed it was something she would like even less than the prospect of surgical alterations. He gestured for Iliana to join him, and when she had seated herself, he told her the rest. "Achieving the level of trust and penetration this operation requires can best be accomplished if you actually believe yourself to be one of them. It will therefore be necessary to suppress your real identity for the duration, and replace it with that of our target."

Iliana stared at him. "I won't know who I really am?"

"Not until you're activated, no," Entek said. "The methods we use will prevent your true memories from surfacing without large doses of desegranine, which must be delivered directly into the bloodstream. When the time comes, one of our people will seek you out to inject you with the drug so you can begin the next phase of your assignment."

"For this to work, you'll need the real Kira alive," Iliana deduced, "at least until you can perform the memory transfer."

Entek nodded. "We're searching for her even now. We've managed to narrow the location of her cell to a stretch of hills on the primary continent of Bajor's northern hemisphere. They're burrowed in like voles. It's just a matter of time before we flush them out.

"As you've undoubtedly realized by now, this is no minor assignment we've tasked you with," Entek continued. "It was tailored specifically to you because of your close physical resemblence to the target. Without you, there is no mission. It's extremely sensitive and extremely dangerous, and requires considerable sacrifice on your part. I'm telling you this because even though I could make this mission an order, I'm choosing instead to make it voluntary."

"Why?" Iliana asked.

"For two reasons. The first is that the memory procedures you need to undergo will stand the best chance of success if you subject yourself willingly."

"And the second reason?"

Entek leaned forward in his chair. "I need to know that you'll take this assignment for no other reason than to do your part in service to Cardassia."

"Absolutely," Iliana said without hesitation. "This I vow." *Now what haven't you told me, my dear mentor?*

"In that case," Entek said, "there's one more thing you need to know." He produced a padd from a small case next to him and handed it to her. She picked it up and saw that the file displayed on its screen was an extract of the intelligence summary for Kira Nerys. She scrolled through it rapidly, committing the details to memory, until one item under KNOWN TERRORIST ACTS made her stop dead.

Gul Pirak's compound. The Order had identified Kira's cell as the one responsible for the bombing.

Suddenly the clarity of self and certainty of purpose Entek had promised her in what now seemed like another life was hers, winking at her from the padd's tiny display, and from the alien face on the conference-room screen. Iliana knew beyond any doubt that everything she had endured the past two years had led her to this. She calmly set down the padd and looked up at Entek, knowing her face betrayed nothing. "When do we begin?" she asked.

Her parents did not take the news well.

Iliana was allowed one last furlough of six days before

the medical procedures were to begin, and she chose to spend it with her family. She could not reveal the specifics of her assignment, of course, but her parents knew that she was being sent offworld on a long-term mission, and it pained them greatly, especially her mother.

"You don't need to do this, you know," Kaleen told her on her third day back home. Iliana was taking a freshly replicated cup of oceanleaf tea to Tekeny's unoccupied study, planning to reread her favorite sections of *The Never Ending Sacrifice,* when her mother came up behind her.

"Better this than fish juice," Iliana answered, taking a sip from the steaming cup as she searched her father's shelf for the beautifully bound hardcopy.

"That isn't what I meant. Your—"

"I know what you meant," said Iliana, finding the book and moving to one of the soft chairs in the study's sitting area. "And you're wrong. I do need to do this."

Kaleen took the chair opposite her, leaning forward restlessly. "Your father has great influence. He can arrange to have you reassigned."

"Absolutely not," Iliana said, shaking her head. "I don't want Father to interfere with my duties. I forbid it."

"Then withdraw from the mission," her mother urged. "You said that it was voluntary. Tell Entek you changed your mind."

Iliana couldn't believe what she was hearing. "How can you ask me to do such a thing? You of all people?" She set down the book and her cup on the low table between the chairs. "I have responsibilities now that I won't shirk, even if I could."

"Don't you dare presume to talk to me of responsibility," Kaleen said. "I'm your mother!"

"Yes, and I'm your daughter," Iliana said. "But I'm not your child anymore."

Kaleen got up and turned away, futilely attempting to conceal her tears as she walked toward Tekeny's desk.

"Mother," Iliana said softly. "I'm sorry."

"No," Kaleen said, her fingers idly touching *Ascension,* the bone carving that rested in the middle of the desk. "If anyone should apologize, it's I. This is my fault. I should have compelled you to attend one of the institutes when you came of age. But I indulged your willfulness, encouraged your independence, gave you a say in choosing your life's direction when you were far too young to make such a choice." She turned back, facing Iliana with tears streaking down both cheeks. "This is the result. I have no one to blame but myself."

Iliana was crushed. "Have I disappointed you so much?" she asked.

"Is that all you think you've done?" Kaleen picked up the carving and held it out to her. "What about what you've done to yourself, Iliana? You were an artist!"

"I was a fool," Iliana corrected, refusing to look at the carving. "And, as I recall, I was becoming something of an embarrassment to both of you."

Kaleen knelt down in front of her. "Only in the way all youthful indiscretions are embarrassing to parents. Your passion, the joy you took in your talent—these things never shamed us. They were the source of our greatest pride."

"But that isn't who I am anymore," Iliana said. "Why can't you be proud of me now?"

"Because you've given up too much! And what makes it worse is that you don't even realize what you've lost."

"I know exactly what I lost."

"No, Iliana, you don't," Kaleen said. "What happened to Ataan was tragic and beyond your control. But what followed was all your doing. You willingly gave up everything that you thought made you weak. And I weep for the day that is sure to come, when you finally realize that the qualities you abandoned are stronger than those you kept."

Iliana blinked. "What did you just say?" she whispered.

Kaleen shook her head, her sadness overwhelming her. She set down the bone carving beside *The Never Ending Sacrifice* and rose to leave the room, touching her daughter's chin before she departed. "I've said all I can, Iliana. You have to follow your heart, as always. I can only hope that someday it leads you back to who you truly are."

Iliana was unable to relax after that. She got up and paced the room restlessly, book and tea forgotten, finding no refuge in the techniques Entek had taught her to lower her heart rate and steady her breathing. Her occasional glances at *Ascension* only increased her agitation, until her only escape was to flee the room entirely. She stormed out the west door of the house, intending to lose herself in the garden. Late afternoon light greeted her. She shielded her eyes, thinking she would find a quiet spot in the shade of the estate's north wall where she could meditate.

"Don't be too angry with your mother," she heard her father say. Tekeny was sitting off to one side on the steps of the stone porch, a glass of *kanar* between his hands. "This is very hard on her. To tell the truth, it's not so easy for me, either."

Iliana sighed and sat down next to him. "That's what I don't understand. I thought this is what you two always wanted for me—to honor my obligations to the State."

Tekeny's lip curled upward. "It's a little more complicated than that, I'm afraid."

"But why? If I'd followed in your footsteps and gone to Dekaris, then gotten a hazardous posting offworld, we wouldn't be having this conversation. Mother admitted as much. It seems the height of hypocrisy to challenge my decision to serve Cardassia through the Order."

Tekeny nodded, acknowledging the point. "As I said, it's complicated." He paused, looking down at his drink. "Do you know why your mother and I agreed to allow you to go to Pra Menkar?"

Iliana shrugged. "Because I finally wore you down?"

Tekeny smiled. "No. The other reason." Iliana shook her head. "It was because we'd both come to feel as you did—that serving our world shouldn't have to mean being contrary to oneself."

"Have you even considered that by joining the Order, I'm being *true* to myself?"

Tekeny said nothing for a long time, until Iliana began to fear that maybe he too was disappointed in her. "May I ask you something?"

For some reason, that simple question, so softly spoken, threatened tears. She forced them back. "You can ask me anything. You know that."

"Is this really what you want?"

"It's who I am."

"But is it what you *want*?"

Iliana lowered her eyes. "What I want doesn't matter. I have a *duty*. I shouldn't have to explain that to a member of Central Command."

Tekeny laughed quietly. "You don't. I understand duty. I've lived my life by it. But as I've grown older, I've come to realize that there are duties that don't necessarily fit the narrow definitions espoused by the Obsidian Order, duties that are just as important. . . . Sometimes more so."

Iliana stiffened. "You should stop talking now," she warned.

Tekeny looked at her with a puzzled expression, perhaps wondering if she would feel obliged to report their conversation. Then comprehension dawned. "You're concerned about their surveillance devices, aren't you? Don't be. Members of Central Command are entitled to some degree of privacy, unless they specifically request otherwise."

Iliana was growing more uncomfortable by the moment. "You shouldn't count on that."

Tekeny smiled. "I don't," he said, and held up his glass, showing her its small, innocuous metal base.

Iliana frowned. "Jamming device?"

Her father inclined his head. "I don't use it often, of course. Just when I'm really determined to keep them out."

"But doesn't the very act of using it give away the fact that you know they could be listening?"

"What can they do? Any protest would require them to admit that they flagrantly disregard the rights of Central Command members. Not a wise move, politically."

"You're playing a dangerous game, Father."

"This is Cardassia," Tekeny said good-naturedly. "Dangerous games are the way of things." He held up his illicit glass to her once again, as if offering a toast, and took a sip of his *kanar* before he continued. "Iliana, I don't want you to second-guess yourself, or to doubt the love your mother and I have for you. I simply wanted to know how you felt about your new life, and what's been asked of you." He held up a hand to stave off her protests. "I know you can't give me specifics about your assignment. I just want to know if you're happy."

She considered simply lying, to make it easier on both of them, but she couldn't. The nature of her work meant that there were secrets she would always need to keep from her parents, but lying to them was a line she was determined never to cross.

Iliana reached out and took one of his hands in both of hers. "I can't answer that. What I can tell you is that I've been chosen for something only I can do, something that really *matters*. I'm part of something now that's bigger than me, and I need to see it through."

Tekeny pulled her toward him and kissed her forehead. "Then be safe," he whispered. "And come back to us soon."

She spent her remaining days at home putting her affairs in order. By the sixth day she had only one last task to see to before she made her good-byes to her parents; Entek had encouraged her to record a message to herself, something that would ease her transition back to Cardassian life after her mission was over, put the time during which Iliana Ghemor would effectively cease to exist into some kind of perspective.

It was strange to contemplate—the idea that she would be someone else for perhaps two years of her life. Strange and a little frightening, given the creature she needed to become. Her only comfort was Entek's assurance that Kira Nerys's memories would be extracted from her mind permanently when all this was over. Iliana would have no recollection of the things she might do while believing she was a Bajoran terrorist; no trace of the monster would be allowed to live on.

She waited until she knew her parents had retired for

the night, when she could make the recording without being overheard. Iliana set up the recorder on her vanity, inserted a fresh isolinear rod, and aimed the device at her workstation across the room. *No, that won't do.* Iliana wanted familiar surroundings, but sitting behind her console would make her seem too remote; she had to connect with herself, to appear friendly and comforting. She changed from her dark suit into a light-colored dress, then pulled her thickly cushioned reading chair out to the middle of the room. Sitting in front of the recorder with her hands folded in her lap, she tried to think of what she could say to her future self that would make the readjustment easier.

"Begin recording," she said aloud. There was a chime of acknowledgment from the device, and she started to speak.

"Hello, Iliana. Welcome home. I've been asked to make this recording for myself—for you—to help my memory recover when I get back. I go in for surgery tomorrow. I'm going to miss Cardassia, but I know what I'm doing is right. The terrorism on Bajor has to be stopped. Father doesn't want me to go. Mother . . . she looks unhappy all the time. I hope someday they understand. I want them to be proud of me."

She paused, hating what she'd said so far, thinking she should just stop and start over. But she decided that this wouldn't work if it seemed rehearsed or scripted. She needed to remain spontaneous, go with whatever came to her.

"You're probably confused, maybe unsure who the real you is. I can relate to that. But I can't know what you've been through, what you're going through now. For me it hasn't happened yet. What I can tell you—what

I think is the most important thing for you to understand during this difficult time—is that there are people in your life who care deeply about you, maybe more than you can know, and you can trust them to help you find your way back.

"Welcome home, Iliana." She smiled reassuringly. "Look for me in the mirror."

The full-body cosmetic alteration Iliana had to endure was carried out in a secure medical facility deep in the bowels of Obsidian Order headquarters. It was long and grueling and painstaking, since it had to escape detection for a prolonged period of time, not just from Bajorans, but from herself. She could be allowed no doubt about her assumed identity. And because it was already well-documented that Bajorans and Cardassians were capable of interbreeding without medical assistance, Iliana's ova were extracted in order to prevent conception during any sexual encounters she might have while on her assignment. Mindur Timot, who had supervised her transformation personally, assured her that her eggs would be cryogenically preserved until her return.

Following the initial surgeries, subtle manipulation of the genes controlling the growth of skin and hair would keep up appearances, while other treatments would maintain Bajoran norms in body temperature, respiration and heart rate, as well as blood and eye color. Prodigious quantities of DNA masking compound—used for decades by operatives who had to conceal their true nature from bioscanning devices—were injected in crystalline form at strategic locations throughout her lymphatic system. The crystals would dissolve slowly over time, maintaining the desired effect for up to five years.

At the end of it all, they wrapped her in a biomimetic sheath that she was told would not only help the alterations to stabilize, but also speed her recovery. "You're a work of art," Timot told her cheerfully during a visit to her bedside, the morning they peeled off the sheath. He seemed absurdly pleased with her appearance. The doctors who performed the actual procedures—and who had accompanied Timot on his visit—were similarly excited, as if she were a newly unveiled statue.

Entek stood in the back of the room, staring at her without expression.

"We've done everything we can for you," Timot continued. "If at any time you're subjected to more than a cursory medical scan, or if you should ever require major surgery, your true nature will be revealed. Short of that, no one will ever have reason to think you aren't Bajoran."

At first, she declined to look in a mirror. She wasn't ready yet to see an alien's eyes staring back at her. The smooth feel of her mutilated face beneath fingers that were far too pale had already been a great shock, compounded by the empty air she found where her neck ridges were supposed to be. She told the doctors as politely as she could that she needed some time alone. Timot and his staff hesitated, perplexed by her reluctance to look upon the fruits of their labors. Entek finally came to her rescue and herded them out of the recovery room, telling her as he left that she would not be required to return to duty until the following day. She offered him a small smile of gratitude as he closed the door, and even that simple act felt strange now in the absence of facial ridges.

Eventually she decided she could put it off no longer. She rose from the biobed and padded barefoot across the cold tiled floor until she stood before the thick curtain that was drawn over the recovery room's wall of reflective glass. With one smooth motion, she pulled the drapery aside and met the stranger whose body she now wore, expecting to be horrified. Instead, she was fascinated. The woman whose frozen image Entek had first shown her weeks ago now stood before her, alive, mimicking her every movement, no matter how subtle. The bizarre copper hair that hung from her head was otherworldly.

She yanked at her patient's tunic and let it fall, revealing her alien body. She had no doubt that the mirror was two-way, that she was being monitored, not just by unseen cameras, but by a team of psychologists, analysts, medics on standby, and probably Entek himself on the other side of the wall. She didn't care. The sight of her new self transfixed her. Different colors, different contours, even different genitalia. She almost laughed.

Reborn again, she thought. *Remade again. It seems I'm destined always to become someone else.*

Nineteen days after Iliana left the recovery room, word came from Bajor: Kira had been captured and was being held at a detention facility in the planet's southern hemisphere, a place known as Elemspur. The massive stone structure was a monastery that the military had converted into a prison facility during the early years of the annexation. An entire level of it had been outfitted for use in interrogations and biological research. One of the rooms on that level was set up with the equipment that had accompanied her on the voyage—machines that would facilitate the suppression and transfer of memories. Iliana was escorted into the room to find Entek overseeing diagnostics that were being carried out by a handful of medtechs. He nodded approvingly when one of the techs showed him the results displayed on a padd, then noticed Iliana standing nearby. He approached her and spoke quietly. "How do you feel?"

"A little nervous," she admitted, "but resolute."

"Good," Entek said. He guided her toward a modified biobed near the room's center, pointing out the different pieces of equipment they would be using and explaining the function of each one. He let her ask questions, and patiently answered them all. When she had run out of things to ask him, his lips curled into a smile, and this time it held no trace of condescension. "Are you ready?"

She nodded as she lay down on the biobed. "Let's get it over with."

Her mentor touched his comcuff. "This is Entek. Where is the subject?"

"On her way, sir," came the reply. *"She gave us some trouble, but we have it under control."*

"What sort of trouble?"

There was a pause before the voice answered. *"She killed one of the guards, sir. And she broke Glinn Tarrik's nose."*

Entek shook his head, looking as angry as Iliana had ever seen him, but he kept his voice low. "The subject was supposed to have been made too pliant to offer resistance."

"Yes, sir. But these Bajorans, they can surprise you. And this one's downright vicious. She's sedated now."

"She had better been given the proper dosage, Calas, or I'll know who to blame. Entek out." He looked down at Iliana and gave her an apologetic shrug.

"Not exactly an encouraging start," she commented, strangely amused.

"Look on the bright side," he quipped. "You'll soon forget all about it."

"Very funny." She found their banter oddly comforting. Intellectually, she knew that was the point; Entek was trying to put her at her ease.

Iliana turned as the room's wide double doors parted, admitting two guards who escorted an antigrav gurney on which lay a semiconscious Kira Nerys.

She was dripping wet and obviously naked underneath a simple sheet that covered her from her breastbone to her ankles. A glinn stormed into the room behind the gurney, the lower half of his face and the front of his uniform stained with blood. "Mister Entek, I demand the prisoner be returned to my custody after the procedure."

Entek didn't even look up; he kept his eyes on Kira as his medtechs took possession of the gurney and glided it toward a pedestal next to Iliana's biobed. "A word of advice, Glinn Tarrik," he said. "Never presume to issue demands to a senior operative of the Obsidian Order."

"That terrorist just killed one of my men!" Tarrik shouted.

"And she bloodied you most thoroughly from the look of it," Entek said as his medtechs locked the gurney in place. "That tells me as much about the quality of the staff at this facility as it does about the prisoner. But if you're very lucky, you won't end up scrubbing plasma conduits when I'm through here. Now get out of my sight, and take your men with you. As of this moment, this Bajoran is the property of the Obsidian Order."

Tarrik looked as if he had been slapped and was now contemplating violence. Instead, he gestured to his subordinates to withdraw. "This isn't over," he snarled impotently, and stormed out.

Entek sighed. "This is why I didn't join the military."

"I think you rather enjoyed that," Iliana remarked.

"I always said you were perceptive."

Iliana turned to look at Kira. The medtechs were attaching neuro-interface devices to her smooth forehead and other points along her cranium. It was eerie seeing her in the flesh, so close. Not a holo this time, not a reflection of her altered face. Here at last was the reality behind Ataan's death, and so many others—a sower of chaos and bringer of misery. Hatemonger and terrorist. Monster.

"What *are* you going to do with her?" Iliana asked.

"After she's terminated?" Entek shrugged. "Her body will likely be filed in the Order archives."

Iliana took no satisfaction from that.

Kira's head suddenly lolled toward her as if drawn to their conversation, but her eyes were glazed, unfocused.

Entek picked up a hypospray. "I need to give you a sedative now, a mild one," he told Iliana. "You'll start to feel very drowsy. You may even sleep a little. That's perfectly normal. Don't fight it."

"All right."

He hesitated. "Iliana . . . I'm going to miss you."

"I know," she said. "Now quit stalling, Corbin."

Entek smiled at her one last time and pressed the hypo to her neck. The sting and hiss passed quickly.

Reality fades in and out. She never loses consciousness, but her perceptions are chaos. Colors swim. People and objects distort. Sounds slow to dull, incomprehensible groans, or blare painfully inside her skull. Moments of clarity come and go, and she clings to these as long as she can.

Gray hands gently affix metal objects to her forehead, her temples, the base of her skull. She hears orders being given, machines turning on, and suddenly someone else's life flashes across the broken landscape of her conscious mind.

She plunges into darkness for a time and floats among shadows. She tries to recall where she is, what's happening, but focusing is difficult. Then she remembers. The Cardassians captured her in the hills, brought her to Elemspur. She remembers being dragged from her cage and being shot with a hypo. *They're gonna interrogate me,* she realizes. But she musn't tell them anything. She won't! They'll have to kill her. She'll die, but the cell will be safe. That's all that matters. *Shakaar . . . Furel . . . Lupaza, Latha, Gantt, Chavin, Bre'yel Mobara Roku klin ornak vaas i'm so sorry i love you all oh prophets FORGIVE ME—*

She hears a sound, muffled, as if through water. She follows it like a lifeline, hears others like it . . . and gradually the sounds resolve into voices. She fights to open her eyes, and sees Cardassians—soldiers, medical personnel, a civilian. One of the soldiers has a face she knows. What—

"—are you doing here, Dukat?" the civilian wants to know.

"This operation is finished, Entek."

Laughter. "It has scarcely begun. And you are outside your jurisdiction. This is Obsidian Order business. You have no authority here."

She tries to move, but her body won't obey her. All she can do is watch through slitted eyes as Dukat swaggers across the room, stepping around freestanding control panels and all manner of complex-looking medical equipment. *Interrogation room?* "On the contrary," drawls the gul. "I am still the prefect of this quaint little corner of the empire, and my authority here is absolute."

The civilian is outraged. "You cannot interfere here, Dukat!"

Dukat shoots a look at the medical personnel. "Clear this room," he tells them. "Now."

The medics all glance at the civilian, then they lower their eyes and file out.

"Listen very carefully, Entek," says Dukat, "because I will say this only once. Leave now. Return to Cardassia and tell Enabran Tain that everything went as planned. Refuse to follow those instructions, and I will inform Central Command *and* your lovely protégée here precisely who was responsible for the failure of the security grid that made Gul Pirak's home vulnerable to the attack, killing him and so many other loyal soldiers of the Union . . . just so that one promising young woman would be turned to the Order."

Entek doesn't move, doesn't say anything. He stares at Dukat for what seems like an eternity before he finds his voice. "You're bluffing."

"Don't be naïve," says Dukat.

"Even if I agreed to this, you cannot expect my superiors to believe my report without Kira's body."

My body. My death.

Dukat moves toward an instrument tray, picks up an empty hypo, and presses it against a bare shoulder belonging to someone—a woman—lying on a biobed next to her. He draws blood. Then he pops the vial and holds it out to Entek. "Make one."

She forces her eyes to focus on the face of the woman on the biobed, sees herself. *Mirror? But I didn't feel the hypo . . .*

Entek hesitates, holding Dukat's stare, then finally he accepts the vial and departs. Dukat watches him go.

"Sir, this one's awake," one of Dukat's men says, sounding very close.

"Sedate her," says Dukat, looking directly at her for the first time. "She has a long journey ahead of her, and she's going to need her rest."

The kiss of a hypospray against her neck. The world fades again. She tries to keep her eyes open, to listen to what the Cardassians are saying, but her eyelids are too heavy. The last thing she sees is Dukat whispering into the ear of her reflection, and she wonders why she can't hear him.

"This is a bad idea, sir."

"You worry far too much, Rokai. You always did."

"If someone should find out . . ."

"It's your job to make sure no one ever does."

"But what if—"

"Sshh! She's waking up. Go. And remember what I told you."

A forcefield opened. A forcefield closed. Footsteps echoed and receded with distance. She opened her eyes and sat up, quickly gathering that she was once again in a detention cell. As dark as the one she'd shared with Yeln and Alu, but some place smaller, cleaner. She saw 'fresher facilities against one wall. She even lay on a bare cot, clothed in a thin, loose-fitting outfit—prison fatigues. The blue glow of the open doorframe testified to the active forcefield between her and the stark corridor outside.

"Good morning," someone said. She turned sharply toward the voice, someone barely visible in the deep shadows. The dim blue shafts of light from the grated ceiling overhead revealed just enough to make him recognizable.

She lunged at Dukat, realizing too late that her equilibrium was way off, her movements sluggish and hard to control. She fell to her knees, right at his feet.

"An excellent beginning," he said.

She stood up slowly, unsteadily. _Drugged,_ she realized. Her teeth clenched. "What do you want from me?" she grated.

"What do you remember?"

No. No games. She spat in his face.

He sighed, slowly wiping off the spittle. Then he took a half step toward her and suddenly the fingers of his right hand were around her throat. "What . . . do you . . . remember?"

She struggled in his grip, choking, her gaze locked on his pitiless ice blue eyes. "I . . . remember . . . every dead Bajoran . . . whose _pagh_ cries out for . . . justice."

Dukat's mouth spread into a smile, then a toothy grin, before finally opening with laughter. He released her and she fell back against the cot. "Perfect," he said, watching her massage her neck. "Simply perfect. Everything I could have hoped for, in fact. I must say I do appreciate your not pretending to be an innocent victim of circumstance. People waste far too much time denying their true natures, don't you think . . . Nerys?"

Kira tried to shake off the fog she felt coiled around her brain. "Not much point to that, is there?" she said, her voice hoarse. "You obviously know who I am. And I've been in this forsaken place for seven days." _Seven? Or was it eight? Nine? Everything after they pulled me from the cell is such a haze . . ._

Dukat's mouth dropped open. "You still think you're in Elemspur, don't you?" There was a chuckle in his voice as he asked the question.

Kira didn't allow her surprise to show. "You've taken

me from one jail and thrown me into another," she scoffed. "So what?"

"Oh, but this isn't just any jail," Dukat said. "You aren't on Bajor anymore. You aren't even on Terok Nor. This is the maximum security facility on Letau, the innermost moon of Cardassia Prime, and this room is its deepest cell. I was the administrator here for nine years, long before I became prefect of Bajor."

"If that's meant to impress me, you'll need to try a lot harder," Kira said. "Whatever you think this is going to get you, you can forget it. I'll die before I tell you anything."

"You still don't understand why you're here, do you? I'm not interested in extracting information from you, nor in seeing you die. Just the opposite. I plan to make sure you'll live a long, long life."

"What for?" she asked. "Don't your people pride themselves on their swift, perverted justice system? Why keep me alive at all?" Her vision was doubling now. She kept blinking her eyes in a futile attempt to clear them.

"Ah!" said Dukat, ridiculously pleased. "The heart of the matter. Yes, it's true: the wheels of Cardassian justice seldom grind so slowly that facilities such as this one are necessary. If you like, think of this place as the exception that proves the rule. It's where we keep criminals with postponed death sentences—condemned prisoners who are suspected of having some value await their execution here, until the State is satisfied that their usefulness is at an end. Letau has more than four thousand inmates here at any given time. In fact, I was responsible for doubling this prison's capacity with the addition of two entire cell blocks." He twirled his finger to indicate their surroundings. "But this particular sublevel was a personal project of mine. The current warden was once my deputy, and he still keeps it available for my use."

She shook her head and the room spun. She grabbed the edge of her bunk to steady herself. "You're wasting your time, Dukat."

He laughed. "Not at all. I have a special interest in your case, and very . . . personal reasons for bringing you here." His expression changed, from being merely sadistic to something much worse. "I watched Kira Nerys grow up, you see, and I long ago made a promise to someone very dear to me that she would remain safe. It was only because of my intercession that you were saved from the fate that awaited you at Elemspur, so that you could find your salvation . . . with me." He moved toward her and slowly unfastened the clasps on his uniform. "You're right about one thing, though. . . . I know exactly who you are."

A savage noise escaped Kira's throat as she flailed pathetically at the empty air between her and Dukat. "I'll kill you," she rasped. Delirious and desperate, she tried to inch away, but was betrayed by the ebbing strength in her limbs. "I'll kill you . . ."

"No. You won't," Dukat whispered as his shadow covered her. "But you have years in which to try."

6

"Nerys, don't leave me. I was such a fool. When the Cardassians started setting fire to the village, I tried to talk to them, to reason with them. . . . Look what they've done to me."

• • •

"Word came from Bajor this morning."

• • •

"What was the count?"

"Five skimmers. And at least—at least—fifteen Cardassians dead. Now that's not a bad day's work, huh? We should celebrate!"

"Yeah, they kill us, we kill them. It's nothing worth celebrating."

• • •

"I think maybe Bajor has driven us all a little mad."

• • •

"We're fighting to live, not fighting to die."

• • •

"You're thinking about him again."

• • •

*"Are you really so ashamed of the person you were?
Is there nothing of her left in you?"*

• • •

*". . . You've given up too much. And what makes it
worse is that you don't even realize what you've lost."*

"I know exactly what I lost."

"No, Iliana. You don't."

She awoke gasping in terror. Again.

Kira sat up on her cot, waiting out the tremors that
racked her body. When she thought she had herself sufficiently under control, she got up and stumbled toward
the basin. She splashed handfuls of water on her face, the
back of her neck, along her arms, stiffening at the chill,
wondering if Rokai was lowering the temperature of the
water deliberately. *Or maybe he isn't doing anything,* she
thought. *Maybe it's just me.*

She peered over her shoulder toward the blank corridor beyond the forcefield barrier, and listened. No
sound, no sign of movement, no change in the monot-
onous blue lighting—no way to know how long she'd
been asleep this time, or what part of the prison day
this was. Her internal clock had become useless a long
time ago against the constancy of her surroundings. She
knew there was no chance she'd get back to sleep now.
Her nightmares were becoming as vivid as her waking world—and in some ways, much more disturbing:
the dreams recalled her days in the resistance, but were
strangely distorted, mixed up with flashes of Cardassian
faces, speaking to her like they knew her.

Spurred, no doubt, by Dukat's last visit, and the sick twist he put on it.

She shook off the memory, took a few sips of the cold water and wiped her mouth on the bottom of her fatigue top.

Kira returned to her cot and stepped on top of it. She took several deep breaths, then raised her arms toward the high ceiling and leapt. She caught the strong metal grating that spanned the top of her cell, threading all ten of her fingers through the lattice and, hanging there thusly, started her daily regimen of pull-ups. It had taken her a while to build enough strength in her fingers to support her entire body weight in this manner, and longer still to turn that ability into a decent workout. But then, time was the one thing she'd been given in abundance.

Four . . . five . . . six . . .

If it weren't for the nightmares, these last few months might have been among the most endurable of her unknown years in Dukat's dungeon. In the corner of her eye, she saw the scratches she'd once made in the stone walls to mark the passing of days during the first six years, before she simply lost the will to count anymore.

. . . Ten . . . eleven . . . twelve . . .

She'd spent her first year in Letau resisting, scheming, testing her prison, looking for ways to escape, for opportunities to kill her captors. By the second year, she knew it was hopeless. Rokai was a shrewd warden; he seldom opened her cell—certainly never while she was conscious. Her food came to her by transporter. He and Dukat were the only living beings she ever saw.

. . . Sixteen . . . seventeen . . . eighteen . . .

She always knew when Dukat was coming for one of

his visits; hours before his arrival, the cell would fill with an anesthetic gas that would knock her out long enough so Rokai could enter safely, bathe her, and inject her with the drug that made her "cooperative." Then Dukat would arrive. With each violation, she prayed for deliverance . . . and each prayer was answered with another rape, another beating, another string of whispers in her ear, vowing that he would continue doing to Bajor what he was doing to her.

. . . Twenty-two . . . twenty-three . . . twenty-four . . .

As the fourth year drew to a close, she made several attempts at suicide. But Rokai always made sure to let none of them succeed. He was ever vigilant; watching her, it seemed, even though she hardly ever saw him.

By the sixth year, she'd stopped counting, stopped praying, stopped caring. Her despair became absolute. She moved little, ate less. She accepted her fate, and for uncounted months thereafter, she thought of herself as one already dead.

. . . Twenty-nine . . .

Until the day Dukat nearly killed her.

She got no warning this time. No gas, no drugs. The usual silence of her prison was suddenly broken by Dukat's angry voice far down the corridor. He was cursing, shouting almost incomprehensibly. She caught words like "withdrawal" and "federation," "wormhole" and "major," but they meant little or nothing to her, and everything else was lost in his rage.

Suddenly he was standing outside her cell, glaring at her. She didn't move, didn't look at him. She was beyond caring, even when the forcefield turned off and he came at her, lifted her by the front of her fatigues and screamed in her face. "It isn't over! Do you understand me? I won't allow it!"

He threw her against a wall. She crumpled to the floor.

"Let them think they've won," he bellowed, kicking her in the gut. "Let them think Cardassia is ready to make peace. In time they'll all learn the grievous error of those beliefs, and of underestimating me. This I vow!" He dragged her to her feet and struck her across the face over and over. When he wearied of that, he grabbed her head in both hands, preparing to smash her skull against the wall.

And the dam began to crack.

Kira lifted her eyes. She peered at Bajor's prefect from beneath her brows, and offered him a thin, malevolent smile. "Bad day, Dukat?"

He froze, too startled to move; she hadn't made eye contact with him or spoken a word in . . . what? Months? Years? It no longer seemed important. All that mattered was this moment, and she seized it.

She flung her arms up and outward, breaking his hold on her head. She pressed her advantage, slamming the heel of her palm up into his face, hard enough to drive the bones of his nose deep into his brain. But Dukat had recovered by then, rolling with the blow just enough to escape its lethality.

Still, the bellow he let out as he tumbled back into the corridor attested to the pain she'd caused him, and to the fact that the forcefield was still down. The blood issuing from his nose spoke to the severity of the injury. Dukat was now as vulnerable as he was ever going to be. She launched herself at him—

And suddenly there was Rokai, standing outside the

doorway, the tall, aging Cardassian's hand on the force-field controls.

Kira collided with the field as it came on. It flashed on impact and she was knocked back, stunned.

Rokai helped up his master. "You'll pay dearly for that, I promise you," Dukat snarled.

Kira nodded toward Rokai, panting. "But you'll always need help to exact it, won't you?"

Dukat looked furious enough to lower the forcefield and go back in—exactly what she was counting on—but once again, Rokai was her undoing. "Sir, let's go! You need to see the medic."

Dukat allowed himself to be pulled away, his expression as he disappeared down the corridor assuring her he'd make good on his threat.

. . . Forty-one . . .

And, of course, he did make good on it—the very next day, and many more times over the years that followed. She supposed she was fortunate that Dukat wanted her alive and healthy; except for that one time, he always seemed to know when to stop, to give her time to heal, to recuperate for his next visit.

But from that moment when her will to fight back had been reawakened, she resolved to endure whatever he put her through. She had found a new reason to survive: to make him suffer for everything he had done, no matter how long it took. She imagined scenarios in which she killed Dukat by degrees.

. . . Forty-four . . .

During that last visit, though . . . his depravity had reached a new low. Just months ago, he had come to her in the appearance of a Bajoran. Even through her drug-induced stupor, she knew it wasn't a flimsy disguise, but a surgical alteration of his entire body. "Now we're a perfect match," she remembered him saying as he took her. And she, unable to defend herself, could only imagine flaying the lying flesh from his bones.

That was when the Cardassian faces started invading her dreams. At first she thought her subconscious was simply dredging up the ghosts of those she'd fought on Bajor. But she could make no connection between the people she kept seeing and her memories of home. And nothing they said made any sense, either. It was as if they were talking to her, and yet not to her. Like the sad woman in that last nightmare.

. . . Forty-nine . . .

She stopped, recalling the woman's voice. She let go of the grating and dropped back to the cot, grasping at the memory. *She used a name. Inna? Yana? What was it?*

As quickly as it came, the memory was gone again. She grunted in frustration and returned to the basin for more water, wondering how much damage her brain had suffered from the years of repeated sedation. Extended periods of drug-free clarity like this one were not unprecedented; there were two or three times during the last several years when she didn't see Dukat for months. Whatever was happening on Terok Nor these days evidently didn't permit him the luxury of sating his sadistic lust upon her as often as he once did.

She dropped to the floor and started push-ups. Kira imagined holding Dukat's head in her cell's forcefield until it burned, or broke apart, or whatever forcefields did to flesh and bone after prolonged exposure.

Someday he'll make another mistake, she assured herself as her arms started to burn with the heat of her exertions. *Like he did the day I broke his nose. And when that day comes, I'll be ready.*

She felt a low, fleeting vibration beneath her palms.

What the hell—? She stopped and stared at the floor. In all the years she'd been here, she'd never experienced such a thing. *Quake?* She realized she had no idea if Letau was tectonically active.

It happened again, a momentary tremor, traveling up from the floor through her fingers. This time she felt particles settling on the back of her neck. She got to her feet and looked up. Dust had been shaken free from the ceiling. With growing alarm, she lightly touched the wall above her cot, then pressed her ear against it.

Oh, kosst . . .

She dove under the cot; it was a solid slab of metal bolted into the wall, and there was at least a chance it would afford her some protection. The room shook, resonating with a distant explosion. Lights flickered. More dust rained from the ceiling. Kira waited, and soon another explosion struck, and then another, each one getting closer.

The next one felt as if it was right above her.

The thick walls cracked, the ceiling grate ripped free along with several hundred kilos of stone and crashed to the floor. The cot buckled against the impact, and the entire sublevel was plunged into darkness.

A dull orange glow suffused the cell—Cardassian emergency lighting—followed by a computer voice over the comm system, *"Warning: main power failure in cell blocks three and four. Emergency lockdown systems unresponsive. Security personnel to riot positions."*

Silence settled over the room. She waited, feeling the walls for more vibrations. None came. She knew she should probably stay put in the relative safety beneath her bunk, but whatever had happened had taken out the forcefield, and this might be her only chance to escape before power was restored.

She crawled out from under the cot, heaving the fallen grate out of the way, and climbed over massive chunks of ceiling. She looked around quickly at the ruin of her cell and spotted a narrow length of metal that had once spanned the width of the ceiling to support the middle of the grate. She pulled it free from the wreckage and hefted it; it was as tall as she was, heavy and blunt-ended. Not the ideal weapon, but it would do for now.

Then, for the first time since coming to Letau, Kira walked out of her cell.

The utter barrenness of the corridor surprised her. Cracks ran along the walls, more rubble and ceiling grates littered the floor, but it was otherwise a featureless hallway. Her cell was located off a dead end, about thirty paces from a point where the passage bent sharply left. She had long known that she'd been in some sort of solitary confinement; what little she'd been able to discern from the forcefield barrier and the interminable silence that prevailed most of the time could only mean she was far from any other prisoners. But it still came as a shock to discover that hers was the *only* cell on this entire level.

The corridor continued beyond the bend for another thirty paces, at the end of which she found two doors. The one facing her had the look of a Cardassian turbo-lift. The other, set perpendicular to the elevator on the corridor's left-hand wall, was a heavy-looking security door with a retinal scanner.

With no expectations, she tried the lift's call button. To her surprise, a soft mechanical hum promptly commenced. The corridor she was standing in, however, was still lit only by the soft emergency lights set into the edges of the floor. *Separate power grids,* she mused. *A safeguard against . . . what?* Kira glanced at the security door again, then looked back the way she came and considered the layout of the place. If the inner wall of the bent corridor defined a separate section that was accessed from the security door, then the space within was at least a hundred square *linnipate*s in area. So what was on the other side?

The hum behind the elevator doors abruptly dropped in pitch. She twirled the metal staff in her hand and quickly adopted a defensive stance, ready to face whatever or whoever might emerge from the lift.

The doors opened, but the cab was empty.

All right, she thought. *Let's see where you go.*

The lift had a touchpad, but no audio pickup. The touchpad had only two obvious controls: "up" and "down." Not exactly standard. Everything about her confinement was looking more and more like something extremely unofficial. Something secret.

Something private.

"This particular sublevel was a personal project of mine."

Kira gritted her teeth as she hit the "up" contact, trying to decide which of her many fantasies for dealing with Dukat she would fulfill when she found him.

The lift ascended slowly, eventually depositing her in a small, hexagonal room. A door stood opposite her, magnetically sealed from the look of it, and smooth except for a crack that ran across its lower left quarter. On the angled walls to the left and right were control panels with rows of monitors set above them. Still Kira heard nothing.

She looked over the consoles, recognizing their configuration. This was a security station of some kind. The monitors offered views of corridors, barracks, cells, even key operational areas. She discovered that she could call up other locations simply by tapping the correct contact, like paging through a book. Several sections came up dark, most notably anything located on sublevel three and sublevel four. Whatever had happened, power was obviously still out on those levels.

Those areas she could see were in turmoil: Cardassian guards ran frantically through them, or took up ready positions at the access points to the cell blocks. She saw damage control teams putting out fires and digging out collapsed rooms, carrying injured personnel to safety. Soldiers everywhere were battling to put down escaped prisoners, or contain them. In places where the inmates had managed to overcome their jailers and arm themselves, firefights were breaking out. Letau was in chaos, and all the Cardassians, without exception, looked scared.

Dukat, however, was nowhere to be found.

He might not even be anywhere near Letau, she thought, resigning herself to the very real possibility that she would need to seek him out, hunt him down. *Fine. But that means my priority is to get off this rock while I still can.*

She located a map feature and called up the layout of the main level, above the cell blocks. Finding the areas of greatest interest to her was then fairly straightforward: the operations center, the armory, the infirmary—all were clustered in the same general area and easily identified. The spacecraft bays were, not unexpectedly, farther removed and fairly isolated.

The question was, where exactly in this labyrinth was she and what awaited her on the other side of this door?

According to base schematics, the room she was in didn't even exist, lending credence to the idea that Dukat had built it and the sublevel where he'd kept her in relative secrecy, long before she'd been brought here. It made her wonder how many occupants of her cell had preceded her, and what had become of them.

She had to assume she wasn't on any of the sublevels; Dukat wouldn't risk putting a room like this too near to the prisoners. She must be somewhere on the main level, but away from areas of high traffic where unauthorized passersby might stumble across it, or see him coming and going. Kira looked at the door, once again noticing the crack that ran diagonally down the bottom left side. She resumed tapping through the camera views of the main level, focusing on areas showing walls that had been stressed by whatever disaster had knocked out the power in the lower levels.

Minutes into her search, she found what she was looking for: a nondescript wall at the back of an alcove, a thin crack showing on the lower right. Kira looked back and forth between the door next to her and the wall on the monitor. The cracks were mirror images of each other; the screen was displaying the other side of the room she was standing in. And sure enough, that same alcove showed on the map as being located in a passageway, halfway between a maintenance room and a T-intersection with another corridor that led toward the prison's operations center. Even though most of the base personnel were probably handling riot control down below, she needed to assume some guards must still be on the main level to protect the more sensitive areas of the facility. She could think of only one way to get rid of most of them at once, and after twenty minutes of searching the security system and bypassing the lockouts, the base computer rewarded her efforts.

"Warning. Main power failure in cell blocks one and two. Emergency lockdown systems unresponsive. Security personnel to riot positions."

On the screens, Cardassians throughout the main level scattered, filing into turbolifts and down emergency stairs. Kira allowed herself a small smile before once more taking up her staff and releasing the magnetic locks that held the door closed. The portal swung open silently and Kira stepped into the alcove beyond. Distant shouting and rapid, diminishing footfalls could be heard between the intermittent tones of the base-wide alert. Kira waited, giving the Cardassians several more minutes to redeploy, listening as a hush settled over the main level—the stillness of a house abandoned.

Then, as she started down the passageway, the silence was shattered.

"Dal Rokai, come in!"

Kira stopped and pressed herself against the wall, just before the intersection. The filtered voice had come from somewhere just around the bend.

"This is Rokai. Report."

Kira's lips curled upward. From the sound of him, Letau's warden must be standing less than ten paces away from her.

"Total loss of containment, sir," the voice said over the sound of weapons fire. *"We've killed at least a hundred prisoners, but some have managed to overwhelm our people and they're arming themselves. You have to send us help!"*

"There's no one left to send! I'm alone up here."

"Then contact Cardassia. Tell them—"

"I can't tell them anything! I haven't been able to raise anyone since Weyoun unleashed the Jem'Hadar!"

"With respect, sir, somebody had better do something soon, because the prisoners are pushing their way to the upper levels! I don't know how much longer we can hold them back!"

"You listen to me," Rokai said, sounding frantic. She could hear him marching in her direction now. "I don't care what it takes, you and your men had better do your jobs and get the situation down there under—"

Rokai stopped talking as he turned the corner and came to an abrupt halt against the end of Kira's staff. She held it beneath the soft tissue underneath his jaw, pressing hard enough to make her intentions clear: any sudden move on his part, and she would drive the broken length of metal straight through his throat and out the back of his neck.

"Your sidearm," Kira whispered. "Remove it. Slowly." She applied more pressure to his skin to to let him know she meant it.

Rokai's narrow, deeply wrinkled face was expressionless as he slowly surrendered his disruptor pistol. The voice squawking from his comcuff kept asking the dal to repeat his transmission.

Kira snatched the pistol from his grasp and pressed the emitter against his cheek. "Now turn off the comcuff," she ordered, "and toss it on the floor." When Rokai had complied, Kira let her staff drop, cushioning its descent with the top of her foot to prevent it from making too much noise when it hit the floor. Then she shoved him hard against the wall.

"I won't waste your time or mine, Rokai," Kira said softly. "You can help me, or I can kill you. Which is it gonna be?"

"You're making a grave mistake," the gray-haired Cardassian said through his teeth.

"Then we've both got a real problem," Kira replied, "because thanks to you and your dear old friend, I have absolutely *nothing* to lose." She ran the disruptor emitter roughly along his left orbital ridge, stopping at the corner of his eye. "Would you like to reconsider your answer?"

Rokai nodded as much as the weapon against his eye would allow. "I'll cooperate."

"How many guards between us and the spacecraft bays?"

"None," the dal said, and in response Kira pressed harder on his eye. "That's the truth," he insisted. "The bays are gone, their ships destroyed with the troop barracks and the power grids. I can prove it."

"How?"

"From ops."

Kira's eyes narrowed. "All right. Show me," she ordered, and spun Rokai toward the intersection, nudging him forward with the disruptor against the base of his skull. Her free hand gripped his uniform at the back of the neck to control his pace. When she saw that the next corridor was empty, she made him move faster, taking a last quick glance at her discarded staff, wishing she could take it with her. She'd liked the way it felt in her hands, its ease of motion when she twirled it before going into the combat readiness stance she'd learned back—

Wait. Back when? I never fought with a staff in the resistance.

In that moment, Kira realized her entire body had been responding to her present situation in ways that weren't entirely voluntary. Her reflexes remembered holding a staff, mastering the techniques of fighting with one, but when she sought those memories, she found nothing. And back in the room behind the alcove, she'd used its control interface to penetrate the base's security as if it was second nature . . . despite the fact that she had no advanced expertise in Cardassian computers—certainly nothing on a level that would enable her to override the most sensitive systems in a maximum security prison.

So how am I doing these things?

Her thoughts were interrupted by the hiss of turbolift doors opening halfway down the corridor, from which emerged three armed aliens dressed in prison fatigues just like her own. Kira kept Rokai between herself and the newcomers; they immediately raised their disruptor rifles toward her.

"Easy," Kira cautioned. "Let's not make any mistakes here, all right? We're on the same side, I think. This man is my hostage, so I'd appreciate it if you wouldn't shoot him."

The aliens were a diverse group—a female Kressari stood at point, flanked by two males, a Tellarite and someone who looked vaguely Vulcan. They refused to lower their weapons. "Well, well," the Kressari said, taking a few tentative steps toward Kira. "Dal Rokai! What an unexpected surprise. How long I've waited for the opportunity to face you without a forcefield between us. And who might your captor be, I wonder?"

"That's far enough!" Kira said. The Kressari halted, her rough, sharp-edged face betraying no emotion, save the changing coloration of her eyes, which had gone from black to violet. "Lower your weapons, and we can talk."

"She's Bajoran," the vulcanoid noted, peering past Letau's warden.

"Good eyes," Kira said. "Now lower your weapons."

"Why should we trust you?" asked the vulcanoid.

"Don't be a fool, Telal," the Tellarite said. "You think a

Bajoran in a Cardassian prison has any less hatred for our jailers than a Romulan?"

Romulan!

"You're the fool, Zhag, if you believe—"

"Quiet, both of you," the Kressari snapped, "and do as she says. Do it, Telal. You owe me." As the Romulan reluctantly joined the other aliens in compliance, the Kressari turned back to Kira. "All right, Bajoran. We've done as you asked. Now what exactly are your intentions?"

"Do you speak for your group?"

"Yes," the Kressari said, and no one protested.

"Then my intention is to get off this moon, and I wouldn't mind some help. Interested?"

"Provisionally," said the Kressari. "What's the plan?"

"Do you know what caused the power failure?" Kira asked.

"No," said the Kressari.

"Then our first step is to determine exactly what's happened, find out what we're dealing with. I was just on my way to ops to do exactly that. Will you back me up?"

"What sort of resistance can we expect?" the Romulan wanted to know.

Kira shook Rokai by the collar, and he answered, "None."

"You expect us to believe no one is in the operations center?" the Tellarite scoffed. "Preposterous!"

"It's true," Rokai maintained. "Everyone else is below, trying to put down the riots."

"He's lying," the Kressari said. "There's no way they'd leave the most sensitive areas of this facility unmanned."

"None of you understands what's happened," Rokai said.

"Then you'd better show us," said Kira. "Right now."

"This is madness," Telal said to the Kressari. "The Bajoran is one thing, but trusting this Cardassian—"

"You might be right," Kira cut in, "which is precisely why I could use the help. Look, it's obvious this place has suffered some kind of disaster. We need to know exactly what happened, and what our options are. Ops is the best place to start. Or does one of you have a better idea?"

No one did.

"Then let's go," Kira said, shoving Rokai forward again. The Kressari fell into step next to her as Kira passed the turbolift, with the others bringing up the rear. Kira noticed that the Kressari wore a burn across one arm of her fatigues. "You three fought your way up from your cell block?" Kira asked.

The Kressari nodded. "We were on sublevel one. We knew something was wrong when we felt the tremors, but it wasn't until a short while ago that the power failed, and we started fighting the guards."

"You're welcome," Kira said.

The Kressari flashed her a sharp look. "You're claiming responsibility for setting us free?"

"I didn't start this," Kira clarified. "Whatever caused the tremors and knocked out the power on the lower levels wasn't my doing. But anyone who made it out of sublevel one and two has me to thank for it, yes."

The Kressari looked as if she was trying to decide whether or not to believe her. In truth, Kira was still wondering if she could believe it herself. "What's your name?" the Kressari asked.

"Kira Nerys."

"I'm Shing-kur. As you may have gathered, the ones behind us are Telal and Zhag."

Kira nodded. "Thanks for not shooting Rokai."

"Don't thank me yet," Shing-kur said, her eyes turning white as she looked at the dal. "I'm still tempted to simply kill him. Every second he lives offends me."

"Believe me, I understand," Kira said. "But we still need him, at least for now."

"And if he betrays us?" she heard Telal say.

Kira let the question hang in the air for several seconds, knowing Rokai was listening to their every word. "Then I'll kill him myself," she promised.

Rokai had told the truth: ops was empty. The cavernous, rhombus-shaped chamber must have been forty paces from end to end, with stations for dozens of personnel . . . and yet there wasn't a soul in the room. Rokai said he could prove his claims from the communications station on the far side of the command center. Kira and the others stood behind him as he seated himself before the wide console and started accessing datafeeds.

"We're wasting time," Zhag said impatiently. "We should be trying to commandeer a ship."

"According to our warden, that isn't an option," Kira said.

"Why?"

"This is why," Rokai said, activating one of the oval holoframes suspended from the ceiling. The scene that sprang to life was one of utter devastation. It was, Kira guessed, an external view of the prison, as seen from a rotating camera atop the operations center. The picture was slowly panning left to show the parts of the surrounding complex that jutted above the rocky, airless surface of Letau. On the outermost edge of the facility, where Kira guessed the energy reactors and the landing bays had been located, a cloud of fine dust was still settling. Beyond it hung the bloated golden orb of Cardassia Prime, filling half the sky. But within the gray nimbus of particulate matter, the dull green remains of a crashed spacecraft were clearly visible.

"A Romulan vessel," Telal said.

"We took several particle beam strikes before the ship crashed," Rokai explained. "The Romulans were forced down. We just happened to be in the way."

"Your people did this?" Telal asked, his voice tight.

Before the dal could answer, Kira said, "Rokai . . . go in tight on Cardassia Prime. Extreme magnification on the upper left."

Rokai complied and the camera zoomed in on a cluster of tiny darting lights that had caught Kira's attention. They eventually resolved themselves into hundreds of starships—Cardassian, Romulan, Federation, Klingon—all in savage combat against two fleets she didn't recognize.

"Finally," Shing-kur breathed.

"Who are they?" Kira asked.

The Kressari's eyes shifted to yellow. "How long have you been here?"

"Just answer my question."

"They're called the Dominion," Shing-kur said. "Invaders from the Gamma Quadrant." Shing-kur paused before continuing, as if she understood that Kira would need a moment to absorb that. "Two years ago they annexed Cardassia and more recently forged a pact with the Breen against the other major powers of the Alpha Quadrant."

"This Dominion conquered Cardassia?"

"No," said Shing-kur. "The Cardassians *joined* them, gave them a foothold in this part of the galaxy. Prime is their center of power here, from which all their offensives have been launched. But for the Allies to have made it this far, this has to be the end. It's the Dominion's last stand."

"And none too soon," Zhag said. "This is the worst war the quadrant has ever known. Billions have died on all sides by some estimates. All because the Cardassians saw the Dominion as their key to conquering the Alpha Quadrant."

"Not anymore," Rokai said. "My people have rebelled."

"Typical," scoffed Telal. "Count on the Cardassians to be fickle in their allegiances."

"That's amusing, coming from a Romulan," said Rokai. "Or are those *not* your people fighting alongside their old foes, the Federation and the Klingons?"

Telal reached past Kira and seized Rokai by the throat. It couldn't have been easy; that wide neck made getting a good grip problematic. But Telal managed it just the same, grasping him under the jaw. "You should not provoke me, *Warden*."

"That's enough, Telal!" Kira snapped.

Telal's eyes were fixed on Rokai, watching him squirm. "I don't take orders from you, Bajoran."

"This isn't about who's in charge. We still need him."

"For what?" the Romulan demanded. "You saw what we all saw. We're trapped here."

"I don't think we are," Kira said. "Now let him go."

Telal looked at her. "You had better be right," he said, and released their former jailer. Rokai doubled over onto the communications console, gasping for air.

"What makes you think he can help us escape?" Shing-kur asked.

"This place has a secret sublevel, with a hidden elevator leading to it," Kira revealed. "I was being held down there until the power went out. It's got a very big security door that needs a retinal scan to gain entry, and whatever powers *that* is still working. Our warden here was heading down there when he almost ran into me—at a time when he had every reason to evacuate, and when he already knew he was cut off from other avenues of escape."

"You think he has a way to get off Letau from down there," Zhag said. "What if you're wrong?"

"She's not," said Rokai. "I can get you all out of here. But I want some assurances."

Kira spun him around on his stool and shoved him back against the console, her weapon against his throat. "No," she said. "No assurances. No negotiations. No deals. I already told you, Rokai, I'm not wasting time with you. You help us, or you die. It's that simple."

"Why are we even bothering to keep him alive?" Shing-kur asked. "You said the door has a retinal scanner. All we need are his eyes."

Rokai looked directly at Kira. "I can give you Dukat."

"Dukat?" Zhag asked.

Kira froze. "He's here?" she whispered.

"No," Rokai said. "But I can show you where he went."

"How?"

"Skrain Dukat?" Zhag repeated. "The gul?"

"The room on the hidden level is a safe house of sorts," Rokai told Kira, speaking over Zhag's questions. "A bunker. But as you surmised, it's also a way off this moon. Dukat used it to depart after his last visit."

Looking like a Bajoran, Kira remembered.

"Kira, what is this all about?" Shing-kur asked. "Why are you so interested in—"

An alarm tone rang through the operations center. *"Warning,"* the computer said. *"Multiple unauthorized transport signals detected."*

The air shimmered across the room as three uniformed aliens beamed into ops, brandishing bulky, blunt-ended energy rifles. "Get down," Kira shouted, pulling Rokai down behind the console with her. The others dove for cover as well, but Zhag wasn't fast enough, and fell victim to a pale violet bolt of energy that burned a hole into his broad chest, killing him instantly. Telal and Shing-kur returned fire from one end of the communications console, while Kira attempted to create a crossfire from the other end.

That was when she got her first good look at the invaders: tall, somewhat reptilian-looking with bumpy gray skin and short, bonelike growths studding their jawlines and the sides of their heads. She failed utterly to hit them. "Who are they?" she hissed.

"Jem'Hadar," Rokai told her. "Soldiers of the Dominion, engineered to kill. You have to keep firing. If you let up, if they're allowed time to concentrate, they'll turn invisible."

You have got to be kidding me! Kira continued firing, sending up sprays of sparks whenever her blasts struck consoles or machinery banks. The Jem'Hadar shot back, but were diving for cover now behind an engineering control station, near the ops center exit, effectively cutting off any means of escape. If Rokai was correct, that was something Kira couldn't permit. She eyed her disruptor pistol, and an idea formed.

"Keep firing!" she told the others. "I need a few seconds." As her allies kept up the assault. Kira released her weapon's maintenance lock and pulled the back half of the pistol apart, revealing the isotolinium power cell within. Using her fingers, she started manipulating the components surrounding the cell, rearranging the three key contacts responsible for generating the forcefield that protected the charged liquid ampoule against accidentally releasing its stored energy in a single unregulated burst.

Energy flow regulator, micro-forcefield inductors, coolant module . . .

Rokai watched her as she worked. He looked . . . fascinated? She ignored him and completed the task at hand. Of course, for her plan to work, she needed to be able to set the charge off from a distance; just tossing it like a grenade wouldn't be enough. She looked at her two remaining allies, realizing she didn't know if either of them could shoot worth a damn. "Listen to me," she told them over the weapons fire, knowing they couldn't avert their eyes from the Jem'Hadar. "I'm gonna throw my weapon across the room. One of you needs to shoot it wherever it lands. Do you understand?"

Shing-kur, crouching nearest to Kira, nodded. "Telal, you take it."

A pale violet bolt fried the control panel near Telal's head. He fired back, telling Kira, "Whatever you're going to do, just do it!"

Kira blew out a breath and lobbed the pistol into the air. It clattered on the floor, coming to rest against the base of the engineering console. Shing-kur laid down suppression fire so Telal would be free to take his shot. Kira kept her head down, hoping the communications console they were hiding behind would withstand the blast.

The Romulan hit his mark. The results were devastating.

The energy discharge whited out the room, the explosion deafening in its intensity and catastrophic in its power. The ops center shook; floor plating buckled and shrapnel flew. Kira felt the comm console come loose from its bolts and rock once before it settled back down.

Silence fell. Dust and debris covered everything. Kira tested her extremities, felt herself able to move, and determined that she was uninjured. "Everyone all right?" she asked.

Rokai was coughing. Shing-kur and Telal stirred where they lay facedown, heads wrapped in their arms. The Kressari rolled over groaning, but claimed she was fine.

Kira poked her head over the top of the console. The Jem'Hadar's side of ops was in ruin, the walls and wreckage coated in splashes of amber. *Blood,* Kira guessed, just before she spotted one of the bodies. Parts of one, anyway.

She exhaled, looking back down at the others. Telal's head finally came up, arching an appreciative eyebrow in her direction. "You're full of surprises, Bajoran," he said. "Where'd you learn to do that?"

Kira opened her mouth to answer, but nothing came out. The answer seemed just on the tip of her tongue, and yet it eluded her. Just like before.

She looked at Rokai, and again he was watching her intently.

"*You,*" she snarled. She reached down and dragged him to his feet. "*What did you do to me?*" she screamed.

"Nothing," Rokai said calmly. "All I ever did was take care of you."

Kira's eyes went wide. Her next words came out as a whisper. "You took care of me?" She snatched Shing-kur's rifle and shoved the emitter against the Cardassian's chest, gritting her teeth as she held it there, trying to will herself to pull the trigger in spite of her need to keep him alive.

"Go ahead, shoot me," Rokai said. "We're all going to die, anyway. Other Jem'Hadar will be here soon. This is the end, don't you understand? The Dominion is killing everyone. They're slaughtering Cardassians by the thousands as punishment for turning against them. That's why they're here. I'm already dead, so you may as well get it over with."

Kira stared at him, frozen. For years she had thought of Rokai as Dukat's brutal enforcer, the shadowy, all-controlling master of Letau. Now he was simply a pathetic old man who understood all too well that his days were numbered.

But there was no way she was going to make it that easy for him.

Telal stepped forward. "Do it," he told Kira, and then raised his own weapon. "Or let me."

"No," Kira said finally. "He doesn't get to decide how this ends." With one swift move, she swung the butt of Shing-kur's rifle across Rokai's face, not hard enough to knock him out, just enough to daze him and to discourage further outbursts. She handed the weapon back to Shing-kur, then recovered Zhag's rifle for herself. "Let's get out of here."

They encountered two more escaped prisoners on the way back to the hidden lift, both of them heavily armed:

One was a hulking, thick-boned Lissepian who introduced himself as Mazagalanthi. His smaller companion, a tan-skinned, white-haired female, was named Fellen Ni-Yaleii, and her people, Kira learned, were called Efrosians. Telal was wary of being joined by more escapees, but Kira believed anyone who had successfully fought their way up from the cell blocks would be an asset to their objective. Shing-kur agreed.

Unfortunately, the hidden lift wasn't built to accommodate so many people at once, especially when one of them was a Lissepian. The two newcomers agreed to wait with Telal while Kira went down first with Rokai, accompanied by Shing-kur.

As their descent began, the Kressari repeated her earlier question. "How long have you been here, Kira?"

"I stopped counting a long time ago," Kira said. "Why do you want to know?"

"From the questions you asked in ops, it's pretty clear you've been here for some time, maybe longer than any of us, and probably in isolation."

"You weren't isolated?"

"No," Shing-kur revealed. "Conditions were brutal and security was tight, but small numbers of prisoners were permitted to interact periodically. New arrivals brought news, and we sometimes overheard conversations among the guards. It wasn't difficult to stay abreast of events in the world outside . . . but it wasn't that way for you, was it?"

Kira didn't answer. She kept her eyes fixed on the back of Rokai's head. The lift began to slow down, then came to a stop. The trio stepped out, letting the elevator return topside to retrieve the others.

Shing-kur took in the security door, then gazed down the dim, debris-strewn corridor. "This is where they kept you?"

Kira nodded toward the passageway. "My cell is around the bend, where the corridor ends. It was the only world I knew from the day I got here to the moment the power failed." She paused, then decided she could put off her next question no longer. "Shing-kur . . . what year is it?"

The Kressari hesitated. "I'm afraid I don't know the Bajoran calendar."

"Do you know the Cardassian one?"

"Yes," Shing-kur said, and then told Kira what she wanted to know.

Something inside her collapsed as she absorbed the information. She felt as if her knees might give out at any moment. Her grip on the back of Rokai's collar tightened as she used him to steady herself.

"Kira?" Shing-kur said.

"Fifteen years," she whispered. "How could it be fifteen years . . . ?"

Shing-kur's pupils turned chartreuse. "I never imagined . . . I'm so sorry." The Kressari's glare became white as it focused on Rokai, who had been staring blankly at the security door since they emerged from the lift. "You should kill him now, Kira. He kept you down here all that time. He deserves—"

"He'll get exactly what he deserves," Kira vowed, regaining her composure. "But first he's going to help me find the one who did this to me."

The lift returned, depositing the rest of their group into the corridor, and Kira ordered Rokai to open the security door. The dal leaned into the retinal scanner, and at once the thick portal rose into the ceiling. Lights within came up automatically as Kira crossed the threshold.

She wanted to laugh. The interior looked like the main room of a lavish Cardassian apartment: extravagant furnishings, artful décor, a sitting area, and a thronelike chair behind a massive desk. A corridor stretching back beyond the desk led to smaller rooms: a luxurious bedchamber with a spacious 'fresher; a storage room containing equipment and supplies of a medical nature; a pantry full of emergency rations and even exotic liqueurs. Fellen found a small armory containing more than a score of energy weapons, plus plasma grenades, body armor, and survival gear of various kinds. A convicted gunrunner for a group of Federation rebels who called themselves the Maquis, Fellen deemed the arsenal "top-of-the-line equipment."

As Kira had suspected, the place was sustained by a dedicated power supply that wasn't compromised by the damage to the prison's main energy reactors. An on-site computer system ran the entire operation, everything from life support to transport inhibitors to the forcefields that gave extra protection to the dense outer walls. Rokai had told her the truth when he called this place a bunker; it was nothing less than a secret fortress where Dukat could barricade himself against the universe if he wished, and for a considerable period of time.

"But why?" Kira asked Rokai while the others busied themselves throughout the bunker. "Why would he need a place like this?"

The dal didn't answer immediately; he was gazing almost wistfully at the great black desk. Shing-kur sat there now, hacking into the bunker's mainframe in order to determine what other resources might be at their disposal in this place. It turned out that the Kressari was quite adept with Cardassian computers—her unusual proficiency, she had explained, was one of the things that had landed her in Letau when she was arrested on suspicion of espionage and conspiracy to commit bioterrorism, four years ago. She didn't say if the charges were justified.

Finally Rokai said, "Gul Dukat understood that the universe is capricious, and that one's fortunes can change quickly, and inevitably will. He was a young man when he first learned that lesson, on Bajor, at the start of the annexation. That particular setback led to his being assigned to Letau as a sort of punishment. But he was convinced he would one day return to grace . . . and he did, again and again. His fortunes were like a pendulum that builds momentum with every swing: each triumph—and each downfall—greater than the last. He was even leader of Cardassia for a time, did you know that? No, of course you didn't. But it's true. He negotiated our entry into the Dominion, and under them he led the Union for almost a year before his fortunes reversed yet again. But no matter what twist of fate he met with, good or bad, he always returned here when he felt the need, to this refuge he created, a place where he could go to renew himself."

"Renew himself?" Kira grated. "That's what you call what he did to me?"

Rokai looked at her, his eyes narrowing sharply. "You were one of his excesses. I tried to convince him not to keep you. I told him it was too dangerous, that *you* were too dangerous. He wouldn't listen. . . . Kira Nerys always was his blind spot."

Before she could respond, a startled sound came from Shing-kur. "What is it?" Kira asked.

"The Jem'Hadar," Shing-kur began. "They're killing everyone." She transferred the images on her desk monitor to the large holoframe on the opposite end of the room, so everyone could see. The invaders had evidently restored power to the cell blocks. Shing-kur had tapped into the surveillance system and was clicking through views of the sublevels, just as Kira had done earlier— only now, the bodies of prisoners and their Cardassian guards were strewn throughout every view as Jem'Hadar soldiers strode among them, shooting anyone they found alive. Kira watched, repulsed and mesmerized at the same time.

Rokai had said they were engineered to kill. The implication was that they existed to serve someone else's purpose. The thought was both horrifying and intriguing. Kira couldn't help wondering how differently things might have gone if only Bajor had had creatures like this to defend it when the Cardassians decided to annex the planet. She studied the way the Jem'Hadar moved, the look in their eyes . . . eyes that projected only death.

That's all they are, she judged. *Death.*

"If there's a way off Letau," said Mazagalanthi, "we need to find it soon."

"Agreed," Kira said. "Fellen, make sure the door is sealed. Telal, Mazagalanthi, you're with me. All right, Rokai. Show us."

The room to which the dal led them was hidden behind a false wall in the back of the pantry, and it was unlike anything Kira had ever seen. She was surrounded by alien instrumentality, but was clueless about its function until she noticed the control pedestal that was juxtaposed with the raised platform that dominated the back half of the chamber: a transporter.

Kira paused at the console, her fingers brushing lightly across the smooth surface. She found the power contact, and tapped it on. The pedestal's slanted circular top lit up in a garish clash of purple and green, as did the rest of the machines in the room. The displays had all been configured to the Cardassian language. The current date came up, along with the date of its most recent transport, confirming that it was last used around the time she had last seen Dukat. And the coordinates—

Kira looked up at Rokai. "Is this a joke?"

Letau's warden said nothing.

"You expect me to believe this thing transported Dukat more than twenty light-years?"

"There are a number of reasons the Dominion has come as close as it has to conquering the Alpha Quadrant," Rokai told her. "One of them is technology that is vastly superior to anything we have in biological engineering, sensors, weapons systems, and teleportation."

"Telal?"

The Romulan, who had been guarding Rokai, looked intrigued. "I've heard of such things," he admitted. "The Dominion supposedly does have a limited ability to beam through subspace across interstellar distances. But I would not trust myself to operate such a device under these circumstances, and I would trust him even less," he finished, sneering at their captive.

"I have some experience with exotic technologies," said Mazagalanthi, who had been scrutinizing the equipment. "I might be able to decipher its operation without having to rely on our prisoner. But I'll need time."

"How much time?" Kira asked.

"Hopefully less than it will take for the Jem'Hadar to discover this place," the Lissepian replied. "However," he added, moving toward her to get a better look at the control pedestal, "I don't believe we should risk attempting to reprogram the coordinates. The safest and most expedient course would be to stick with the presets—go wherever the last transportee went."

"That suits me fine," Kira said. Telal volunteered to stay and assist the Lissepian, and to see what he could find out about their destination. Kira left them to their work, pushing Rokai out at gunpoint.

When they were through the pantry, she asked him, "So Dukat's Dominion masters gave him a subspace transporter as a reward for being a dutiful puppet?"

"They knew nothing about it," said Rokai. "During his time as leader of Cardassia, Dukat undertook a number of secret projects that involved quietly acquiring samples of 'misplaced' Dominion technology."

"He was planning to turn against them," Kira realized. She laughed bitterly, shaking her head. "More schemes. More deceptions."

"Anything he did was out of his sense of duty to Cardassia."

"Keeping me in order to feed his sick appetite was his duty to Cardassia?"

"As I said . . . you were one of his excesses."

"You make it sound like he couldn't help himself," Kira spat. "That's not an opinion that's going to prolong your life."

They arrived back in the main room. The dal shrugged. "You or the Jem'Hadar—what's the difference? What can you do to me beyond what you've already threatened?"

"I've had fifteen years to think about it," Kira reminded him. "Don't tempt me."

"And how much thought have you given to what's changed in those fifteen years?" Rokai asked. "You have no idea what's awaiting you out there."

"I'm way past the point of caring about what's out there," Kira said. "Except Dukat."

"Kira," Shing-kur called from the desk. "I think I've found something you need to see."

Kira steered Rokai behind the desk so she could get a good look at its shatterframe display. On it was an image of herself . . . except that she had shorter hair, and she wore a red uniform emblazoned with the symbols of Bajor. The image was labeled COLONEL KIRA NERYS, BAJORAN MILITIA.

Kira frowned, wondering what would motivate anyone to create a fake image of her. She turned to Rokai. "Explain this."

Rokai shrugged. "I don't know anything about it."

Kira studied his face. "You're lying," she decided. "And I think that's the first lie you've told since I took you captive. But why would you feel the need to lie about something like this?"

Rokai said nothing.

"It was part of an unrestricted cache of data," Shing-kur explained. "Included in it were several files about some Starfleet and Bajoran personnel—including you—along with a Cardassian intelligence summary on Bajor."

Kira looked at Rokai again to gauge his reaction. He gazed back at her impassively.

"Show me the summary," Kira told Shing-kur. The Kressari did as instructed, allowing Kira to read through a brief history of the occupation. It was skewed toward the Cardassians' perspective, of course, but the historical highlights right up to the year of her capture tracked with her memory: the attack on the Kiessa monastery, the Kendra Valley massacre, the construction of Terok Nor and Dukat becoming prefect, the raid on Pullock V and the liberation of Gallitep, the various attempts on Dukat's life and even the bombing of Gul Pirak's compound—it was all here, all accurately dated, if not objectively described.

Moving beyond the history with which she was familiar was a revelation, however: seven years ago, the occupation had finally ended; the Cardassians withdrew, leaving Bajor weary and deeply wounded, but finally free. It gave Kira a brief sense of elation to know that the resistance had finally beaten back her world's occupiers . . . until she learned of Bajor's alignment with the Federation and that body's subsequent years of interference in Bajoran affairs. Bajor had welcomed the arrival of the long-prophesied Emissary and the opening of the Gates to the Celestial Temple . . . but the Emissary was an alien, a Federation officer and the new commander of Terok Nor! According to the report, this same individual had provoked the Dominion's decision to invade the Alpha Quadrant, leading directly to their involvement with Cardassia and a second occupation of Bajor—something this supposed Emissary had allowed to happen—and to the war Shingkur had described, which the Federation and its allies were staging from the Bajoran system itself.

How could her fellow Bajorans have traded one group of overseers for another? How could her people have allowed themselves to be duped into believing one of those new taskmasters was Touched by the Prophets?

How could everything I've gone through have been for nothing?

She found part of the answer in the personnel files, one of which belonged to "Colonel Kira Nerys," the first officer of Terok Nor, serving under the man who was supposedly the Emissary—a woman who looked like Kira, claimed Kira's name and past as her own, and who for the past fifteen years had lived a life that Kira had not . . . now as a servant of the new order, betraying everything Kira had fought for.

"An agent," she realized, then turned back to Rokai. "Your people sent an agent to pretend she was me, didn't they? That's who that person is. She's part of some conspiracy between the Federation and Cardassia to keep Bajor weak and submissive."

Even as she said it, she was gnawed by doubt, and with every second that passed, her agitation grew. The awful thought that she had been replaced by someone else was coiling itself tighter and tighter around her mind, constricting her ability to think straight, strangling her very soul.

"There's a restricted cache in the same sector of memory," Shing-kur informed her. "It's huge. But I can't access it without a code key."

Kira's attention returned to Rokai. "Give her the code." .

"I don't know it."

"That's another lie." Kira raised her weapon and shot Rokai in the leg. He howled in agony and fell to the floor, clutching his blackened, half-incinerated knee. "The code. Now."

Rokai grimaced against the pain, forcing a string of numbers and keywords through his clenched teeth. Shing-kur entered them, and the desk answered with a tone as it opened a new menu of files. "That's odd."

"What now?" Kira asked.

"There are scores of files here, but they all have the same name; they're differentiated solely by their dates."

Kira peered past her shoulder, frowning at what she saw displayed on the desktop screen: a single name appearing over and over:

ILIANA

Kira blinked, mouthing the word under her breath. It was the name from her dream; the name her mother had used when—

Wait—what? Where had *that* come from? Her mother was Kira Meru, dead many years now. The woman in her dream was Cardassian!

"Don't you dare presume to talk to me of responsibility. I'm your mother!"

"Yes, and I'm your daughter. But I'm not your child anymore."

Her heart was pounding. "Open one of them," she said.

"Which one?"

She looked at the dates alongside each appearance of the name: all of them were from the last fifteen years. "It doesn't matter."

Shing-kur accessed a random file, one bearing a date from nine years ago. It was an audiovisual recording. Kira immediately recognized her prison cell and realized she was seeing it from a surveillance camera she never knew existed. She gasped at the sight of herself, nude and dazed and sobbing, screaming helplessly as Dukat moved toward her.

"My Gods," Shing-kur breathed, and quickly cut the playback. "Kira, are you all right?"

Recordings. He made recordings. He kept them.

"*I know exactly who you are.*"

She looked at the file names again.

"*What do you remember?*"

She closed her eyes. *It's not true. It can't be true.*

"*And who is this lovely creature?*"

"Kira?" Shing-kur prompted.

"*What do you remember?*"

No. She felt herself trembling. *No, no, no, no, no—*

"*Are you really so ashamed of the person you were? Is there nothing of her left in you?*"

"*What do you remember?*"

"*But that isn't who I am anymore. Why can't you be proud of me now?*"

"*What do you remember?*"

"*I don't believe in ghosts.*"

"*But my dear Iliana . . . you are defined by one.*"

"*What . . . do you . . . remember?*"

"Kira!" Shing-kur shouted.

"Kira Nerys," she whispered. She opened her eyes and locked them on Rokai, who still lay on the floor, watching her from beneath the ridges of his eyes.

She brought her foot down hard on what was left of his knee, the cracking sound loud and clear even over his wails of agony. She struck him across the face with her rifle. "Say it!" she commanded. "Say my name!"

Rokai's body folded up in misery, his breathing ragged. "Iliana, please," he moaned. "I can help you."

"*I'm Kira Nerys!*" she screamed, and shot him in the face. She kept on firing until there was nothing left of Rokai above the shoulders.

The water fell against her in frigid sheets, numbing her wherever it struck. Where Rokai's blood had spattered her, the icy spray blasted it off, the dark gray-red flecks vanishing into the metal grate beneath her feet.

She leaned heavily against one wall of the transparent shower stall, her hands flat against it, the tangled mess of her long red hair hanging over her eyes.

"I don't understand," came the voice of Telal, muffled by the roar of the water, but still reverberating through the stall well enough to be heard. "Did she experience a breakdown?"

"I'm not sure what to call it," she heard Shing-kur say. "All I can tell you is, she saw some files that strongly suggested she was the subject of some obscene Cardassian deception against Bajor, and it pushed her over the edge. She killed Rokai, then staggered into the 'fresher, stripped off her clothes, and got into the shower. She hasn't moved since."

"And now?"

"Now I'm just waiting. What's the progress on the transporter?"

"Mazagalanthi is making some final tests, but he believes we'll be ready to beam out of here soon."

"All right. You and Fellen raid the storage rooms. She should be almost finished with the armory. Load up with as much as you can. I'll take care of Kira." A pause. "She's the reason we've made it this far, Telal. I'm not simply going to leave her."

"We can't wait forever."

"I know. Go. I'll be there."

For several minutes after that there was only the white noise of the water. Then the icy spray abruptly ceased, leaving only its echo in her ears.

"We need to go," Shing-kur said.

At first she refused to move. Then slowly she turned

and met Shing-kur's vermilion gaze. There was a tricorder in the Kressari's hand. "You know."

Shing-kur nodded. "How much do you remember?"

She looked down at her hands, studied her skin—her
pale Bajoran skin. Skin without ridges, without scales . . .
without truth.

"Everything," Iliana answered.

"You're shivering," Shing-kur noted. She pressed
a touchpad on the wall. Several hot white lights in the
ceiling came on, targeted at the stall. It was a heat meant
to invigorate a Cardassian, and it embraced Iliana like an
old friend as it drew moisture from her lying skin.

"The others?" she asked.

"I haven't told them. And I won't," Shing-kur said. "I
figured that after the last fifteen years, you ought to be
the one to make those choices."

Iliana watched as steam rose from her arms.

"I want you to know I'm still with you," Shing-kur
added, "no matter who you are."

Iliana looked at her. "Why?"

"Because I think you want the same things I want,"
Shing-kur said. "Revenge, and your life back."

"My life?" Iliana's eyes narrowed. Still covered in
beads of moisture, she left the stall and stopped in front
of Shing-kur. "Which life?"

The Kressari was at a loss to answer her.

"Bajor is turning into the very thing I remember trying to prevent it from becoming," Iliana continued. "Cardassia is being decimated as we speak. Maybe they both
deserve their fates. There's nothing left for me on either
world." She spread her hands, inviting Shing-kur to look
upon her. "This is what I have left."

"But, Iliana—"

"Don't call me that!"

Shing-kur blinked, startled.

Iliana turned away from the Kressari's intense stare and went into the adjoining bedchamber. She headed directly to the replicator and, speaking Cardassian, she ordered up undergarments, boots, and a casual brown suit for a woman of her height and build. She dressed quickly while Shing-kur watched her from the doorway.

"I'm sorry, I—I don't understand. You said you remember everything."

"That's right," Iliana said, "I remember everything. I remember growing up as part of the ruling elite on an arid planet so poor in natural resources that we needed to annex our inferior neighbors to keep our proud civilization going. I remember believing I could change the world just by following my dreams . . . and how, in the end, it was the world that changed me.

"But I also remember being a child born into a world of brutal enslavement, where the value of our lives was measured in how much ore we could mine for our vicious alien overseers. I remember the thrill I felt with every Cardassian butcher I took down, the self-loathing that followed each kill, and the decision I made to go on fighting in spite of it. I remember praying to my gods for the clarity and resolve to do what was right, and I remember the mass graves at Gallitep.

"I remember Ataan Rhukal, the man to whom I had given my heart, who was murdered in a despicable terrorist bombing on a pathetically backward planet, and how I joined the Obsidian Order just so I could go on living with myself. And I remember the night I crept through the shadows to set the explosive that took his life.

"I remember Dakahna Vaas, one of the best and bravest fighters in the resistance, someone I loved, and how losing her almost destroyed me. And I remember my satisfaction when I killed her for the Obsidian Order.

"But do you know what I remember more than anything? I remember how for fifteen years I was locked in a box, the occasional plaything of the most sadistic creature I've ever known. And now I understand it wasn't just my body that was raped for those fifteen years. It was my mind, and the very memory of me. *Both* of me. He took everything. My freedom, my friends, my dignity, my faith—everything except my identity. My sense of self, my certainty about who I was—that was the one thing I could cling to when I had nothing else.

"I'm not giving it up now, Shing-kur, not again, not after all I survived. I'm Kira Nerys, and no one, *no one,* is taking that from me."

"And what exactly does Kira Nerys intend to do next?" the Kressari asked.

"I'm going to find Dukat and punish him for what he did to me."

"And then?"

"Then?" Iliana closed the final clasp on her tunic and considered her reflection in a nearby mirror. She liked what she saw. "Then I'm going after the rest of them."

"Nice suit" was Mazagalanthi's only comment as Iliana strode into the transporter room. The towering Lissepian lifted his double-pointed chin as he peered down at her with his tiny, deep-set eyes.

Shing-kur arrived shortly thereafter. Both women were similarly outfitted, having replicated large backpacks and shoulder bags loaded up with everything Telal and Fellen had not been able to pack. Iliana, however, had one additional item. At her request, Shing-kur had transferred the complete contents of Dukat's personal database to an isolinear rod, which now resided securely in an inner pocket of Iliana's jacket. Shing-kur had told her that in addition to the caches they'd already discovered, the database contained a veritable treasure trove of military intelligence, security files, even Dukat's own reports and personal logs going back forty years—and it was Iliana's intention to read every word at the earliest opportunity.

Telal approached them, scrutinizing Iliana carefully. "You appear recovered."

"Drop it," Iliana said. "Mazagalanthi, is this thing ready?"

Standing at the control pedestal, the Lissepian nodded his great head. "The unit is fully charged and all systems are at optimum. We can leave at any time."

Iliana cast a glance at the stage, which was already half-filled with silver cases, overstuffed satchels, and piles of loose equipment. "How confident are you that we aren't going to overtax the transporter's mass limitations?"

"Completely," said Mazagalanthi. "I inspected the activity log. There are records of far greater loads than this being beamed, and always to the same location. As far as I can tell, this unit was never used to go anywhere else."

Interesting. "Fellen, how are we set with plasma charges?"

"I'm carrying six," the Efrosian answered. "There are fourteen more in one of the chests on the platform."

"Set four of them on a five-metric delay and place them around the room where they'll do the most damage."

"Understood," Fellen said, and quickly went to work.

Telal arched an eyebrow. "Burning our bridge behind us?"

"Aptly put," Iliana agreed. She turned to Shing-kur. "You took care of the computers?"

The Kressari nodded. "Six more charges inside the mainframe and elsewhere will detonate in thirteen metrics. There won't be much left of this place at all after that."

"Good," Iliana said.

"And once we're away from here," Telal pressed, "then what? We all agreed to join forces and follow your lead in order to escape this place, but beyond that . . ."

"That's up to each of you to decide on your own," Iliana told them. "I've got business to take care of that has nothing to do with any of you, and I'm not expecting anyone to stick with me once we beam out of here. But if you do," she added, glancing briefly at Shing-kur, "then I vow to make it worth your while." She looked at each of the others in turn. "I don't know who you were before Letau, and I don't care. The way I see it, who we used to be is dead. This is our chance to start over."

No one spoke. Then Fellen announced that she was done setting the plasma charges, and promptly started handing out fresh weapons. "We'd better be ready for anything. I hate the idea of transporting blind."

"What do we know about our destination?" Iliana asked as she ascended the stage.

"The planet Harkoum," Telal said as he and the women joined her on the platform, followed quickly by

Mazagalanthi after he initialized the transport sequence. "Remote, relatively isolated, and sparsely populated. Primarily a scattering of industrial complexes, mostly long abandoned. In short, a good place to hide."

"No," Iliana corrected just before the beam took them. "It's a good place to begin."

END OF SIDE TWO

TO BE CONTINUED . . .

About the Author

Olivia Woods was born in Cape Town, South Africa, where she also spent her early childhood before moving with her parents to Ireland. At the age of fourteen she came to live with her extended family in the United States and began her torrid and enduring love affair with all things *Star Trek*. She currently resides in upstate New York with her spouse and daughter.

Acknowledgments

There are a number of people to whom I'm grateful for helping to make this book possible.

First, there's Paula Block at CBS, whose deliciously twisted idea for what really happened to Iliana Ghemor tipped the first domino;

All the authors of the previous *Deep Space Nine* novels set after the TV series, but especially the ones who laid the groundwork for Iliana's return: J. Noah Kym (*Fragments and Omens* from *Worlds of Star Trek: Deep Space Nine, Volume Two*), David R. George III (*Olympus Descending* from *Worlds of Star Trek: Deep Space Nine, Volume Three*), and David Mack (*Warpath*);

The writers on the television series, especially Robert Hewitt Wolfe for "Second Skin" and his collaborators on the follow-up episode, "Ties of Blood and Water," Edmund Newton and Robbin L. Slocum;

Steve Breslin in Pocket's production department, for patience and understanding above and beyond the call;

And finally, my editor, Marco Palmieri, for throwing me into the deep end.

Side One quote from "Waltz"
Written by Ronald D. Moore

Side Two quote A from "Ties of Blood and Water"
Teleplay by Robert Hewitt Wolfe
Story by Edmund Newton & Robbin L. Slocum

Side Two quote B from "Waltz"
Written by Ronald D. Moore